The Journal of Mrs Pepys

Portrait of a Marriage

The Journal
of Mrs Pepys

Portrait of a Marriage

Sara George

ST. MARTIN'S PRESS
NEW YORK

THOMAS DUNNE BOOKS.
An imprint of St. Martin's Press.

THE JOURNAL OF MRS PEPYS. Copyright © 1998 by Sara George. All rights
reserved. Printed in the United States of America. No part of this book may
be used or reproduced in any manner whatsoever without written permission
except in the case of brief quotations embodied in critical articles or
reviews. For information, address St. Martin's Press, 175 Fifth Avenue,
New York, N.Y. 10010.

Library of Congress Cataloging-in-Publication Data

George, Sara.
    The journal of Mrs. Pepys : portrait of a marriage / Sara George. – 1st
U.S. ed.
        p. cm.
    ISBN 0-312-20554-6
    1. Pepys, Elizabeth, 1640-1669—Marriage—Fiction. 2. Great Britain—
History—Charles II, 1660-1685—Fiction. 3. London (England)—History—
17th century—Fiction. 4. Pepys, Samuel, 1633-1703—Marriage—Fiction.
I. Title.
PR6057.E55J68   1999
823'.914—dc21
                                                        99-101082
                                                            CIP

First published in Great Britain by Review/Headline Book Publishing, a division
of Hodder Headline PLC

First U.S. Edition: May 1999

10 9 8 7 6 5 4 3 2 1

To Ruth and Daisy

And to the memory of
Margaret George
1924-1998

The Journal of Mrs Pepys

Portrait of a Marriage

1659/60

∞

31ST DECEMBER 1659

This is the last night of the year and I have sat here alone by the fire while my dear husband is out and about, and in thinking over how much has happened in the last twelve months I have resolved to keep a journal, and it will be private. I shall keep it hidden, and it will be mine alone and I shall say whatever I like. So that on days and nights like this it will be company of a sort.

I'm not just angry about Sam spending so much time in taverns – though I am – but I miss him when he's not here. We still have pleasant evenings together, reading, Sam playing his lute, and when he takes me out I think he's proud of me, but so often it's business and I'm not allowed to go. It seems to me that for every ounce of business, there's a pound of pleasure. Sometimes when I'm alone for hours on end I have to pinch myself to be sure I'm alive. Or I wander round the house and can't settle to anything.

Now I shall be able to settle to my journal. I know that I'll be uninterrupted for some time yet. These sorts of days have their familiar rhythm.

My first concealment will be to write it in French. That will keep it from Jane, at least, and Sam's French isn't nearly as good as he'd like to imagine. My father may have been unable to provide for me as he wished but he was a Frenchman and he made me fluent in his language and no one can ever take that away. Then the pages can go under the bottom mattress of our bed. Sam would never dream of turning a mattress, and Jane doesn't do it without being told, so my journal should be safe enough. And when I visit my parents I can store the pages in my old carved box where I have some other trifling keepsakes that I can't bring to my married home.

I have to conceal it because I want to write from my heart. Sometimes that will mean writing things I don't want Sam to read. I am blessed with good friends – I shall run across the yard tonight, through the snow, to see the Hunts – but I find I can tell one person one thing and another something else, but there's nobody who knows it all. I think of it as unburdening myself to a dear friend, one who won't judge, or betray. And I'll know that I'm alive because my life is written down.

So . . . here I am . . .

My name is Elizabeth Pepys, born Elizabeth St Michel at Bideford, Devon, on 23rd October 1640. I'm nineteen years old. My husband Samuel is a tally clerk at the Exchequer and he'll be twenty-seven next month. Our little maid Jane Birch completes our household. No children, alive or dead.

I had thought, during Christmas, that there might be a chance this time, but after seven weeks my hope proved to be false. It was worse being at the time of the Nativity. Such a long time we've been waiting, so many disappointments.

I met Sam when I was fourteen, just after my family had returned from two years in Paris where Papa had failed to claim his inheritance. Sam was mad for me at once, couldn't bear to wait. And I was mad for him. Sometimes I wonder whether he thought there was more money in the family than was the case, knowing that my mother was descended from the Cliffords, Earls of Cumberland, but in any event I brought him nothing in terms of a dowry.

Our earliest years together were hard. I'd not quite turned fifteen when we married. I had no idea how painful the physical side might be and how it's in the nature of a man to be insistent. I missed my parents and my brother Balty. I was overwhelmed by the sheer drudgery of looking after two people in our condition. We were living in a garret at the top of Lord Mountagu's lodgings in Whitehall Palace. The Pepyses are distantly related by marriage to the Mountagus and over the years the Pepyses have served them in various ways. Sam had to look after the establishment in Whitehall and attend to my Lord's business while he was away at sea, or in the country at Hinchingbrooke.

I had only to look after our room and our selves but it seemed as though it was never done. I carried endless buckets of coal and water up to the top of the turret. We couldn't afford soap to wash clothes so I had to use lye and my hands were so raw I cried with pain. And vanity. I've always been proud of my white skin. I don't know whether Sam appreciated the effort. As his mother had been a washerwoman in a grand house in her youth perhaps it seemed I was fussing over nothing. (Of course we don't say washerwoman, we say laundry maid to Lady Vere.)

We were as poor as church mice and our entertainment was largely had by talking and reading to each other. And Sam would play his lute and sing to me. Those were sweet times when I didn't mind being poor. Yet there always seemed to be enough money that when the mood took him Sam was able to meet his friends in various taverns and be merry, judging by the state he came home in. It wasn't how I'd imagined marriage would be. Those nights were long and lonely and I half expected someone to appear and sweep me away to my real life where there were no dirty clothes or boozy breath.

But deep down I knew there'd be no rescue, so instead I escaped. One day when there wasn't a scrap of food left in our cupboard, and no money, and he'd been out for hours, I wrote him a letter about my unhappiness and left our home to go back to my parents. I can't say that they were overjoyed at my return – I think having me safely married was a weight off their shoulders and they didn't like my giving it up so soon. It brought home to me that they were poor and I was an extra mouth that could have been fed by someone else.

I still thought Sam was charming and energetic and intelligent, I just couldn't bear to live with him. I was too young and he was too insensitive. At first he was furious but then he learnt that if he wanted me back he would have to woo me, not shout at me.

That was when I first met Captain Robert Holmes. I've always had a weakness for military men – my earliest memories of my father are of a tall, dashing soldier coming home from fighting in France or Ireland. Robert had fought for Prince Rupert and now he was rising fast in the Navy. He was also a good friend of Lord Mountagu's. I was constant enough to Sam that nothing serious happened between us, just lingering glances, a few illicit words, a gift or two. The little silver necklace is still in my old box at my parents' house. Sam's baseless jealousy had been one of the causes of our separation but now I was quite content for him to hear that Captain Holmes was paying attention to his wife. Sam was miserable but he tried so hard not to be angry that I was touched. He told me I was such a beauty that every man in London must want to be my servant. He begged me to let him be my protector again and I very happily agreed.

So we resumed our married life and by now, in addition to his duties for Lord Mountagu, Sam had a position as a clerk in the Exchequer. It wasn't a job that made use of his talents, or one with great prospects. He spent his time receiving and paying out money, cutting wooden tally sticks for the exact amount. But it meant our income was a little more, enough that in the summer of 1658 we were at last able to rent our own home and we moved into our house here at Axe Yard.

I felt drunk with possession. I scrubbed and polished and arranged and rearranged our few things. Our maid Jane, not much more than a little girl then, joined us at that time and is with us still.

The candles are guttering and my hand aches from writing. It's time for bed.

The landlord comes for the rent and Sam hasn't got it. He takes him down to the office to borrow it from there. Then he has to arrange payment for Lord Mountagu's soldiers, then he has to walk in Westminster Hall to hear the latest news of the Army and Parliament and General Monck. He rushes in for his dinner then has to see some Exchequer colleagues about paying out money. I don't understand why this has to be done in a tavern.

But it gives me a chance to write a little – I know he won't be back before supper – so I'll try to be grateful for the opportunity, not angry.

We've been very sociable for the last few days – when the weather's so cold there's nothing more enjoyable than staying in, having long dinners and playing cards with friends and neighbours. On Twelfth Day itself we dined at Cousin Thomas Pepys's – pleasant enough though the venison pasty we were promised turned out to be beef which we thought rather mean. In the evening we supped at Cousin Strudwick's with most of Sam's family. There was the traditional cake – a very fine one – with the bean and the pea hidden in it. When it was cut Cousin Strudwick got the bean so he was King for the night, and Sam's sister Paulina – or Pall, as we have to call her – got the pea, so she was Queen. And she made the most of it, boasting and gloating in the graceless manner we've come to expect. There's no love lost between her and Sam, he's irritated by her and thinks it's no wonder she's still unmarried at twenty.

It was quite a relief to leave and walk home arm in arm, with a link boy lighting our way. There was a great frost – the city looked strange and clean and there was no smell because of the cold. The whiteness everywhere made the flames of the torch spread much wider light than usual, made the buildings sparkle, and the sky was so clear that the stars blazed. We were laughing, and warm with food and drink. We were happy.

By Sunday there wasn't a coal in the house and I had to spend the whole day at Salisbury Court with Sam's parents. He's worried about how to pay the rent because all his money is tied up with his Uncle Robert at Brampton so he hasn't dared lay out on coal. At least his parents' house is warm, though it means listening to his mother ranting and raving. His father's so good with her it makes me ashamed of my own impatience. But sometimes spending almost every Sunday with them tries me beyond endurance and I long to be either in my own home or somewhere else entirely.

The talk at dinner was all of General Monck and his army marching down to London. We all know that he's the man who'll decide things, but nobody knows whether he'll support the hated Rump Parliament or the free Parliament that everyone wants. It's a strange time. The Rump still has the power and people are very careful what they say. And everyone knows that a free Parliament would eventually mean Charles being restored as King, but that's unmentionable yet.

15TH JANUARY

There's been a great thaw and everywhere is filthy. The melting snow reveals that dead rats and piles of rubbish have not miraculously disappeared. Mr Hawley came to say Sam must repay the rent money to the office at once.

Sam's been out and about to the point where the other day I'd had enough. He'd been out all morning at the office, where there was little to do, then to the tavern, and returned at noon to collect me for dinner at the Wades', which was quite enjoyable. Then we went to see Kate Stirpin, Mrs Pye's maid, and as usual Sam could barely keep his hands off her. As soon as we arrived home he said he was going out again, and I said where were we going and he said not us, just him. I asked why and he said it was business, and I said I knew that was a lie, he was going to see Kate, or he was going to a tavern. He said he'd go wherever he chose, and I said it wasn't fair to leave me on my own while he was out carousing, and he slammed the door and walked off. So I followed him to Whitehall where he saw me and turned round and was furiously angry and walked me home and said he was going to see how Lady Jemima did, which is part of his duty to Lord Mountagu, and he would be pleased if I would mind my own business, and off he went again. Jemima is my Lord's young daughter and while she's having her crooked neck treated Sam is required to see to her well-being. I can't argue with that.

I gave up and went to the Hunts. If John Hunt weren't such a Puritan . . . and if we were shipwrecked on a desert island . . . and if we weren't both married . . . But we are, and I'm very fond of Elizabeth Hunt too and they're both unfailingly good to me. There's always some supper and kind words when I feel neglected. Elizabeth was at her mother's that night and John said if he were my husband he'd never expect to enjoy himself without me. I made sure I stayed there until after Sam came home – which was a lot later than if he'd only visited Miss Jem.

But today it's Sunday and we're very pleasant at home with each other. A neighbour's dog barked all through the night and even the snow falling hadn't muffled its sound, keeping us awake for a long time so we slept late. Sam took physic yesterday for his costiveness, so he must be at home today near the pot while it takes effect – no question of going to church. We didn't even have to visit his parents. I made us a good little dinner and we kept the fire blazing, never mind the cost, and Sam talked about his money worries because the office want the loan repaid. Also it snowed heavily, so even more reason not to go out. I have to confess I avoid going to church when I can. Mr Milles, our vicar at St Olave's, is a good enough man I suppose, but I find the Church of England a cold thing after Mass in Paris when dear Father Fogarty was my priest and he always had a twinkle in his eye and that warm Irish accent.

I love Papa dearly but sometimes I do wish that he'd felt able to continue as a Catholic and not become a Huguenot. And not just because that cut him – and all of us his family – off from his worldly inheritance, but also because I lost the inheritance of the Catholic faith. (Though I must say that if he'd had his family money, life would have been a great deal easier for us all – perhaps they wouldn't have been as eager for me to be married so young.)

But I know that for me to be a Roman Catholic would be a great hindrance to Sam in his career, Catholics being hated here as much as they are. I don't press it, but neither do I embrace Mr Milles and his interminable sermons. I think that on days like this, when we are quiet and at peace together, talking and reading, and having our family prayers together in the evening, we are worshipping in our own way and Our Lord will understand.

END JANUARY

Of course the next day – being a washing day – was quite different. Jane and I have to get up at two in the morning to put the water on to boil and even if I go back to bed for a couple of hours it makes for a grumpy start. Then all day the house is full of steam and there's all the heavy work of lifting a month's worth of dirty linen in and out of tubs and emptying the tubs and filling them over and over and wringing it all until your wrists ache and your hands feel as though they'll drop off. It didn't surprise me that Sam was out all day but when he rolled in at eleven o'clock, merry from the Green Dragon and the Golden Lion, he got short shrift. Seeing his humour was falling on deaf ears – we'd been washing for fifteen hours by this time – he soon went to his closet to do some paperwork (the diary he thinks I don't know about). When he went to bed at one o'clock Jane and I were still – washing.

The next day was spent ironing and folding the tablecloths very carefully into the press so the creases would be perfectly straight when they were laid on the table. Sam follows the superstition that a wrinkled crease – 'a coffin' – means death to one of the diners, so Jane and I take great pains over it.

At least it meant we had clean cloths for our grand dinner at my Lord's lodgings, which he'd given us the use of while he was away. I thought it was a slightly uncomfortable combination of guests. We invited Surgeon Pearse and his wife Elizabeth whom Sam thinks is a great beauty, wit, etc, etc. They'd asked us to dinner a few days before and we'd arrived not quite in the right mood because I had new pattens over my silk shoes and I kept slipping in the rain and Sam was cross because we were late. Then there was a lot of drinking and people got riotous and it ended up with a mock wedding with everyone pulling off the bride's and groom's ribbons in a very bawdy way which neither of us cared for much. One good thing about Sam and me is that we both more or less agree on what we find seemly and what sluttish. Most of the time.

Our guests, apart from the Pearses, were Sam's family: mother and father, brother Tom and Uncle Fenner with his wife and two daughters and their husbands – the Joyce brothers. Two brothers who married two sisters. We love to hate these young men. William Joyce is loutish but sometimes quite comical, while his brother Anthony is not quite as loutish but much more stupid. Sam loathes them both. At least they're his family, not mine.

We spent all the day before our dinner in preparation. I was larding pullets and making tarts until eleven at night. Sam laid the cloths, which he does very well, very precisely.

Our menu was a dish of marrow bones, a leg of mutton, a loin of veal, three pullets and two dozen larks, a great tart, a tongue, a dish of anchovies, a dish of prawns, and cheese. It was a fine dinner and Sam was impressed with my cooking and said so, which warmed me enough that I could withstand Elizabeth Pearse telling me how beguilingly simple my gown was, while showing off her own rich lace. She was as beautiful and as condescending as ever — eight children and the figure of a girl . . . Sam has no idea how much women can communicate to each other with the raising of one eyebrow. Sometimes men need beating about the brow to see what is transparent to any woman. She has good taste, but more important she has the money to lay out. If I had as much, I could do as well. At least she couldn't be high with me about the food because I count myself a good cook and my time in France taught me more than most Englishwomen know.

William Joyce didn't disappoint us with his behaviour. Having started off cheerful and merry he became more and more drunk and quarrelled with his wife and her parents. He and the Pearses and Tom stayed after everyone else and then went on to a tavern and Tom told us later that despite it being at William's insistence he made them all pay their share. Sam was delighted at how typical this was. The talk, when it wasn't William ranting, was of General Monck being very near London with his troops. It's said that he'll support the Rump, but nobody quite believes it. When everyone had gone, Sam attended his employer to write out a couple of documents while Jane and I cleared up, then he came back and we sat by the great log and ate leftovers and felt pleased with ourselves, and so home.

∞

MIDDLE FEBRUARY

Great and little events all mixed up. The Rump's army regiments mutinied. There were soldiers in all the streets refusing to leave town until they'd been paid. As though in sympathy we had nothing in the house to eat but pease porridge.

The next day the regiments of foot took over Somerset House and the regiments of horse were sent to dislodge them, but instead they all joined forces and now the whole army in London was in mutiny. The apprentices were crying out for a free Parliament, and some had been arrested. The Strand was full of soldiers and there were drums beating incessantly everywhere. Sam had to go to the Exchequer to pay out what there was so the officers could disband their troops. Of course there wasn't enough.

He brought Cousin Jane Turner for dinner, having

ordered a shoulder of mutton and a bottle of wine to be sent home. They'd just watched General Monck's forces march through Whitehall – stout men, well equipped and well disciplined.

But the shoulder of mutton he'd ordered arrived barely warm, let alone cooked, and we had to stew it. Even in the midst of revolutions we have to wait for the meat to cook. So while we waited for it to cook some more we designed a posy for a ring that Mrs Turner will have at Cousin Roger's wedding. And every now and then we'd hear bands of soldiers calling for a free Parliament and we'd look at each other and try to imagine what was going to happen next.

That night Sam and I, in bed, heard a single drum beat, all night long, and we wondered what it meant.

The days run into each other. It becomes safe to express hatred of the Rump. The boys in the street are shouting 'Kiss my Rump' instead of 'Kiss my arse'. The weather is warm and spring-like despite being so early in the year. I have to kill the turkey Mr Shipley had sent us from Hinchingbrooke because Jane will never kill anything. I learned about that sort of thing from my early life in the West Country – the trick is to be resolute and do it quickly.

The City refuses to pay any taxes to the Rump Parliament. The Rump orders General Monck to march from Whitehall to the City and tear down its defences.

In our yard the pigeons are breeding in the warm weather. Sam has a terrible boil under his chin. Dear importunate Balty has brought me a sweet little black spaniel bitch and I shall call her Fancy. Our sleep has been disturbed because she keeps trying to get in bed with us and I can't refuse her, but Sam says she's flea-ridden and has to stay outside our bedchamber. So she howls at the door all night and I get up and let her in and Sam complains and so we go round and round.

Meanwhile, General Monck marches to the City and arrests nine leaders but his men refuse to take down the defences. Sam was rushing in and out (mostly out) with rumours and news. Against the Rump's orders Monck marched his men out of the City and back to Whitehall. He held all the power but everyone was on tenterhooks which way he'd go.

Then the next day, it was a Saturday, Jane came racing back from an errand and shouted 'Free Parliament, he's called for a free Parliament' and we hugged each other and danced round the kitchen. Then we ran into the street and hugged our neighbours and even soldiers and strangers. Sam was in Westminster Hall when the news came in and he said as it spread, it was so strange to see all men's faces suddenly turning to joy. Later he was at the Guildhall when Monck came out and there was a huge roar of 'God bless your Excellency'.

As night fell, the bonfires began. Sam came home for me and we walked abroad together. In King Street alone, at the end of Axe Yard, we could see eight bonfires, and from Strand pier we counted thirty-one. All the church bells were ringing and boys were carrying rumps of meat on sticks to burn on the fires. It was such a sudden, common joy, all the people felt it – it was what everyone wished and our faces were red and smiling in the firelight, and people crying God bless to the soldiers and giving them money and drink. The butchers at the Maypole in the Strand rang a peal with their knives before they sacrificed their rump. It was the suddenness of it and the greatness of the celebration – past imagination. We walked as far as the New Exchange in Covent Garden and then home, very tired and happy. We thought it was the beginning of something wonderful. I never expect to see so much fire at one time again in my life.

1ST MARCH

Of course such great joy can't last. In our case by the very next evening we had high words in bed when Sam threatened to throw Fancy out of the window if she didn't stop pissing everywhere. It isn't her fault, I'm training her but it will take time for her to learn. The trouble is that Sam can't bear disorder of any sort in the house.

On Valentine's Day I awoke to hear my Lord's lawyer, Mr Moore, talking to Sam in his closet, so I went in and claimed him as my Valentine, being the first man apart from Sam that I saw in the day. I haven't had my present from him yet but these are busy times. There seems every chance that now there is a new Parliament Lord Mountagu will be in favour again, with a good hope of employment. But it's two sides of the coin – poor John Hunt fears for his post in the Excise because he's known as a Puritan and his wife Elizabeth was even a relative of Oliver Cromwell's.

Sam was twenty-seven last week. I dearly hope that if my Lord Mountagu is favoured by a free Parliament it will help Sam too, in his humbler way. I know that he's capable of more than he's doing now, and will show himself so if he's given the chance.

∞

19TH MARCH, HUNTSMOOR, BERKS

From wishing to being . . . Everything has happened so quickly. Within a day of my last writing, Lord Mountagu had been offered and accepted the post of General-at-Sea. Within a week my Lord had asked Sam to go to sea as his secretary. He promised to do him all the good he could. We lay awake for hours talking over what it would all mean for us. Suddenly everything's changing, there are all sorts of hopes. In the meantime news came from his Uncle Robert in Brampton that he would make Sam his heir and leave him the Brampton house and land. It wasn't altogether a surprise, except hearing of it at this time, with so much else happening.

Of course Sam agreed to go to sea with Lord Mountagu. His main problem was that it meant being away for several weeks and he was very reluctant, indeed positively determined against leaving me in London on my own. He says it's not safe. I think he's more concerned about the Captain Holmeses of this world. There was some considerable dispute but in the end I had to agree to go to the Bowyers at Huntsmoor (where I'm writing this now).

Before that there was a busy, happy week of preparations for Sam's voyage. I was making him caps and Jane was knitting stockings. He spent a whole Sunday at home without even putting his neckband on, getting things ready. We did lots of shopping at the Exchange and he was sweet to me and more than usually considerate. One day when he'd already dined out he came home and I had a mind for some cabbage and he said I must have it and sent out for it at once. Another day we bought a salmon for eight pence and dined on it together at the Sun. He made his will and promised me all his worldly goods apart from his books (except the French ones, which I was to have). We had a farewell dinner at his father's and the next morning bade our adieus in bed. We were both tearful at the thought of parting. I think we do love each other very dearly, in spite of our arguments.

All our valuables were locked in the dining room and I took the key with me. Sam accompanied me and Jane to Holborn where we took the coach to Huntsmoor, with William Bowyers, the oldest son, escorting us. I'm grateful to the Bowyers for taking me in, but they are an old couple and I'm already missing life in London.

∞

26TH MARCH

I'm sure about the date today because it's the second anniversary of Sam's operation for cutting his stone. I thought about him a lot this morning, how brave he was and how frightened we both were. Afterwards he promised Mrs Turner that he would always give a dinner on the anniversary, in thanks for his deliverance. Last year we did but with Sam being at sea now it's impossible this year.

It was a bitter cold winter that year which always made the pain worse. He was in such dreadful agony that an operation was his only recourse despite the terrible pain and the danger. We were still living in our turret room then and it was impossible to have it done there so Cousin Jane Turner offered her hospitality at Salisbury Court. Mr Hollier came on the appointed day and he was very fast but it's a dreadful procedure – up through the cods and into the bladder, cut and scoop – and even biting on the leather strap Sam couldn't help but groan and I couldn't bear to watch, just kept stroking his head. Mr Hollier took out a stone the size of a tennis ball. Then it was over and I held Sam's head up while he sipped a drink of lemon juice and syrup of radishes which soothed him. We both gave heartfelt thanks to God for his survival.

He made a complete recovery. But the strange thing is that Mr Hollier operated on thirty patients that year, all of whom survived, but then he operated on four more, all of whom died. After that he never performed it again. Sometimes, at the very back of my mind I wonder if the operation could have anything to do with our being childless, but I'd never say it because Sam wouldn't believe it and if he did it would hurt him terribly.

I long for news of him – I haven't had any yet. God speed him. Life in the country is like it always is in the country, we have our meals, we visit neighbours, we go for a walk or we don't go for a walk according to the weather. I wish I were back in London.

MID-APRIL

Letters at last, and fifteen shillings. They came via Balty who'd just left Sam on his ship, the *Naseby*. It seems their departure was delayed by the high March winds and there was a great tide as well so that King Street and our house in Axe Yard flooded. It was fortunate all our things were locked upstairs in the dining room. Sam says the talk is open now that the King will return.

Being Secretary to the Generals of the Fleet has meant Sam's suddenly being courted by all and sundry for a favour here, a place there. And where he's been able to oblige, people are happy to express their gratitude. And he's addressed as Esquire now.

Eventually the *Naseby* joined the fleet in the Hope and when they passed the Vice Admiral's ship they exchanged such abundant gun salutes that all the windows in his cabin were broken by the retort. (I thought it might have been more prudent to save the gunpowder for an enemy, but then I'm no General.) They lay at anchor above Gravesend and Sam wrote that he was heavy-hearted because he hadn't heard from me and was apprehensive for me. It made me feel warm and loved, makes me smile when I read the words again.

Balty had visited him to ask for his help in finding a place, which knowing Sam's low opinion of my brother I hadn't much hope of, but in fact Sam made the request to Lord Mountagu who was very civil and promised Balty a letter to Captain Stokes. I so hope something comes of it and he'll stick at it.

Sam had one bad day of seasickness, even though they were at anchor, when the sea got up very rough. In the middle of it my Lord sent for him to eat oysters, insisting they were the best he'd ever had, and poor Sam had to set to and eat them. Oh, the pains that must be endured for advancement.

MID-MAY

I've been ill with a fever but I'm better now. Sam wrote so sweetly, telling me who to go to for money if I needed it, though I haven't so far. There's not much to spend it on here.

On May Day there was a maypole on the Green — the first time they've been allowed after all these years of Puritan rule. An old lady who remembered the dance from her childhood taught the children how to do it and they looked so pretty, weaving in and out with their ribbons. It seems strange that such an innocent pastime was forbidden for so long. Everyone was saying that the King would surely return, it was bound to happen. It was exciting to say the words that would have been treasonous a few months before. Late in the day news reached us that Parliament had voted for his restoration and there was great rejoicing, bells pealing and a bonfire.

Strange how things go – eleven years ago they were happy to execute King Charles I and now they're happy to ask his son back as Charles II. It seems that my Lord Mountagu has been in correspondence with the King and the Duke of York during their exile and Sam says their letters to him are in the most familiar style, as though to a friend. He's delighted at my Lord's good condition and so am I, for it can't do Sam any harm to have as his patron a man who is a confidant of the King.

Sam is to be of the party that goes to Holland to escort the King back to England. My Lord told him to order silk flags and scarlet cloths to decorate the King's ship and to order a barge and trumpeters and a set of fiddlers.

They've sailed and must be nearly at Holland by now. I long for him to be home and us to have our life in Axe Yard again.

∞

END MAY

I've been ill but am better. I've been up to London with the Bowyers and come back again. The country is the same as ever. Sam, however, has been at the heart of things. They anchored off the Hague and he spent a week on land, says it's a very neat town in every way. He went to Delft too, and has bought me a very pretty basket of Delft ware. The Duke of York came aboard on the 22nd and the King on the 23rd. In the course of the gun salute Sam managed nearly to get shot in the eye by standing too close, but in the end no harm done although it was sore for a few days.

He says that the King walked the quarterdeck and talked about his escape after the Battle of Worcester, nearly ten years ago. He'd walked through the mud for four days and three nights in a pair of rough country shoes that made every step painful. And at one inn he was recognised by the landlord, who hadn't seen him for eight years, and at the same time not recognised by a soldier from his own regiment at Worcester. At another inn the landlord kissed his hand privately and wouldn't ask who he was or where he was going but blessed him. Once he shared a piece of bread and cheese out of a poor boy's pocket, another time he had to hide in a priest's hole for days on end. It seems incredible to think that the King of England suffered all this – and that Sam was there at the first public telling of it.

He's spoken in person with the Duke of York who's promised him his favour. As they came into Dover the King's dog shat in the boat which made them all laugh. My Lord Mountagu has been invested as Knight of the Order of the Garter for his loyal service during this time and he's given Sam £30 out of the 1,000 ducats the King gave him for the ship's company. Our star is rising – I long to be back at home with him.

Mid-June

While I was staying in London at Sam's father's we had the Joyces for dinner and the brothers are doing well in their tallow-chandler business and growing very fine and proud. Someone suggested that Sam might be knighted for his service and they nearly fell off their chairs laughing at the idea. When I told Sam later he said he didn't give a fig for them and he counted himself much happier with me and his estate than they were with theirs.

My Lord has told Sam that if things stay as they are between him and the King then he and Sam will rise together. Only they must be patient for a while. It's rumoured that my Lord will be made Master of the Great Wardrobe which is one of the most important Royal household appointments and rewarded accordingly.

Sam wrote that his heart was troubled that my health was not as constant as before. Mr Cook, my

Lord's servant who carries our letters, must have told him this because I haven't made much of it when writing so as not to worry him. And I'm perfectly well now.

At last, on Whit Sunday, we met again after nearly two months apart. We had to stay at his father's because our house wasn't ready yet after being empty for such a time, so we all dined together at Salisbury Court and then Sam and I went for a walk in Lincoln's Inn fields on our own. We walked in the shade under the trees because it was so hot, and he was infectiously full of news and plans and ideas and we were cheerful and merry together. There were fashionable people strolling around and when I admired one lady's dress Sam promised that if all went well I should have one as fine, and I know that his ability and hard work will provide it one day, if he just gets his chance.

It was a sweet but short time because he had to leave to attend my Lord, but he was back in time for us to go to bed together and have great pleasure as husband and wife.

16TH JULY

We were supposed to move today but it's raining too hard. So much has happened in the last month but now, with everything packed, there's nothing more to do here in Axe Yard. I'm eager to go, but there's still a little sadness in walking through the empty rooms, hearing them echo, remembering the times we've had here in our first proper home.

It was on 23rd June that my Lord told Sam that he had the promise of a post for him – Clerk of the Acts of the Navy Board. The salary alone would be £350 a year, and in addition he would be in a position to grant favours to the suppliers of everything from candles to masts to clothing. Sam says this must make our fortune over the years (though he doesn't intend to be greedy and he'll always choose what's in the King's best interest).

Three days later he was offered £500 to desist from his Clerk's place by a merchant who wanted it for himself but though Sam felt he had to consider the offer it didn't take long to decide he'd be better off keeping it. He and Lord Mountagu went to see Mr Coventry, the Duke of York's secretary, who promised to dispatch the business of the Clerkship. Everyone was congratulating Sam as though he already had it but it still wasn't official.

On the 29th of June he got his warrant from the Duke of York to be Clerk of the Acts and all seemed to be plain sailing until he heard that a previous holder of the post, a Mr Barlow, still held the reversion of it and was coming up to London to look after his interest. This plunged us into gloom for it looked as though all the bright prospects might yet be lost. My Lord told Sam to get possession of his patent as soon as possible and he'd do all he could to keep Barlow out. Then Thomas Turner of the Navy Office joined in, offering Sam £150 to share the patent with him and advise him how to get rid of Barlow. Sam decided to refuse this offer as well.

In the middle of all this Jane sprained her ankle and was completely lame. Sam took on a little boy to help out. Dinners still had to be cooked – I killed six of our pigeons for one of them.

The Privy Council ordered the new Navy Board to meet even though their patents weren't issued yet. Sam was named as one of the officers, but Mr Barlow had an appointment with Mr Coventry to put his case to the Duke of York. However, he turned out to be a sickly old man who didn't intend to take the post himself and that made us feel a little better. The next day Sam went to see the Navy lodgings beside the Navy Office in Seething Lane and he said even the worst house was very good. He moved into the Navy Office and began work by taking an inventory of all the papers and books, but still worried that the appointment could even now be given to Barlow.

On 9th July he spent nearly all day drawing up the bill for his appointment. On the 10th he received his warrant from the Attorney General (and we went to the rich and noble Roder wedding and of all the beauties there I was thought the greatest, which pleased us both very much). On the 11th his warrant was turned into a bill, signed by the King. Meanwhile there was much jostling for the Navy houses and Sam was desperate to make his appointment official so he could lay his claim. The other officers had already received their patents and we were on tenterhooks that Sam's would be too late and all the houses would be gone.

On the 12th he started as early as possible at the Privy Seal, gave them his bill and they granted him a Privy Seal writ for his patent. Now all he had to do was to get his patent formally written out and sealed by the Chancery. But Mr Beale, the Deputy Clerk of the Patents, was too busy to do it himself, so Sam ended up running up and down Chancery Lane trying to find a clerk who could write in Chancery-hand but none of them had time to do it. What made it more urgent was that Mr Barlow had called at the Chancery threatening to make a stop in the business. Then Sam had to go to a meeting at the Admiralty and it wasn't until eleven at night that he found a clerk who promised to write out the patent by the next morning.

He started early again on the 13th, finding the clerk still in his nightgown writing it out. Sam took it to the Chancery and got a receipt for it then took it to Mr Beale for a docket, but Mr Beale was unwilling because he said it was badly written (just because he hadn't done it himself) so Sam with much importuning got the clerk to come and finish it properly. Then he went to a meeting at the Navy Office where he was allocated a house but he was still frantic to get his patent sealed. He went back to Mr Beale who now had the patent ready to be sealed by the Lord Chancellor. They went to the Lord Chancellor's and by dint of pressing every influential name he knew, but mostly my Lord's, Sam succeeded in getting his patent sealed in only two hours. He came home to collect me and some money and I waited for him in the coach while he went in to pay Mr Beale his £9. It was a wonderful warm day and I had the coach door open and suddenly Sam was running to me and flung himself and his letters patent on my lap and I was overjoyed.

And then we drove through the streets in the sunshine, babbling to each other about what this would all mean and Sam directed the hackney to Seething Lane and showed me the Navy Office and, next to it, what will be our new house. And I was mad for it at once.

It's part of a very big old house that's been split up. It's much finer than our house in Axe Yard, the ceilings are higher and there are more rooms. We have a cellar and a back yard and a big garden which all the houses share, with walks and fruit trees and all manner of flowers. Above the first floor there is a large flat roof which will be lovely to sit out on because it's high enough to give us a view of the river and the first thing we'll do is build a door from the house on to the leads so we can use it. Although it's in quite good condition the house still needs a lot of work doing to it and my mind is full of ideas for improvements. In truth I can't think about anything else, I'm besotted with it. I started packing as soon as I got home.

We ended that night with great quiet of mind, eating bread and butter in bed.

MID-AUGUST

Mr Barlow eventually appeared. He was old and consumptive and just after whatever gleanings he could get. He settled for £100 a year, and by the look of him it's not going to go on for ever. Elizabeth

Hunt helped us move in. All our things from Axe Yard were sent by cart and we went by coach and spent the day unpacking. In the evening we went out to the nearest cook's and bought a quarter of a lamb and ate our first meal, a poor one because the lamb wasn't cooked enough. Sam had to leave to attend my Lord Mountagu (who is now created the Earl of Sandwich for his service to the King).

The next day our household was increased when Will Hewer came to live with us. He is to be Sam's clerk at the Navy Office and his manservant at home. He's not quite eighteen, well-bestowed in appearance and most respectful to me. I begin to feel like the mistress of a growing establishment, for there's now Sam and me, our maid Jane, the little boy Will, and Sam's man Will Hewer. This all means more food bought, cooked and cleaned up, and of course more washing. In addition, Sam working at the Navy Office right next door to our house means he's nearly always home to dine, and often with guests. I'm very happy with this, but it is a much larger house and there is a great deal to do at the beginning – trying to replace broken irons from the kitchen range for a start, so I have something to cook with.

But the first time that we had family prayers on a Sunday night, with the candles lit in the dining room and with Will Hewer reading a chapter from the Bible and Sam reading from the book of Common Prayer, I knew that all the work was worth it and I thought that this was my home, these were my people, and I loved them with all my heart.

Sam was out a good deal on business and I was working every hour of the day on getting the house

straight so it wasn't a great surprise when my old
trouble recurred and I collapsed into a week of pain
and illness. It was the abscess on the lip of my thing
again, that I had when we were first married. After
a while Sam sent to Dr Williams for some ointment
and he was a bit annoyed when I wasn't cured the
next day. Sometimes husbands seem to take their
wife's illness as a personal affront, though Sam's
much more sympathetic in this respect than many
other men. But then I was well again and we had
pleasant times visiting friends, though Sam drank too
much wine and was then ill himself – at which I was
sympathetic, and I think he learnt a lesson of sorts.

He's been trimmed by the barber at home for
the first time, and he loves to have Jane or little
Will comb through his hair at night. Moving here
hasn't meant any fewer nits, unfortunately. When
he's home in the evening he likes all the family to be
here and was furious with Will Hewer for staying out
till ten o'clock. I found him weeping that he'd upset
Sam and I interceded for him and made it all smooth
again. He's a willing young man, but as master of the
family Sam has to be strict with him, he says.

SEPTEMBER

Now that we're living the other side of London, as
far east as you can get before the Tower, we travel
much more by water. The Navy has its own boats and
boatmen of course. Sam drops me off at one steps or

another to go shopping while he's about his business, if he has to go to Whitehall or Westminster. Often his father accompanies me, if I'm laying out on pewter or something like that. For Sam it's a question of my safety and also having a prudent person there – he doesn't really trust me with money. But last week he was caught out when he'd given me 50 shillings to buy stuff for a new petticoat and his father persuaded me to buy a really fine cloth and some beautiful lace so it came to £5, double what we'd agreed. I went to him at the Privy Seal and confessed it very sweetly and he couldn't help but give way. When I wore it for the first time he said it was very fine but no great show because the cloth was pale and the lace was silver thread. I don't think about making a great show when I buy clothes, I just buy the best quality I can afford and I think there's no harm in colours being subtle. But I didn't say that because it was a Sunday and I try to keep that a peaceful day.

Even so there was a row later on about me leaving my clothes all over our chamber, but I'd had to make dinner for Mr Creed and Sam's brother and when that was all done I didn't want to start tidying up at once. John Creed is clever and knowledgeable – though a sanctimonious puritan – and Sam loves his conversation. However, Mr Creed is in Lord Sandwich's service too and is Sam's principal rival for my Lord's favour, but Sam will never admit that this rivalry sets him on edge, so he must find fault elsewhere. (Me.) But it blew over pretty quickly and we ended the day walking together very pleasantly in the garden.

The other thing that was occupying my time was

that my dear little Fancy has whelped. I was frightened for her because the dog she was with was so big I thought she'd die giving birth. But no, four lovely puppies. I can't help but spend time playing with them. We have had many gifts: four dozen bottles of wine from Captain Bun, a vessel of Margate ale from a purser, a beautiful Turkey carpet and a jar of olives from Captain Cuttance, and especially for me a pair of fine turtle doves from one of Sam's clerks. Sam says it's important not to make any formal acknowledgement of these gifts, but I think my journal is safe enough and sometimes, after all the years of penny-pinching, it feels like manna from Heaven is falling on us and I can hardly believe it's true. Not that we're anywhere near rich, but we're much easier than we've ever been before.

And that makes everything else easier because Sam's out a lot and I'm left to myself. But there's enough to do – finding out that our little boy Will had been stealing took up a great deal of time. Mr Jenkins had left a letter with half-a-crown in it for Sam to send to his son, but it disappeared and the only person who was there at the right time was Will. The next day, before Sam went to work, we both interviewed him about it but he denied everything with such confidence it was hard not to believe him. But later Will Hewer came and told me there was 6 shillings missing from his closet. We searched all the obvious places and eventually I spotted it while I was relieving myself in the house of office, hidden in a crack in the wall. At last, the boy confessed and Sam saw his father who agreed to take him home and never mind the indentures. But that night, while he was still in our house, Jane thought she heard noises downstairs and I was terrified that he was going to come and attack us and kept shaking all night. He went the next morning, sobbing, but tears come cheap to some.

I was asked to be a godmother to Elizabeth Pearse's baby – I suppose she wants to be friendlier for whatever reason – but Sam advised against it because she's profligate and it could mean a great deal of expense so I just stood as proxy for Lady Jemima. It was the first occasion that I've ever worn patches: a tiny diamond, a crescent moon and a heart. I put one on each cheekbone and one near my mouth where there actually was a blemish to be concealed. The blackness shows up my white skin. Sam looked rather taken aback but Jane and Will Hewer both said it looked very well. Elizabeth acknowledged it too, though there had to be a jibe later about how men adored the fashion because it was so much cheaper than a whole new gown. She was wearing a new gown, of course, as well as patches.

Sam's brother and father came to see the new house. Sam was out but I was able to entertain them myself to wine and anchovies. I love having a store cupboard and a cellar that are beginning to be stocked. His mother didn't come because she's been ill for some time with the stone.

Sam has been teaching me music which isn't one of my strengths, but he says I'm much more apt than I think. Harmonious times! All our books have arrived from Axe Yard and he's never happier than when sorting and arranging his books, it makes him calm and content. Though this has not been true in the day when the workmen are here. For the last two weeks the joiners have been laying a new floor in the dining room and making cupboards, and their laziness and the mess they make drive him mad. The house is in a sorry pickle and there's a lot more to do yet.

Even so he brought our neighbour Sir William Penn back for dinner after church last Sunday. He's a Commissioner of the Navy Board and so a colleague of Sam's, a Bristol man who's spent most of his life at sea. He seems sociable but Sam thinks he's cunning. He admired the pearl necklace that I finally persuaded Sam to buy me after many promises. It cost £4 10s but Sam admits to being worth nearly £200 now so I think he can afford it.

The King's younger brother, the Duke of Gloucester, has died of smallpox. It seems as though death is all around. In the last month Aunt Wight has had twin girls, Cousin Strudwick a boy and a girl, and Cousin Scott a boy and all five babies have died. I've been sitting with Sam's mother in her illness and sometimes it all seems like sickbeds and burials for me while Sam's having merry dinners and late nights out. Well, now all the babies are gone please God there won't be any more deaths for a time.

OCTOBER

I saw the Duke of Gloucester's coffin brought down Somerset House stairs to go by water to Westminster. As befitting a grand person it was at night, and the light of all the burning torches reflecting in the water was an awesome sight. And the thought that they would all be plunged into the ground, making sudden darkness. But off with death and on with mourning, which is quite a different matter and very much the mode for fashionable ladies. Sam gave me fifteen pounds to buy mourning for us both then grumbled because I hadn't got good enough value. The trouble is he wants things but it's almost a physical pain for him to have to part with the money for them.

There was a big family dinner at Cousin Scott's. I couldn't believe she'd buried her baby ten days before and now gossiped with her friends so easily. I suppose if you are with child you have to steel yourself to not being attached until the child has a reasonable chance of life, a year perhaps. I don't think I could bear it.

The household has been enlivened by the arrival of young Wayneman, Jane's brother, to be Sam's new boy. Jane has been teaching him how to put Sam to bed, viz. how to comb his hair, where to put his clothes, how to wash his feet on special occasions, how to wash his ears when he wants it done, how to lay out the clean linen for the morning, and so on.

The household has also changed with the arrival of the plasterers. If it was bad before, it's ten times worse now, to the point that I had to make up a bed in the kitchen for me and Sam to sleep in because there was nowhere else habitable in the house. Perhaps the strain of all this was why he gave Will Hewer such a great rebuke for coming in late. I helped to smooth things over the next day. The chief plasterer was called Edward Goodenough and there were endless jokes about the work being or not being good enough. But by the end of September the plastering was finished, with the workmen being cajoled until eleven at night and Sam finding enough drollery in the situation to keep them cheerful.

So that was fine and the kitchen looked so handsome that we couldn't regret the trouble, although everything upstairs was in the most foul state. On the 1st of October the painters moved in. I bought a bed and furniture for our chamber which Sam liked, and I've ordered hangings and curtains. It will be wonderful when it's all finished. In the meantime we live in a hand to mouth sort of way, setting up camp wherever in the house the mess isn't too bad. It seems to have been going on for ever, though it's only just over a month so far. We hope that in another month it will all be over.

Sam's brother Tom has been in trouble with their father. He stayed out all night and then his father wouldn't let him back in to the house so Sam's been trying to make peace between them. He told Tom to mend his ways and warned his father that if he didn't let Tom back he'd just go to ruin outside. Poor Tom, with his stammer, I don't altogether blame him for finding his pleasure where he can. He's supposed to take over their father's tailoring business at some time in the future but I can see trouble there. It's strange how two brothers can be so different in their character and abilities: Sam so organised, always trying to be in control of his life, while Tom drifts and relies on providence to find him a safe berth.

Sam told me a saying that Lord Sandwich's father had written in a book: that if a man married a wench whom he had got with child he should as well shit in his hat and put it on his head. This was about the Duke of York having got the Lord Chancellor's daughter with child. It will cause jealousy at Court if the heir to the throne marries the daughter of the man holding the highest office in the land. Sam says my Lord Sandwich has grown very indifferent in religious matters since being at Court. Lady Sandwich is quite a different matter, all that a lady should be and a sweet, tender soul. Sam dined with her and she reassured him that his Uncle Robert of Brampton is definitely making him his heir.

There was a nasty row between us. He'd been out most of the day and had witnessed General Harrison being hanged, drawn and quartered because he'd signed the death warrant of Charles 1. When Sam and I were first getting to know each other he told me that he'd been quite a Roundhead when he was a boy – at sixteen he'd witnessed the beheading of Charles 1 and had said that day that if he had to preach on it his text would be 'The memory of the wicked shall rot'. These are clearly not words that would commend him to the present King who has ordered a solemn Fast Day on the anniversary of his father's death.

Perhaps this all gave him unquiet thoughts. By the time he arrived home after dining at the Sun he was in a mood to find fault and the fault was that my things were lying about. I'd been trying to sort out what was clean, what was dirty, and what should have been clean but was covered in plaster dust. I hadn't finished so things were strewn about. He shouted about my slatternly ways, I shouted about his time in the taverns. He kicked out furiously at a pile of clothes and in doing so kicked the little Delft ware basket he'd brought me back from Holland and it broke into pieces.

I cried out 'Oh' but I didn't cry any tears. I felt as though something else had broken too, but I couldn't put a name to it. He was very, very sorry. I looked at the broken pieces and thought that things done can't be undone. It was a heavy, sad feeling. This time, by chance, I'd won, but there was no joy in it.

The next day, a Sunday, we were tender with each other. We'd been invited to dine with my Lady at the Wardrobe. (My Lord was dining with the Lord Chamberlain.) She was very gentle and respectful to me, as one woman to another. I talked about the mess from the builders – which Sam was uneasy about because he likes everything to appear perfect to outsiders – and she said she expected exactly the same herself because they are soon to begin extensive alterations at Hinchingbrooke. I like her in all her ways, she seems to me to be a naturally good woman.

NOVEMBER

Will Howe (always a good source of information because he lives with the household) says my Lord is very melancholy because he's lost a great deal of money at cards. Sam dined with them at the Wardrobe and says now he's the Earl of Sandwich he's become the perfect courtier – talks very high, wants a French cook and a Master of his Horse. When my Lady said she'd accept a good merchant, even if he was a citizen not a gentleman, as a husband for Jemima, he swore he'd rather see her with a pedlar's pack on her back. I don't suppose it will quite come to that.

This last fortnight has been wearying. My abscess has come back in the old place making it impossible for me to lie with Sam. Dr Williams has sent ointment that soothes it a little and pills that make me sleepy. I spent my twentieth birthday in bed, reading and dozing. Sam had stayed at my Lord's the night before and was out all day and home very late so it passed unremarked, as usual. But a week later, when I was still ill, he brought home a beautiful old missal and sat beside me and read the prayers that I remembered from when I was at school in Paris at the Ursuline convent and it gave me such pleasure to hear the old words again and know that he wanted to please me.

The house has been up and down. The dining room was finished at last with green serge hangings at the windows and gilt leather on the walls. It looks excellent. The next day, going down to the cellar to show a workman where he wanted a window made into the yard, Sam stepped knee-deep into a pile of turds and found that our neighbour Mr Turner's house of office was full and overflowing into our cellar. It took five days before the men came to clear it and when they did it took them all night. I stuffed rags sprinkled with rosewater under our bedchamber door to try to keep the smell out – not very successfully. Then it was just a question of the workmen making the window, which meant great bangs and thuds ringing through the house.

No sooner was that all finished than our new neighbour, Lady Davies, started up. She's a very proud woman, always talks high. Her husband is also a clerk in the Navy Office and the first thing she did when she moved in was to seal up the door from the leads to our chamber. 'The leads' is part of our kingdom, even though the bulk of it overlies their lodgings, but there had never been any dispute over access until she moved in. Sam was so mad about it he couldn't sleep but when he went to the Comptroller's office to complain, they were all too scared of her to dare to meddle. I'm sure Sam will sort it out somehow – he generally does when things matter enough to him.

The days are so short we have to get up by candlelight. We went to the Pearses' and Sam said he had no objection if I wanted to wear patches. I smiled and thanked him, not reminding him that I'd taken it upon myself to wear patches at the christening two months ago. Men must believe they are masters in their own house.

Gunpowder Plot Day was very much observed this year with lots of bonfires and fireworks. We watched through the windows, and then Sam spent the evening learning about the law from Mr Moore while I sat and sewed, half listening, feeling content. But it couldn't last. Next day we had a row about my little Fancy fouling all over the house and he wanted her kept in the cellar at nights and I refused and wouldn't give in. Mastery is all very well but when it means cruelty to innocent creatures I get upset. We were still a little strange with each other the next day – hardly surprising since his first words on waking were 'Oh, all night I dreamed you were dead.'

It was no joy then to hear from old Mr Bowyer that my brother Balty has left his horse at grass with him in Huntsmoor, citing his family connection with Sam, who was troubled by Balty's boldness on this score and so was I. I visited my parents the next day to lock away some more pages and told them they must talk to him about it. Nothing had come of the letter to Captain Stokes. I know Sam thinks my family is a burden on our marriage, not an asset. That's why I never let him come with me to see them, not that he would want to anyway. Papa has a tiny pension and my mother has a little money from the sale of the house at Bideford, though I doubt there's much left now. They struggle to maintain their gentility. Sometimes, selfishly I suppose, I resent them for not having done better with their lives. Both are of good family, both are intelligent and yet somehow they've failed, and though I love them and want to support them, I'm not willing to be dragged down in their failure. I'm determined to make my own life, as far as I can. Sam fears any generosity towards them will unlease insatiable demands.

But I'm not the only one with a difficult family. I'm very fond of Tom but I have no confidence in his future. And as for his awful sister . . .

It's suggested she should come and live with us – as a servant. I can accept Pall into our household on that basis, and Sam won't consider any other. We'll see what comes of it. Things are going quite smoothly at home at the moment. I've bought a dozen napkins

— our first ever — in a diaper pattern. I tried out the oven with a variety of pies and tarts (the first time the house has been clear enough for me to use the kitchen freely). They burned, but now I have a better idea of the oven's heat so I'll know next time. There are always workmen around. The latest job is to make a doorway from the garden into the entrance. In addition, the washing — oh, never mind, that's always with us.

We visited Lord and Lady Sandwich at the Wardrobe and Sam had other business and had to leave, but I stayed and was able to assist my Lady by interpreting for her while she hired a French maid. I suspect this is my Lord's idea since Lady Sandwich has very little French to speak of. By then it was dinner time and I was invited to dine with them. On my own account! Without Sam being there! I must say my Lord is very gallant when he chooses to be, almost flirtatiously so. I gave him no encouragement in this, being too fond of his wife.

We've also been taken up by our neighbours the Battens — Sir William and his young second wife, a grabbing sort of woman she seemed to me, although he was pleasant enough, a Somerset man. We were both made much of when we went there for supper. In addition I was admitted to the Queen Mother's presence chamber where I was able to stand behind her as she dined, and it was strange to see her footman dip his own bread first into all her dishes, that she might not eat anything bad.

Sam thought I was much more beautiful than Princess Henrietta. All in all, not a bad month.

December

Sometimes he's so unreasonable and like a child in his temper. He beat Jane with a broom until she cried because she didn't have his clean linen ready for Wayneman to lay out for him. He stayed out all day and came home late and fuddled. The next day, Sunday, I'd cooked roast mutton for our dinner and he refused to eat it because the sauce was too sweet, so he just picked at the dish of marrow bone. Of course this had nothing to do with feeling ill from all the wine he'd drunk the night before. A few days later he did it again, came home late and drunk and was vexed that Jane was only just returning from an errand for me, and made it the excuse to go to bed in a great pet.

On this occasion I didn't really care because at last I've got the second volume of *Le Grand Cyrus*. I've read the first volume in French and I've already got the third volume in French and it's taken all my strength not to read them out of sequence. But Mr Kirton sent word that he had the second volume, in English but that doesn't matter, and I practically ran all the way to his shop to get it (and put it on Sam's account, but he never minds when it's books). So instead of troubling myself with Sam's moods I can be in ancient Persia with the valorous, handsome Cyrus, trying to rescue his beloved Mandane from her third? fourth? fifth? abduction by one of his rivals. He is the ideal prince, who loves the victory in battle but not the blood, who is absolute master of his passions, who is serene and sure of himself, gentle and courteous. And I know that Mandane will be snatched from under his nose and he'll have to fight his way to her again. And there are a thousand pages in this volume and another eight volumes to go. What immense pleasure. Sam can go to bed in a pet as often as he likes if it means I can sit by the fire in my closet and read to my heart's content.

Things at home smoothed over, as they do. We went to a very good dinner at Mr Pearse the purser's – he'd asked Mr Pearse the surgeon as well – and their wives. Had an excellent chine of beef and many other dishes and a lot of wine. It was dark by the time we left and we walked home by lantern but the wind was so strong it was hard to make our way and the shop signs rattled on their chains so fiercely we thought at any moment one must fly off and hit us. Tiles were being blown into the street and we were very glad to be back in the safety of our own house.

Early the next morning Sir William Batten called Sam to him and told him the *Assurance* had sunk at Woolwich in the gale, twenty men drowned.

Lady Batten decided we must see this sight so we went down to Woolwich by barge but it was very rough and she was so scared on the water that I wondered why she'd wanted to come at all. (But she is the kind of person who always has to be more scared/surprised/amazed than anyone else.) When we got there it was a very sad sight, only the upper deck and the masts visible and the thought of all those poor sailors drowned below. It was Captain Stokes's ship so I thanked God Balty's attempt at employment there had been unsuccessful. Lady Batten was of course deeply affected by it all. She insisted she was much too frightened to return to London and I had to stay with her for two nights until the water was calmer.

Sir William Batten and Sam had gone back the same day and Sam seemed to have missed me when we were all reunited at Lady B.'s house for dinner. Another guest was Captain Robert Holmes – I haven't seen him for a long time – and he managed a couple of rogueish glances despite Sam being there and asked me if I ever wore a certain necklace. And I said it was a treasured possession, but nothing about whether I wore it or not. He's commanding an expedition to West Africa. I always knew he'd do well. But I'm sure Sam is a much better husband than he could ever have been.

Meanwhile the workmen have been painting the parlour, then gilding it and then painting the arch over the door, and Sam kept on and on at them so that they'd be finished by Christmas. The Princess Royal has died of smallpox. Poor soul, it was only a few weeks ago that I'd watched her eating and drinking, perfectly sound, in the presence chamber. (Yet in truth I was more concerned with getting the workmen out.)

But by Christmas Day we were clean and clear and we had Tom to dine with us on a good shoulder of mutton and a chicken. I'd decorated the dining room with holly and ivy and rosemary – it looked very pretty. We both went to church in the afternoon and dozed through a very dull sermon and then Sam spent the evening in his closet reading Bishop Fuller's *Church*

History and playing his lute and I spent the evening in my closet reading *Cyrus*, even though it was a holy day and I should have been reading something worthier.

And now it's the last night of the year. Sam has been out all day and I don't expect him before bedtime. He sent Wayneman home earlier with a cat for me from Sarah, my Lord's housekeeper. He's supposed to be a splendid mouser so I hope he'll earn his keep, we're overrun with them. I wish the Hunts were still across the yard and I could run over to them. The Battens are friends, but not in the simple, good-hearted way that the Hunts are.

So much has happened this year – except the one thing that would have made my cup overflowing – but I pray God that Sam and I may continue our life together in good health and contentment (most of the time).

1661

January

We started off the year with a breakfast for Tom, Sam's father, Uncle Fenner and the Joyce brothers. (Uncle Fenner told Sam's father he was so concerned with the way William and Mary Joyce were always fighting each other that he had a mind to see them divorced.) Anthony Joyce's only child had died that morning but he insisted on coming and seemed merry enough. We had a barrel of oysters, a dish of tongue and a dish of anchovies, with plenty of wine and beer. At noon we went to Cousin Thomas Pepys's for dinner where we dined with more of the family, Dr Thomas, the Strudwicks and the Scotts. There was only ordinary meat, no venison, which we thought a poor show for a man of his estate. Then we went to Surgeon and Elizabeth Pearse for supper where we had a carbonade of calf's head but so raw we couldn't eat it. I couldn't help pointing out the dark tide mark on her neck to Sam. He said later she was such a slut in her personal habits he couldn't enjoy her food. This comment gave me a quite ridiculous feeling of satisfaction.

Pall joined the household but Sam wouldn't let her sit at table with us so she understood without any question that she was here as a servant not a friend or companion. Accordingly she didn't join us when on Twelfth Day we went to the theatre with her brother Tom and then supped at Cousin Strudwicke's, but Sam gave the servants a shilling to buy a cake for themselves. When we cut our cake, the pea was cut in half and I shared the title of Queen with Mrs Ward, but we couldn't find the bean at all so we elected Dr Pepys and made him send out for more wine. Arriving home we found the servants had invited neighbouring servants in and even young Mr Davies, Lady Davies's son. Apparently she takes it ill that I don't visit her but I don't see why I should be civil to someone who is so uncivil herself, even though the matter of our access to the leads has been resolved.

Sam and I have had rows about me not being neat enough now I have two servants. One time when he came home after an overnight trip to Chatham he found the monkey loose and flew into a terrible temper and beat her till she was half dead. I don't understand how sometimes he can walk through the door and have lost his temper before he's even taken his coat off.

But there've been happy times as well. We've had our first proper dinner since being here, with the Battens and Sir William Penn and Captain Cuttance. The only problem was that the chimney in the dining room smoked and Sam was rather taken aback that the food and wine and candles cost him £5. Two days later we had the Pearses and Captain Cuttance and Lieutenant Lambert who was with Sam on the

Naseby when they went to Holland to bring the King back. He confessed he was lately married so we had some fun pulling off his ribbons and garters, though not to excess.

I went to a merry dinner at the Hunts'. Sam was dining with Lady Sandwich so he called for me later – walking in just as we were playing forfeits and their French lodger was kissing me. It was innocent enough fun, Sam had to admit there was nothing in it, but an incident like that makes him realise that he has a pearl of some price in his keeping. That sounds vain but I have to believe I'm worth something.

We've seen lots of the Battens, dinners and suppers backwards and forwards, and Lady B. and I went to see Oliver Cromwell's corpse being hanged at Tyburn. It – he? – it's hard to know – had been embalmed and was shrouded, but recognisably a man. We didn't stay until sunset when they brought him down and cut his head off to be impaled at Westminster Hall. His body was buried under the scaffold. What an end. For most of my life he was the Protector and now he's worse than nothing, the birds pecking his skull clean.

FEBRUARY

We've been talking about perhaps going into France this summer. I would so love to see Paris again. I remember walking down the streets, so innocent, the last years of my childhood, and the smell of polish in the convent. Too short a while. I liked the calm order of those days and the richness of the Mass, Father Fogarty's thick black hair and his deep strong voice. I wish my father had let me stay there longer.

In the end I even came to revere Sister Pauline, who threw my work in my face with, 'These aren't hemming stitches, they're eagles' claws.' Inwardly I growled, but within a few months I could sew beautifully and her severity gave me that skill for life.

We had an excellent Valentine's Day. The evening before, Sam had sent for me to come to Sir William Batten's where he was at supper and we all chose our Valentines for the next day. I chose Sam which pleased him no end. On the day itself we got up early and Sam knocked on the Battens' door and when Mingo their blackamoor came to answer it Sam asked if it was a man or a woman and Mingo put on a funny voice and said a woman, so Sam pretended Mingo must be his Valentine which caused some merriment. Then Sam went in and claimed Martha Batten, their daughter, as his Valentine, and Sir William came out and claimed me as his.

At ten o'clock we all embarked on the Navy barge and went down to Deptford to see how Mr Pett's yacht that he's building is coming on, and then we continued to Woolwich, to Captain Brown's ship, the *Rosebush*. He's Sir William's brother-in-law so we were very well received and had a fine dinner that had been cooked ashore. It was the first time I'd ever been on a sailing ship – they were soon to leave for Jamaica – and Sam showed me over it as proudly as if it were his own. It was pretty to hear how he came out with the proper names for all the different bits – the fruit of his recent study. He was proud of young Wayneman, too, who carried a sword like his master and was referred to all day as 'young Pepys'. (Sir William Penn's boy is called 'young Penn' but Wayneman is much smarter and better looking.) All the talk was of who the King will have for his Queen and whether Lent will be able to be observed as strictly as the King wishes, because the poor people cannot afford to buy fish and will have to buy some meat or starve.

We came back again by barge when it was growing dark and it was calm but very cold on the river. Sometimes the Navy seems like a big family and I love it.

Sam took me and Martha Batten to the Exchange to buy her Valentine gift. He spent 40 shillings on one pair of embroidered and six pairs of plain white gloves for her. While he was in a spending mood I ordered a lustrous silk suit for myself – I'll need something to wear when I watch the Coronation procession. My Valentine, Sir William, sent me half a dozen pairs of gloves and a pair of silk stockings and garters. There are scaffolds being set up all along the Coronation route, and even though it's another two months yet, there's a feeling of great cheer in the streets.

∞

April

There's plenty of time to write because I'm staying at Salisbury Court with Sam's parents while the workmen are making a new staircase at home. I stayed there for the first week but in the end the noise and dirt were beyond bearing so I moved here with Pall. And here I'm stuck for the moment, with my mother-in-law alternately moaning (about the maid, about the laundry, about the dog – there's always something) or screaming at her husband or Tom or Pall about her hard life, their lack of gratitude, her ill health, etc, etc. She doesn't attack me directly because we have an understanding that we don't get on, so we simply avoid or ignore each other. Pall, of course, is not a servant here but the daughter of the house and she takes every chance to flounce around in her ungainly way. Poor Tom's stammer is always worse when he's with his family, but he can't help that.

So it's not altogether surprising that Sam chooses not to lie here himself. He must stay at home to supervise the workmen. He looks in to Salisbury Court when it suits. That is, when he's short of a supper elsewhere.

I should try not to be so cynical. He isn't all of my life.

I've had my teeth scaled – very painful but effective, they're much whiter. What else? We saw a lot of the Battens and we had the Stone Dinner to celebrate Sam surviving his operation three years ago. Elizabeth Hunt is terribly worried about John's position, I fell over and hurt my knees, my mother has been ill, Sam has been away on a jaunt to Chatham on which Lady Batten was allowed to accompany her husband but Sam chose not to invite me to join them. And so round to him again.

∞

APRIL GOES ON

It all came to a head, thank goodness. His brother John had come down from Cambridge and on Good Friday morning at seven we both went to Seething Lane to see Sam. He was polite, but sent us on our way because he had to go to the office. I next saw him on Easter Sunday when he appeared at Salisbury Court for dinner. After dinner he must be off to the Temple to hear another sermon and then he saw Mr Moore and went to my Lord's with him. There he heard Mr Barnwell was in town to bring my Lord's children to see the Coronation so he must drink with him at the Goat for a good while and then he turned up here for supper.

And all through supper we were awkward with each other, and Pall was gloating and Tom trying to make things better but making them worse. And we were picking holes in each other's coats – it was mad, we both knew it but we couldn't get ourselves out of it.

Sam: Then you won't be wanting me to stay the night?

Me: It's not what I want, it's what you want.

Sam: If you want me to go then I'll go.

Me: If that's what you want to do.

Sam: If it's what you want me to do.

Me: But I think it's always really what you want to do.

Sam: Then I'll go.

I ran up to my chamber and fell on the bed and wept.

But then I lifted my head up and heard the rain at the window and thought of him walking home through it and suddenly I had to be out in it myself, out of this suffocating house and with him, and I ran downstairs and out of the door (his mother shouting 'You'll catch your death, then you'll be sorry'; Pall standing shocked and silent for once).

I didn't care about any of them, running through the rain in the dark, holding my skirts up, I couldn't be stopped, nobody got in my way, nobody tried to take the wall from me, the rain cooled my heat so I could simply run. I heard the signboards swinging overhead, red light from latticed tavern windows shone out on the raindrops, they looked like rubies and I thought this is my life, here, now, with him. Though I knew what his route would be I was afraid of losing him and when I came out on to Fleet Bridge and saw him ahead of me, bowed against the rain, I thanked God and ran up to him but he didn't hear my voice in the wind so I plucked his sleeve and he looked round in alarm and then he saw it was me and a look came over his face – a look that is all why I love him – and he held me very tight and we kissed and told each other our love.

Back at Salisbury Court nobody dared say a word. Sam said that we must go to our chamber to take off our wet clothes and that is what we did and Sam shut the door very firmly and we resolved our differences in the way that couples have done since Adam and Eve.

Since then he's stayed the night much oftener. Even so, we spent the days of the King's Procession and the Coronation apart. I got up very early so Jane could dress me in my new lustre suit. Sam watched the Royal entry with the Penns and the Battens, while I went to his Cousin Charles in Fleet Street where we had an excellent view. The route ran from the Tower to Whitehall, and all along it the buildings were hung with beautiful tapestries and all the streets were gravelled. The finery of the King and the Court was beyond imagination – gold and silver threadwork with diamonds everywhere, in the end it hurt our eyes to look at it. Even the horses wore jewelled cloths. It must have been a great emotion for the King to receive the adulation of his people after his privations and exile but he didn't show it, just smiled calmly. My Lord the Earl of Sandwich smiled up at me as he rode past – his suit alone cost £200.

The next day, at the Coronation, Sam managed to secure himself a place in the Abbey, though not one where he could see the actual crowning. Like many other ladies, I had a seat on the scaffolding in Westminster Hall from where we could watch the King dine. His retinue was the same as the Procession the day before, but even finer, if possible. He entered wearing his crown and carrying his sceptre, with his nobles in their ermine gowns. The Barons of the

Cinque Ports held a canopy above him with little bells on the fringes. Eventually they all reached their tables and sat down. The Lord High Constable, the Earl Marshal and the Lord High Steward appeared on horseback and stayed mounted throughout the meal. And then there was the dramatic appearance of the King's Champion in full armour on horseback while a herald proclaimed that if anyone denied Charles Stuart to be King of England, here was a Champion that would fight him, and at those words the Champion flung down his gauntlet. This happened three times as he approached the King. (Needless to say no one took up the gauntlet.)

The dinner went on until six. One thing happened that was slightly disorderly, when the King's footmen somehow got hold of the canopy and the Cinque Port barons tried to wrest it back and the bells were tinkling like mad. I couldn't help finding it funny. Apparently the King ordered the footmen to be sacked and imprisoned. The rain, which everyone had been fearful of, had held off for two days and it seemed miraculous timing that just when the King had left the Hall to enter his coach, the heavens should suddenly open and there was the most terrific thunderstorm. Some take this as a good omen and some as a bad one. I just think there was a thunderstorm.

Sam came to find me and we went to the Bowyers' afterwards, with a lot of other company, and stood on the leads waiting for the fireworks but there weren't any that night. But the City had almost a halo round it, with the bonfires. I was to stay the night with the Hunts – we knew in advance it would be impossible to get a coach – and when we got to Axe Yard there were three great bonfires burning and lots of gallants, men and women, who insisted we must drink the King's health, kneeling, which we did. They drank prodigious amounts and after a while I retired to bed. Sam stayed the course and reported that several of them simply fell down on the ground, dead drunk.

So that was the Coronation, and I feel privileged to have lived in this city at this time and to have seen such a glorious sight.

MAY

An early summer evening. The last night of a five-day trip to Portsmouth made with the Hayters and John Creed. The men making payments and conducting sales of surplus goods, Mrs Hayter and I walking on the ramparts. Everywhere most respectfully received. Good meals, games of bowls. We're in Guildford, staying at a very pretty inn with a big garden. A fine dinner. Afterwards we sit outside and Sam and John Creed spend the afternoon seeing who can jump best over an old wall. Inevitably what begins as a game becomes a competition – though unacknowledged – and they both get hot and tired.

We have our supper in the summerhouse. A scent of May blossom. The beginning of the long, warm summer evenings. White roses in the twilight, honeysuckle tumbling over the roof. But there's a sense of weariness, we've all seen too much of each other. I'd like to be alone here with a book.

The conversation turns to Elizabeth Pearse, of all the stupid things; sitting in this rural tranquillity and we have to bring her in, the essence of artifice and city tricks. Is she a beauty or is she not? Is she or isn't she a slut? Sam calls her a slut as though that excuses his freeness with her. He says I'm a fool to be jealous.

(She's pregnant again.)

It's almost as though we love to argue about her, like picking at a scab. And John Creed is present, enjoying this silly married couple's dispute. And that makes both of us more emphatic than we might have been, as though we're each putting our case up for his judgement, although he's much too clever to take sides.

Things didn't get any better when we arrived home and found that no progress whatever had been made on the house while we were away. It was still a filthy mess so I was despatched to Salisbury Court again. But this time I only stayed two nights. Having been away from it all for a week I couldn't bear listening to his mother's mad pettiness and Tom arguing with his father all the time and being disrespectful to him. As well as all this I had a terrible toothache so I had to go to the dentist and have it drawn – agonising pain and a terrible crunching noise and I felt so bad afterwards that the only solace I could think of was to be in my own home, no matter how disordered it was.

And it was. And by now I felt my abscess coming up again in the old place and Sam was furious with me for turning up in such a state but I ignored him and took to our bed and I don't know which end of me hurt most. I stayed in bed for four days while the hole in my gum healed but the abscess got worse and worse and the pain drove me mad until it finally burst and the matter started coming out and the relief was wonderful. Dr Williams sent over a wad of cotton to put in the wound to keep it open and let everything drain out, and Sam inserted it for me, so gently.

And now at the end of the month the joiners have finished and I've recovered, and that's good enough.

JUNE

It's been so hot it's stewed my brains. I've passed the time in a sort of haze though Sam has been busy seeing my Lord off to Portugal to collect Catherine of Braganza, the King's bride. He's supposed to sort out Tangier as well, I think.

We've had some beautiful evenings sitting and walking out on the leads. (The vile Lady Davies has been despatched to Ireland with her husband so there's no trouble from her any more.) One night Sir William Penn joined us in his shirt and we stayed out till midnight drinking claret and eating fish roe and bread and butter, singing and Sam playing his flageolet. The scent of the garden wafted up, the Madonna lilies still white in the gathering dusk – it was barely dark when we went to bed, the evening seemed to stretch out magically. And the damask roses and our herbs and the new pots of pinks all joined to smother the smell of the city. It was like a little time in Heaven.

The news at the end of the month was that Uncle Robert Pepys of Brampton is very seriously ill with dizziness and Sam's father has gone down to look after his affairs. Sam, his heir, said thoughtfully, God's will be done. And what else can one say?

We have moved our bedchamber to the room we once called the nursery. God's will be done.

July

The news from Brampton was that Uncle Robert seemed by fits stupid, or drunk, or speechless. He wasn't expected to last long. We had a good supper at the Battens' – venison pasty, all very merry – and the next day the news arrived that Uncle Robert was dead. Sam left for Brampton as soon as he could, for once not worrying about leaving me on my own in London. When he arrived, the coffin was smelling so badly he had to have it put outdoors and watched over by two men. His aunt – the widow – was in bed, hysterical, having been left nothing. (It seems Uncle Robert never forgave her for not producing the £200 jointure she was supposed to bring to the marriage. These Pepyses don't forget debts.)

The will, as expected, leaves the house to Sam's father and then to him. Then there are various bequests and legacies, which are outnumbered by the debts and the whole estate's in the most awful pickle and is going to take a long time to sort out. Sam says Hinchingbrooke is all in a state of dirt because of the building work there, which my Lady confirmed when she came to visit me while he was away. She said she'd love to be in the country now but it's impossible for a while because of the mess.

Sam was back in London in time for us to celebrate my Lord's birthday while he was absent in Portugal. We were invited to dine with my Lady at the Wardrobe, and among others there was Lady Jane Ferrer, Captain Ferrer's wife. She's the sister of a Scottish earl and her family disinherited her for marrying beneath her. A lively, charming lady. I only know Captain Ferrer by repute so far – that he's my Lord's newly appointed Master of Horse and that he was involved in a stupid wager with Sam that ended with him for some reason leaping off a very high balcony – the greatest and most desperate frolic he'd ever seen, Sam said. Although Captain Ferrer didn't break anything he injured his back so badly he couldn't walk for several weeks. When I asked his wife how he did, she just raised her eyebrows and slightly shook her head in the manner of one who knows that with a husband like that there are still many bridges to cross (not to mention balconies to jump off). I am slightly intrigued by him to tell the truth, perhaps more so because we haven't met yet.

We took my Lady's daughters, Jemima and Paulina, home with us for a visit. For once we went under London Bridge which I'm usually too afraid to do. Even though it was very calm and the river was at standing water, the currents swirling round the piers looked so treacherous that it needed all of

Sam's confidence to calm us. In the event it was so easy that we took the girls back the same way. But even Sam admits that he wouldn't do it at high water and gets off and walks round like everyone else.

Home has its own problems, or rather Sam's family. His sister Pall took the opportunity of Uncle Robert's death to suddenly pretend a great affection for him, and Sam's absence at Brampton was the occasion for her to become lazier and prouder than ever. In addition Tom insists that he will only set up business in Salisbury Court, nowhere else (assuming their parents now retire to Brampton). Sam thinks the house is too big for him and he won't make a go of it. On top of that his mother is spending money hand over fist in quite unrealistic expectations of her lot from Uncle Robert's estate.

The only time Sam – and thus the household – is truly happy is when Mr Goodgroome comes to give him his singing lesson. At those times we are all content to know that he is home and in good humour. And the singing sounds quite good, sometimes.

August

Our friends – to some extent – and neighbours, Sir William and Lady Batten, took us to Walthamstow for a day in the country. He has a house there, left to him by his first wife. The occasion was to visit a neighbour there who was lying in. Sir William Penn was also of the party and Peg, his daughter, just returned from

Ireland (and not at all the beauty she was said to be, to Sam's disappointment). While we were there we heard a story from the nurse's husband that Lady Batten was a certain man's whore, and that he'd left her his estate. We knew she'd been left an estate but nobody had known the details, and try as we might, we couldn't find out more. It comes as no surprise to me that she's been any man's whore – I care for her less and less the better I know her.

We've been able to do my Lady some service. Her eldest son fell sick of the smallpox and she was very concerned to move her younger sons away from him. As a rule they would have gone down to their country house at Hinchingbrooke but the building work there makes that impossible at the moment. Her Ladyship asked me to dine and we settled very quickly that Lord Hinchingbrooke would stay with her at the Wardrobe, where she could nurse him, and the three younger brothers would come and stay with us at Seething Lane. What made it all the more troubling was news that Lord Sandwich was severely ill with a fever, ashore at Alicante. My Lady wasn't told of this, for being about to give birth it was thought she couldn't bear any more strain. When the news came that he was recovering, only then was she told, and wept tears of fear and relief. Young Lord Hinchingbrooke was getting better as well and within a few days my Lady was brought to bed of a healthy girl, her tenth child. Thank God they all go well.

I missed the boys when they went. We had some merry dinners at home and I took them to see the lions in the Tower. Even better was seeing the baboon Captain Holmes brought back from Guinea. It looks so like a man we thought it must be a monster got by a man on a she-baboon. They say it already understands much English and might in time be taught to speak.

The day they left, news came that Aunt Fenner had died – the mother-in-law of the Joyce brothers is the only way I can think of her, she was unremarkable otherwise. We went to the burial of course, a lot of people there but a pretty mean affair. We wore our own mourning clothes to do Uncle Fenner the honour of letting the world think he had bought them for us but William Joyce wasn't slow to complain about his father-in-law's meanness in giving us nothing, not even a pair of gloves. We left as soon as we decently could and went to Aunt Wight's for supper. (An excellent Westphalian ham.)

It's been all family this month. A possible wife has been proposed for brother Tom. She's the daughter of a Mrs Wheatley who offers £200 with her, though she fears her daughter may be too young. Sam says the girl is well-favoured but modest and would do very well for Tom. A good wife would certainly be the saving of him. And a good husband would be the saving of Pall. As it is, she makes us mad and Sam's determined that she must leave us – which means high words with his mother and father. And then my family intervened in our life in the shape of Balty in desperately poor condition, begging me to ask Sam to find something for him and I have tried my best, tears etc., but I know that Sam's reluctant to get involved because he's afraid there'd be no end to it. But when I wake up in the morning Balty's problems are the first thing on my mind – this is not a cheerful start to the day.

I'm told Lady Batten looks askew on me because I don't buckle to her. Good. I haven't much regard for women who make their way by battening (how very appropriate) on to successive men.

Not as good: that our maid Jane Birch has left us after three years to go back to her mother in the country. Even though Pall has done her best to make her lazy and spoiled, I doubt that we'll easily find her like again. We all cried. But sometimes people must go away to grow up. I know that from my own life.

The dog days of August are always a wearisome time; this year the city was stinking in the heat as usual but there were also strange fevers everywhere. Sam's office had no money to conduct business and Ned Pickering reported the Court had no money to pay bills but plenty for drinking and whoring.

One satisfying thing happened to me though – just me. We went to the theatre and I met Thomas Somerset again.

The last time I saw Thomas was in Paris when I was thirteen and he was a fine looking boy with the noble manners you'd expect of Lord John Somerset's son and now, eight years on, he's a fine looking man. He saw me first and came over and was full of compliments for how the little girl had grown into a woman. I introduced him to Sam who made it very plain he didn't intend to further the acquaintance. The play was a French comedy, very poorly done – Thomas and I kept exchanging glances of private merriment at how bad it was (but very carefully on my part). He asked me how I spent my time and I said I kept my house and cooked and went to market –

and that I would be at the New Exchange on Monday buying some goods for myself.

We left before the farce, Sam said it was so bad it was making him physically sick. I didn't show what a good mood I was in. It lasted all weekend. There was a huge rainstorm on Saturday night and on Sunday morning we found that one of the gutters was blocked and the rain had got in and ruined some of the ceilings. Even the prospect of having the painters in again didn't trouble me.

I got up early on Monday and spent all morning baking pies. (If my housewifery is beyond reproach then perhaps I'm allowed to talk to an old friend without my husband's disapproving presence.) When I got to the Exchange I saw him at once in the upper gallery, but I pretended I hadn't, and waited for him to catch sight of me as I walked round the booths downstairs, looking at ribbons and lace and gloves. And then what should happen but I turned a corner and there were my Lady's daughters. They fell on me for advice about a lace collar Jemima wanted to buy, so we went to look at collars and suddenly he was there, remarking on the coincidence that we should meet again so soon. I think I was composed enough not to blush. He thoroughly charmed the girls, even the ill-disposed Paulina, to the point that they wouldn't leave us and he insisted on asking their help in choosing a little bracelet (of linked silver rings) for him to give me. It wasn't quite how I'd imagined it would be but in the end I was glad that everything was above board and I could show Sam the bracelet in all innocence. I was still with the girls when we parted from Thomas at the Exchange, so nothing further was said, just how very pleasant to have met you again, things like that. I went home feeling half happy and half not.

However I was happy enough when Pall and Sam's mother finally left for Brampton where they'll live with his father. I know there are worries about Tom taking on the business at Salisbury Court, but it will be a great relief to me to have the rest of them out of the way in the country.

Sam and I went to Bartholomew Fair — I always think of it as marking the end of summer. We saw the Italian dancing on the tightropes and the women doing tumbling tricks and the monkeys on sticks. On our way a French footman intercepted me and asked if I would meet a certain person tomorrow at a certain small inn and I said I would. Sam was deeply suspicious of course but I said it was simply an arrangement to see a friend — he cannot deny a lady that freedom. It troubled him, but then I'm endlessly troubled with his staying out and being free with ladies so I didn't make anything of it, either to gloat or to apologise.

The next day Uncle Fenner came to us for his morning draught of ale and then took Sam to see dying Aunt Kite. They seemed to expect me to cancel my engagement and go with them. She's the widow of Sam's mother's brother, a butcher, and since I have very little to say to his mother I have even less to say to her sister-in-law. I'm satisfied I've done my duty in terms of his family, so I went off to my assignation with a clear conscience, leaving Sam troubled and angry.

It was raining, I couldn't get a coach and my hair

was glistening wet – like diamonds, Thomas said – when I finally arrived at the inn where we'd arranged to meet. We dined together and talked of the old times in Paris, people we used to know, the places we went to. It was all without guile, just that I couldn't have talked so freely or enjoyed myself so much if Sam had been there.

Thomas leaves London tomorrow. It has been a pleasant interlude for us both and no harm done and there's an end of it. The main thing that made me want to see him again was that he reminded me of that time before I was an adult, those idyllic last years of childhood in Paris, when it seemed anything in the world was possible.

SEPTEMBER (UNENCUMBERED BY ROMANTIC FIGURES FROM THE PAST)

The sun begins to sink lower in the sky.

Balty's been round, looking as fine as hands can make him, with a French servant in tow. This is typical of him – from rags to riches overnight, and back to rags again soon enough if I know anything. He came to tell us that he had a new mistress, young, handsome and rich, and he was determined to marry her. He took me to visit her. On the way I asked him how he had acquired his fine clothes and he was evasive, he'd done someone a service. The young lady was all that he claimed but she had in addition a guardian who seemed to me most unlikely to give her to an unpropertied man with no income. As usual, nothing will come of it.

We've been to Brampton so Sam could sort out the copyholds on the lands left him via his father, in the will. Various members of the family are making different claims and it's driving him to complete vexation. I went with him on the spur of the moment, riding side saddle all the way. I fell off on the first day but no great harm done. A merry supper at Ware and slept soundly but woke the next day very stiff and sore. The second day's riding was much harder, the road bad and muddy and I took another fall, this time into the dirt, and felt very miserable and Sam got impatient with me. Sometimes my strength just seems to give out – he acknowledges I'm an excellent travelling companion as long as I'm well, I just can't be well for long enough.

Sam went to the local court and saw stewards and bailiffs and agents and relatives until everything was more or less decided. Much more interesting for me was the game of what alterations I'd make to the house and how I'd furnish it if it were mine and money were no problem. Sam likes playing this too – sometimes we lie in bed in Seething Lane and imagine we've been given the house next door as well as our own and we talk about which walls to pull down and where to have the staircases. So far as the Brampton house went we could make real plans so we decided to start with the kitchen and knock out two or three old cupboards to make a decent sized pantry, and block off one of the doorways so we can have a dresser made to fit. That will do to be going on with while we think about the rest.

On the way back we stayed the night at Welwyn and for the first time slept in the same room but in two single beds. We were very tired but even so I woke several times with the noise of the rain and people moving about, yet each time I felt wonderfully contented and floated back down to a deep sleep. In the morning we both agreed it was the best night's sleep we'd ever had. (But I think we won't make a habit of it at home.)

My Lord sent melons and grapes from Portugal, the first melons I've ever seen. I would never have imagined one single piece of fruit could be so big. We ate some when the Penns dined with us on Sunday, and we supped with them and Sam drank so much wine during the day that he was too drunk to take prayers at home that night in case the servants realised his condition. The first time we've not had family prayers on a Sunday night.

Lots of firsts, and another one is that I'm to have singing lessons with Mr Goodgroome.

OCTOBER

Servant problems. They don't like the Somerset cheese – too hard for them. Unfortunately we have a large round of it and I'm determined it will be eaten before I buy any more. Doll works quite well but is always angry, can't hold her peace. Nell is droll and lazy. Mary left after a month. Will Hewer has taken to wearing his hat indoors, like a gentleman. Sam called it a proud trick and gave him a sound lesson in respect for his master and mistress (though he thinks well of him in most ways and I don't find him disrespectful at all, indeed I'd be very sorry to lose him).

It's interesting that the sound lesson was given after a trying episode between ourselves. We'd dined at the Wardrobe – that was no hardship, with a good venison pasty and my Lady feeling merry and looking well after her lying-in. Then Sam and I went to the theatre to see *Love and Honour* (he for the third time this week and I think it was one time too many and he was angry with himself for wasting his money). On the way out we bumped into Eliz Pearse and her friend Mrs Clifford (both in paint and patches while I'm still in mourning for Uncle Robert and my mourning suit three months old and so worn Sam's ashamed to be seen with me). Oddly enough I would much rather encounter my Lady, the Countess of Sandwich, in these shabby clothes than I would Mrs E. Pearse. My Lady has no need to mock.

Sam of course had to stay and talk and talk and talk to them until I thought I would go mad and I insisted on going home but he made it clear he was discontented. And when we got home that was the moment he chose to give Will Hewer his lesson in respect. It's all of a piece.

We celebrated our sixth wedding anniversary – the religious not the civil. We had a pleasant night together but not quite as merry as we'd intended because Sam had a swollen testicle which happens to him now and again, we're not sure why. I made up a poultice according to Dr Burnet's instructions: a good handful of bran, half a pint of vinegar and a pint of water all boiled together till thick, then a spoonful of honey added and all wrapped up in a cloth and laid on his cod, repeated several times over the next two days. It worked.

I went to my Lady's to dine and ended up staying the night, sleeping with Mlle le Blanc, the girls' governess. I get on with her very well. We talk in French, things that we might not say in English. (My Lord's roving eye for example.) My Lady is very forthright that Sam must be made to buy me more clothes, and I'm in complete agreement.

NOVEMBER

Sir William Penn came to supper after the theatre with Sam and they sent for his son William to join us – he's just been sent down from Oxford for inciting a riot against surplices. We were merry until very late. Young William is a fine looking youth, very intense about his Puritan beliefs, but in a rather charming way, as though his hair curls against his best effort. I'll be interested to see what path he takes in life. I think whatever he does he'll make his mark.

My Lady has spoken delicately to Sam about laying out more money on my clothes – he has promised me a laced gold-thread collar.

Another Sunday spent mostly apart, with him too fuddled at the end of it to take family prayers in the evening. The next day I collected some samples of lace and went to the Wardrobe to show them to my

Lady. We spent hours looking over them and looking at her clothes and talking about a lady's requirements. She urged me to choose the lace without regard to cost, she said I deserved the one that would make me happy. I think she knows that life with Sam isn't always easy (though I never specify, and wouldn't). I was looking forward to seeing how Sam would react when he turned up, and he didn't disappoint.

My Lady brought out the piece we had chosen and pointed out the delicacy of the thread work. He agreed that it was very fine. We all know that he's a man who prides himself on his discrimination, it's what makes him a gentleman, and he'd die rather than appear anything else to my Lady. But he knows that discriminating taste costs more than plain. After some more time spent admiring it he said that I must have it. He had no choice.

So it came to the burning question – how much? – and he tried to make his voice casual but it came out slightly strangled. My Lady told him £6 and there was a wonderful pantomime of expressions on his face as he swallowed a gulp and pretended to be surprised it was not more, but the strain in his voice showed he thought it was far too much. Never mind, the moment was served.

Later, at home, there was muttering about the dire consequences of his prodigality. But why is it only my expenditure that is profligate, when he spends far more on himself? What is truly absurd is that when the collar has been made and I'm wearing it he'll be proud and delighted at how fine I look and the compliments I get. So why is it so painful for him to lay out money for me, as though it's the final breach in the wall and we'll be overrun by poverty and dishonour?

But I have my collar, that's the main thing. John Hunt admired it when he called on me. (Sam was put out when he came home and found us sitting together in the bedchamber but he calmed down when he realised it was washing day and there was no fire anywhere else so we didn't have any choice.) I wore it later that day to a christening at Cousin Scott's and again to a dinner at the Dolphin with the Battens and Captain Cocke and his wife, very merry with music and dancing. And of course I showed it to my Lady at the Wardrobe and Captain Ferrer was there too, so I met him at last and he was just as dashing and charming as I'd imagined and he paid me extravagant compliments (the famous lace collar, very fine, but not as fine as the skin beneath it, etc.). After dinner he and I and Mlle le Blanc met Sam at the theatre and during the hour before the performance I felt as fine as any lady there.

December

Ups and downs. Staying in bed late on cold mornings (while Parliament is sitting, the Board doesn't meet until the afternoons). A good new servant, Sarah, but Nell more cross-grained than ever. Sitting for our joint portrait by Mr Savill. A good likeness. Strange how a picture of yourself makes you feel more real suddenly – proof that you were alive at such a moment and this is what you looked like. Good dinners at home – Captain Cocke sent me a jar of gherkins, the first I've ever seen, delicious. We ate some raw with brawn and I've used some chopped fine in a sauce. It was a sad day when we ate the last one.

A good breakfast: Captain Ferrer comes to take his leave. He's going to Lisbon with the fleet that will meet the Earl of Sandwich and escort our new Queen home. He's with a German who is a footman to my Lord though apparently he deserves much better. I'm still in bed. The German is an accomplished lute player and they come up to my bedchamber and he plays on Sam's lute, beautifully, while Robert Ferrer teases me about the lace collar, why I'm not wearing it in bed, even more beautiful without it, lovely, silly stuff and I feel like the cat that's got the cream.

They leave me to dress and I put on my favourite loose morning gown and when I come down there's a breakfast of mince pie and brawn and wine and we're all very merry and at last the gentlemen make their farewells. Sam and I fall to talking of other things and not fifteen minutes later there is a commotion outside the door and the German falls back into the house, covered in blood. What's happened? He fears Captain Ferrer has been killed by some watermen at the Tower Stairs. Sam and I look at each other in alarm and Sam runs to Tower Stairs while I care for the German who is shaking. I dress the wound on his head and hold his head against my breast and pray that Robert Ferrer isn't dead. It feels strange to have a man in my arms who isn't my husband. This man's body is longer and thinner, even the curve of his spine is different. Sam comes back with the story: the watermen were rudely pressing Captain Ferrer to take him to his vessel, he struck one of them with his cane, they struck back, the German drew his sword and they both got soundly beaten. But in any event Captain Ferrer has got away and has managed to reach the boat that will carry him to the fleet waiting in the Downs.

Sam gives the German a clean cravat and a crown for his purse and sends him on his way. End of remarkable breakfast.

On the family front there is a possible wife for Tom in the shape of Mr Townsend's daughter. He's Clerk of the Wardrobe. We'll see what happens.

Captain Robert Holmes was at church. I was wearing my gold-laced collar, he was wearing a gold-laced suit. We glanced at each other once or twice, smiled, remembering old times. Sam took care to remind me it was time for us to leave to go to a friend's christening.

Arguments about the servants' sluttery, even on Christmas Day.

Late nights with the Penns, playing cards.

Always a hard time of year — the celebration of birth.

1662

∞

JANUARY

On the first day of the year Sam awoke with a
terrific start and hit me a great blow on my face
with his elbow, waking me with the pain. He was
so apologetic it was almost worth it. I try not to
think of it as an omen.

We've seen a lot of the Penns, taken their
children William and Peggy to the theatre, suppers
and cards till late at night, culminating in a Twelfth
Day dinner to celebrate Sir William's eighteenth
wedding anniversary. An excellent chine of beef
and eighteen mince pies in a dish. The Battens
were there – we've distanced ourselves from them
lately – and, of more interest to me, Captain Robert
Holmes (now a major but I still think of him as a
captain). Poor Sam was beside himself with jealousy
and determined to prevent any undue friendliness,
but he needn't have troubled himself because I found
the Captain's manner a little too assured, as though
he would trade on our former acquaintance to be
freer with me than I wished. It was all a long time
ago and feelings change. And behaviour that seemed

charming when he was thirty-four doesn't seem as charming at forty.

I reassured Sam but it didn't prevent Will Hewer from catching his displeasure. When we got home and he was told (by Nell, who took great pleasure in her task) that Will was already in bed, having vomited and complained of a headache when he came back from the Dolphin, Sam ordered him to be woken and was very angry with him for being drunk. I can't help thinking this is the pot calling the kettle black, it was Twelfth Day after all.

Within the family Uncle Fenner has remarried – a very ugly midwife – and they had a mean wedding dinner which we had to go to. The Joyce brothers have proposed a wife for Tom but she would only bring £200 with her and Sam pointed out that since it was possible he would have no child and thus leave his money to his brother, Tom might reasonably expect a wife with more.

I think this is the first time that not having a child has entered his calculations. It gave me a sad, cold feeling, as though a distant hope had died.

FEBRUARY

We would have liked to, but couldn't, refuse the Battens' invitation to their third wedding anniversary dinner. (Sam is increasingly annoyed at his incompetence and corruption – they favour different suppliers and Sam's merchants at least offer good quality at a good price while Batten's are the people who reward him best.) Whatever the case, they're colleagues, so we went. The atmosphere was different from the Penns'; Batten being an old man with a younger wife somehow makes for a certain lewdness. There were three venison pies, with the middle one an oval cut out of the other two and there was great mirth over getting the middle piece, with people stealing a spoonful to feed to other people. Mrs Milles stole a piece for Sam – I thought she was a little free for a minister's wife – and at the end of it Mrs Shipman filled the pie with at least a pint and a half of white wine and drank it off. An unusual sight, though I doubt she would have liked to see herself in a looking-glass at that moment.

Later that night we went with my Lady to a fine supper at Captain (Major) Holmes's lodgings in Trinity House (excellent lobsters) and all that business in the past seemed quite forgotten until we were leaving, when he murmured, 'Ah, Elizabeth, if I'd met you before you were married,' and I just smiled. When we got home late we could hear the noise still going on at the Battens' next door, great shrieks of laughter at tearing the ribbons off the mock bride and groom, but we'd both had enough by then and went to bed.

Thinking about it, we've been in rather good agreement for most of the month. We went to see *Rule a Wife and Have a Wife*, very funny, and Sam was able to feast his eyes on the King's mistress, Lady Castlemaine, for a whole hour before the performance. Looking at beautiful women simply gives him great joy, just like his love of music.

And Lady C. is certainly a beauty – her skin was wonderfully radiant. But the talk is all of what will happen when the Queen arrives, whether the King will give her up or not. She showed no sign of being troubled by it.

We've had a new coal hole made and the cellar cleared and now it's clean and tidy Sam's more pleased with it than anything else we've had done in the house. Another little piece of order in an untidy world. The next day he stayed in his chamber all day close to the pot because he'd taken physic and I decided that although I didn't exactly feel ill I also didn't feel quite well enough to go to church on my own. We had a lovely quiet day together, sitting by the fire, talking about the clothes I'll buy at Easter (he's giving me £20). At family prayers that night I felt fortunate in my lot, and contented.

Valentine's Day was quite amusing because the painters came in very early to gild the pictures so I had to walk round with my hands over my eyes in order not to see them, until William Bowyer arrived to claim me as his Valentine and I could truly say he was the first man I'd set eyes on that day (apart from Sam but that doesn't count). We managed to spend another comfy Sunday at home because we both had colds but there was a hiccup when I asked Will Hewer why he wasn't going to church with the maids and he said he wouldn't be treated like a slave with no will of his own and he could decide for himself where and when he would go to church. I had some sympathy with this and didn't mention it to Sam but one of the servants did and the result was Will got a severe chiding.

But on the whole the household has been contented. The new pictures have been arranged in the dining room and on his twenty-ninth birthday Sam declared himself as happy a man as any in the world.

∞

Stone Dinner

First course: two stewed carps, six roast chicken, a jowl of salmon.

Second course: bitter tansy omelette for Passover, two calves' tongues, cheese.

We had a man-cook in to dress it.

Guests: Cousin Jane Turner of course, who gave her hospitality for the operation, and her daughter Thea, Cousin Joyce Norton, their friend Mr Lewin.

Talk: Officer in King's Guard killed in duel. What will happen with Lady Castlemaine when Queen arrives. Singing.

∞

A picture of Easter Sunday

The house is clean and clear. It's a bright day in late March. Sam goes to church in the morning while I dress and supervise our dinner. Jane Birch has come back, thank goodness, though she won't take a penny under three pounds a year, but we both think she's worth it. She's cooking a shoulder of veal in her usual neat way and we're chatting about her family. The light falls on her plump neck and busy hands, almost like a painting.

Sam comes back and our dinner is handsomely served to us. Afterwards we both go to church and I sit in the pew below Sam's, right at the front, to stop Lady Batten and her daughter taking precedence as they try to in their arrogant way, and they look very put out at seeing me there already and later I look round at Sam and we smile. Then we go home and it's a fine afternoon and we walk in the garden which is beginning to look verdant, the honeysuckle green already and the fruit trees in bud, lots of primroses out and the violas just beginning. Sam tells me he is worth £500 now. He says that if we live frugally and he can become worth £2,000 we will have our own coach.

After an hour or two the breeze turns cold the way it does in late March and suddenly all the warmth is gone from the day and we go inside and have a good supper of lobsters and crab. (Peggy Penn has sent the crab and we can't work out the reason because we've been less friendly to them lately.)

We have our family prayers by candlelight in the dining room.

To bed and Sam and I lie together as man and wife.

∞

April

Sam is making an alliance with Sir George Carteret
who's the Treasurer of the Navy Board and the man
in charge. Carteret doesn't like Sir William Batten's
slovenly ways but he approves of the way Sam works.
As Sam says, it can't do any harm for the future to
have Carteret's interest on our side. Even so, he and
Sir William spoke very amicably about the plan to
have the roof of our building raised – we reckon it
will give us an additional four rooms, and him the
same. The mess, when it happens, will be – don't
think about it, it will be worth it.

Our maid Sarah has been sick of the ague for
weeks and Sam persuaded me I should take her to
Brampton for a change of air. But he was a little
bit too keen to take me to Paternoster Row to buy
me things for going away and I started to become
suspicious. Why was he suddenly so concerned for
Sarah's health? I determined not to go to Brampton
but sent Sarah off on her own. Eventually he had
no choice but to admit that he was leaving the next
day on a ten-day jaunt to Portsmouth with Batten
and Penn and none of them were taking their wives
so there was no question of me going too. Of course
he doesn't call it a jaunt, it's official Navy business,
to pay the men what is owed them. I have to accept
it but we parted coolly this morning.

But it's given me time to myself. The Hunts are
making a great fuss of me and I have visited my Lady

several times. Today I had dinner with my parents and walking back in the afternoon the sky was a clear, pale blue, with white clouds scudding across it and I suddenly remembered the sky over Bideford when I was a little girl.

The sky was bigger then. It was immeasurably high, stretching out over the sea to a horizon that lay at the end of the world. In that bright, cold light everything seemed possible. Balty and I would roam the countryside for hours, playing soldiers, gathering nuts and berries, stealing apples. Sometimes my father was there and he'd tell us stories of his noble Anjou family and how one day he would reclaim his lost inheritance. But often he was away, fighting in France or Ireland, and when he returned, the joy, the staying up late to sit on his lap, looking at the little curiosities he'd brought us back.

Balty and I adored him. We loved his whimsies, the ideas he produced to make our fortune, sometimes practical, sometimes so fantastic we would shriek with laughter. And on quiet, candle-lit evenings my mother would try to explain her descent from the Cliffords, and Balty and I would never understand the details except we knew that in some mysterious way we were kin to the Earls of Cumberland and in our minds we imagined that our future was peopled with guardian angels.

All that was a long time ago, when we were children. I've never seen a sky like that again, and I've stopped believing in whimsies and guardian angels.

The merry month of May

Sir George Carteret tells Sam he's vexed that William
Coventry has been appointed as the new Commissioner of the Navy Board. He doesn't like Sir
William Penn either. I'm required to visit Lady
Carteret to cement Sam's relationship with her
husband. I do, and together with Lady Sandwich
we go in her coach to Hyde Park and drive round
in a great company of fine ladies and gentlemen. It
was very pleasant because it had rained the night
before so there wasn't the usual dust cloud from
all the horses and carriages. The talk was of Lady
Castlemaine intending to lie in at Hampton Court
which means she'll be there when the new Queen
arrives, which none of us thought right.

When the Queen arrived at Portsmouth all the
bells were rung here and bonfires lit but there was
no great feeling of joy – people don't like the pride
and luxury of the Court. It hasn't taken the King
long to spend the good will he was greeted with.

We dined at the Wardrobe with my Lord's
housekeeper, Sarah, who loves to gossip. She told us
that the King spent every night at Lady Castlemaine's
last week, and the night of the new Queen's arrival at
Portsmouth, when there were bonfires outside every
house, there was none outside hers, which was much
commented on. And that they sent for a pair of scales
to weigh themselves, and she being with child was the
heavier. Afterwards we saw the privy garden where

her linen was laid out on bushes and strung between the trees to dry, incredibly fine smocks and petticoats hemmed with the richest lace. But now the King has left her to join the Queen and when we saw her at the theatre she looked as beautiful as ever but very sad and I couldn't help but feel for her a little, the way people are slighting her already.

When Lord Sandwich finally returned he told us Queen Catherine had been reclusive on the voyage from Portugal, never venturing out of her cabin, but liking to hear music played next door. She seems a kind and pleasant lady – though her Portuguese women are plain, and still wear farthingales which went out of fashion here thirty years ago. And now the King is with her at Hampton Court and said to be well enough pleased with his bride. She brings as her dowry Bombay, Tangier and £300,000. Now we must wait for her to produce an heir. As to her happiness with such a husband, has anyone warned her to expect a string of mistresses? But fondness and respect go a long way in a marriage, I hope she'll have that at least.

I found out from the maid of a friend of a friend that Elizabeth Pearse had been in Portsmouth at the same time as Sam and they had dined together (in company). It's strange he never thought to mention it.

JUNE

We had to sleep with three chests of Portuguese crusados in the cellar – about £6,000 – until they could be taken to my Lord's. Sam was so busy he seemed to have forgotten they were there but when I said in bed how terrified I was of thieves he called the maids to get up and light candles to scare them away. I said we could just as easily get up ourselves instead of waking them but he insisted it was their job.

He's been quite concerned about discipline within the family this month – he was annoyed at Will Hewer walking home from my Lady's with his cloak flung over his shoulder like a ruffian. (I thought he looked quite fetching.) Sam asked him where he learnt to dress in such an immodest way and he said it wasn't immodest and Sam boxed his ears. Young Wayneman has also been in trouble, though more justly, for we found all the whey gone and knew it must be him but he lied through his teeth until Sam whipped him. Even then it took more whipping until he finally confessed he'd drunk the whey, and hidden a candlestick in his room, and pulled up flowers. Poor little silly, stubborn boy.

Balty came to tell me he was married! To a lady called Esther who is promised a dowry of £500! He wanted me to ask Sam what he should do with the money to their best advantage. Sam said time enough to think about that when he had the money in his hand. It's true, Balty has

been known to count his chickens before they're
hatched.

∞

Summer at Brampton

It's much more tolerable with my Lady in residence
at Hinchingbrooke. I couldn't argue about coming
down here. Once the workmen took off the roof
to make our new top floor the house was virtually
uninhabitable (and of course as soon as the roof was
off, it poured with rain and the ceilings below were
ruined and will all have to be redone when the other
work is finished). I've been here for weeks with
Sarah and Wayneman and of course Sam's parents
and Pall . . .

∞

A ride with Captain Ferrer

It's a clear, golden day in early September. My Lady
has asked me to dine at Hinchingbrooke. Captain
Ferrer is there. After dinner he proposes we should
all go out for a ride but my Lady wants to rest. So he
and I ride out together and canter to Brampton Wood
where the cobnuts are ripening, and we ride through
it slowly and stop in a clearing where the light falls
through the leaves, dappled. Our horses stand close

together. I feel as though I'm in a story from *Cyrus* – a young man and woman in a glade, away from prying eyes. Captain Ferrer has a horseman's body, his thighs hard, his back straight and strong, no trace of the injury from leaping off the balcony.

We chat of this and that – the improvements at Hinchingbrooke, how well my Lady looks now my Lord has returned, Lady Castlemaine's continuing hold over the King – and then he says the King is not the only man who has the desire for a mistress, and my skin begins to prickle and I am very still. I sense he is about to make a proposition to me. And so he is, but not the one I expect.

Distantly we hear the sound of girls' voices singing, the milkmaids coming home with their pails full. He suggests we move to the edge of the wood to watch them. We're under a tree looking out at the maids. He says they make a pretty picture. I agree.

But not as pretty as another one he can see.

I lower my head, smile.

There is someone we both know who thinks me the most beautiful woman in London.

(Not himself then?)

If he were to say that my Lord, the Earl of Sandwich . . .

My eyes widen and for a moment there is a sort of surging feeling inside and the idea 'Mistress of an Earl'. Jewels, lace, silk gowns . . .

Then I'm listening to words – unparalleled beauty, great admiration, utter discretion.

And I'm watching the milkmaids, their song carried on the soft afternoon air, and I think about

Edward Mountagu, first Earl of Sandwich, aged thirty-seven, well enough looking and with some other quality that only power and title can bestow. And there's no hesitation in my heart and I'm glad, it's a testament to my happiness that I would not for a moment imperil my marriage for what would be a trifle. And I'm just not the woman who could flaunt another man's wealth in my husband's face. And it would break Sam's heart.

And how would I be able to look my Lady in the eye again?

So I thank Captain Ferrer for his kind words and I'm conscious of the honour his Lordship does me but I must refuse, and he beseeches me to think again but I tell him I'm quite resolved and he says that's what he feared I'd answer.

So if you won't take the Earl, there's no hope of you taking his servant?

There is one of those looks between us and I laugh and say he knows that I can't.

He smiles back and says my beauty gives him no choice but to try.

The milkmaids are past us now, heading home, their voices dying away. We canter back into the low golden autumnal sun and I feel alive and desired and desirable and beautiful and young and happy. And when we return I'm able to greet my Lady with an open eye and a clear conscience and I'm driven home in her carriage, through the green lanes of Huntingdonshire, smiling to myself.

Not that most days are like that. More often it's Sam's parents at each other's throats because of his mother's unreasonableness, and Pall driving us all mad with her airs and petulance, and Wayneman playing the rogue with all sorts of silly tricks and Sarah constantly complaining and quite unable to do my hair properly. But Sam has written affectionately, seems to be keeping himself busy and out of mischief, working hard and studying mathematics – he's almost mastered the multiplication tables. He has an increasing regard for William Coventry, while being careful to keep in with Sir George Carteret. He's worried that Sir John Mennes, who's moved in next to us, is claiming our best chamber as belonging to his property, and trying to block our access to the leads. Oh, let me get back to the view from the leads of the sun setting over the river . . .

Autumn

When I did return, it was to be met on the road by Will Hewer – I was almost surprised at how very pleased I was to see him. He seems to have grown up a lot in the two months I've been away, he looks taller and is more assured in his manner. He took me to Tom's, who gave me a great welcome, even crying, dear silly man. Then Sam arrived, great joy, merry supper and a most pleasurable and companionable night – it had been a long time. We snuggled together while I told him all the Brampton news, that our first alterations on the house work very well, that my Lord has drawn up a plan for further alterations we might make. And he told me his news, that he has a good reputation at the office, my new closet is finished, the prospect of a wife for Tom. The ordinary stuff of our married life. But such a nice warm glow the next day.

(I mentioned my ride with Captain Ferrer in a very light way, making nothing of it, so that if his father spoke of it I would already have told him.)

Captain Ferrer himself appeared a few days later. He showed us the scars from his latest escapade, when he'd reprimanded one of my Lord's footmen and struck him, whereupon the footman drew a sword and nearly severed his fingers. He had his familiar rogueish smile, but no hint of the business of Lord Sandwich.

The same day a gentleman whom I'd travelled up with from Brampton, a very charming man, a Mr Pimlott, came to call and Sam made a great deal of him. He has been very considerate lately, though even so the return to everyday life and what that is really like has been hard for me. In the country I forgot how much of my time I spend in London waiting for Sam to come home, sitting alone while he's engaged in his important work — I know it's work, not wine or women or cards — I can't argue with it, it's our living and a good one but a lot of the time it leaves me, how can I put it, standing to attention with nothing to do. And then when the troops are mutinous . . . Sarah is very difficult, although she can still work well when she feels like it. Sam only sees her working, he doesn't hear the muttered asides, how she rushes to bear bad news and stir ill-feeling. It's driving me mad to have her in the house all the time but Sam won't hear of her going away. Meanwhile I'm trying to trade off having dancing lessons against going into the country again next summer.

Sam had to go to Brampton Manor Court to do more business on the will, vexatious enough to make him almost mad. I was happy enough to stay in London doing what I could to get the house straight while the plasterers and painters worked on it. Mr Goodenough, who's worked on this house ever since the Navy bought it, says definitely that the room we have as our best chamber belongs to our house and not the Mennes'. It was only ever lent to next door, and in the division of the original house it was always intended to be part of ours.

I spent my twenty-second birthday alone, apart from the servants and the workmen who were here. Sam spent all day in the office apart from visiting Sir William Penn (sick of the gout) and Sir William Batten (just sick). He came home late for supper, well pleased with his hard work.

I am pleased with his work too but sometimes I feel I am turning into a shadow, that I barely exist.

And then the next day is a happy one when life is full and content. In the morning we lie late in bed, talking and sporting, then Sam goes to the office for a while and makes a quick trip to the dockyard at Deptford to further his idea of keeping books of all work done. He's home in time to supervise the cooking of a dish of tripe covered in mustard that he saw done at Lord Crew's, and he's very pleased with it and calls for wine to drink.

Surgeon Pearse turns up to join us and tells us

that he has the offer of being the Royal surgeon but he's unsure what to do because the King is so difficult. He won't acknowledge any of the Queen's ladies, particularly the English ones, for fear that they'll tell the Queen how he behaves with Lady Castlemaine (whose hold, it seems, is undiminished). But the Queen's own surgeon has told Mr Pearse that the Queen knows of the King's behaviour and since she can do no good by taking notice of it she ignores it. At the same time she's rumoured to be pregnant. That will do her no harm – the King loves his bastard children and he would surely love his legitimate heir. But the people don't like his behaviour, and they don't like the fact that we've sold Dunkirk to help pay Court debts. The Court is running scared, although it doesn't change its ways.

Talking of all this made me feel as though I were at the centre of things, as though our house was a place where people who know what's happening in the world come to talk it over. (Though something we didn't discuss in front of Surgeon Pearse was the fact that Sir Charles Berkeley, as soon as he was made Privy Purse, offered Eliz Pearse £300 a year to be his whore. Surgeon Pearse told Sam this himself and Sam thought it was very funny.) I'm glad no mention of money was made when Captain Ferrer propositioned me so I can remember it as a pleasant might-have-been rather than the buying and selling of flesh.

Yesterday a neighbour's maid poisoned herself because she was crooked. Mr Milles got to her before she died and that was the only explanation she could give. Sam thought this was extraordinary behaviour, but a hunch-backed girl with no prospect of marriage, I think her explanation was enough.

∞

NOVEMBER

One needs pleasant memories, they're almost like good friends. I'm so lonely sometimes that the day seems to last for ever with nothing to do but talk to the servants and since I can't abide Sarah any more there's not a lot of choice. There are very few people I know that I can call on in my own right (apart from family). The Hunts, of course. Eliz Pearse, I suppose, the friend I love to hate. She insisted I had two perukes made from my own hair and although she was pushy in the way she urged it, she was right, they look very neat. But I've no wish to see her too often. I like Jane Ferrer but our paths don't often cross. I don't have much to say to Cousin Jane Turner.

As for Lady Batten, she'd love us to be neighbourly but I detest the woman. She called Sam to her the other day and complained that I'd spoken unhandsomely of her (the maids gossip to each other of course) and that our maid Jane mocked her when she called to her maid Nan. It's true, I've heard her. Lady B. screams out 'Na-an' and Jane echoes it, 'Na-an', and all the servants laugh. Sam had Jane up to our chamber to reprimand her for this disrespect but he couldn't stop a smile breaking through.

But the tenor of my days is loneliness and the answer to it is so simple it drives me mad that Sam won't countenance it. I need a waiting woman of my own, a young lady from a decent family who will be my companion, someone to talk to in a way that I can't talk to the servants, someone who knows how to dress hair, someone I can go to the theatre with. It's hardly an extravagant request for a lady in my position. Sam's had his own footboy in livery since we first moved to Seething Lane, nearly two and a half years now, but the idea of spending an additional £10 a year for a woman for me is anathema to him. Things came to a head when two young sisters whom Balty knows came to see me to ask if I knew of any positions for waiting women and offering their services. Sam was furious things had gone this far and we had a terrible row. He won't listen to reason when his temper is up so I'm going to write to him to try to make him understand.

My dearest Husband,

Our recent harsh words to each other give me no joy. Please believe me that the intention of my life is our mutual happiness. I know that when we speak in anger we are both so full of our own case that we don't always listen to what the other is saying. I'm writing to you now calmly and I hope you will be able to read it calmly so you can understand my situation.

Sam, I know that you work immensely hard to maintain us all in a manner we could hardly have dreamed of when we were first married.

I know that all our prosperity is due to you. You have been kind enough in the past to call me a prudent housekeeper who ensures your money is not squandered and this has been my contribution to our present estate.

I know I brought no dowry to our marriage except my great love for you. I respect the value of your money and I wouldn't ask for a waiting woman simply to confirm my position as the wife of a prosperous gentleman.

The truth is, Sam, I'm lonely most of my days. I know that your position means you must be at the office or out and about seeing people most of the time, and that even when you are at home your desire to master every detail of your business means you will spend a lot of time alone in your closet studying your mathematics and law and shipbuilding, amassing the knowledge that makes you so well-respected by your peers. All of this I accept. But while you're so absorbed, I am wondering what I'm to do for the rest of the day. If we're in the middle of rehanging a chamber and I'm fully employed in sewing and adjusting and making things just right then that occupies me and time doesn't lie heavy, but other times . . . Other times I wander round the house and I touch the hangings, I touch the walls, the doors, the furniture, our precious objects, and I'm not even sure I'm alive, I have to believe in myself through these things that we have made together. This is a sad state to be in, like some rootlesss plant. I must have things to do, I must have someone to talk to or I'll go mad.

Sam, the expense is not so terrible, it will add less than a pound a month to our housekeeping bills, as well as her food, but young girls don't eat enough for that to be a great consideration. It would contribute greatly to my happiness to have my own woman. Won't you consider it?

I wish to assure you that I am at all times and in all circumstances your devoted, faithful and obedient wife,

Elizabeth

I made two copies of this: one to keep with my personal papers where I could retrieve it easily if there was an argument over exactly what it said, and the other I sent to him at the office by hand of Will Hewer who knew that something was up between us but he didn't dare ask and I didn't tell.

And the upshot was that Sam said I could have one of the girls whom Balty recommended, Winifred, and she will come next week. This news has put Sarah's nose out of joint so much that she's given notice. Very good. Sam's cross about it because he thinks she's a good chambermaid, which is true in some respects, but he doesn't have to spend all day suffering her pettish moods.

So. The painters have finished at last and the servants have been working hard to make the house perfectly clean. Winifred and Balty came to dine and once he'd heard her sing, Sam was more than reconciled to her coming, in fact couldn't bear the thought of her not coming. He's started calling her our 'petite marmotte' because her red hair and something about her teeth make her look like a pretty little squirrel. I've been preparing her chamber and rearranging things all over the house. I've altered the old dining room hangings to fit Sam's study and it looks very neat now and he's pleased. It's been snowing. The canal in St James's Park has frozen over and I saw people sliding over the ice on their 'skates', they're called, a Dutch invention, a sort of metal rod on the bottom of the boot. They looked so graceful, I could never have imagined people could move in such a way. The snow makes everything clean and quiet. My house is in order. I'm to have my woman. I'm happy.

DECEMBER

Well, nothing is for ever. Balty brought a message that Winifred couldn't come when we expected her because of some business of her mother's so we had to wait another week. When she did finally arrive she proved to be good company, and I noticed that Sam immediately started spending more time at home.

She lasted two days. This business of her mother's meant she would have to spend more time away on that than she spent with me, and if that wasn't acceptable she'd go. So she went. Sarah left the same day, in floods of tears. Jane cried, Sam nearly cried. The house seemed quiet and empty afterwards and we were all melancholy that night.

But life goes on. Jane is promoted to chamber-maid and our new cook-maid Susan is settling in. She's another of Balty's recommendations — Sam says he'll try not to hold that against her. Her timing isn't perfect yet. Sam came home to dine one day, unexpectedly bringing Mr Coventry with him, the man he respects above all others. He'd invited himself for dinner and when they arrived at two o'clock the leg of mutton and the capons weren't done enough. Sam carved expertly to ensure our guest had the cooked bits and Mr Coventry seemed pleased with his dinner but after he'd gone Sam was mad with rage at me and Susan. I can see it was an unfortunate day for dinner to be late. The truth was I'd spent too long reading *Cyrus* that morning, lost in a world where there are no servant problems or meals to be cooked. Of course I didn't admit that.

We made friends again. He bought me a beautiful copy of Ovid's *Metamorphoses* and we read it together by the fire. We agreed my kitchen accounts at £7 a month. I spent Christmas Day in bed with the usual. Sam dined at my bedside on roast pullet and plum porridge and he sent out for a mince pie because I'd been too ill to make any and I don't trust Susan yet. I made up for it the next day, baked a huge batch.

We're to spend a few nights at my Lord's lodgings and I'm to be admitted to the Queen's presence chamber. Sam's mortified that I haven't got a good winter gown — everyone else will be in moire while I shall have to wear taffeta. I think I'll manage to endure it, but I'm glad Sam realises at last that my clothes don't match my position.

Perhaps the new year will bring a new gown.

Next time I write it will be 1663.

1663

∞

January

We veer from the contented to the enraged. At the turn of the year while we stayed in some splendour at my Lord's lodgings we were happy together of course. His housekeeper Sarah was reasonably sober (part of the reason we were there was that my Lord was worried she was becoming a drunkard and wanted Sam to have a word and keep an eye on her) but as always a wonderful source of gossip. She described Lady Castlemaine's miscarriage at a dinner when she cried out that she quickened and she was undone, and all the men were made to leave the room while the women attended her.

Sam took me to the Queen's presence chamber, where she was playing cards with her maids of honour and the King's bastard, the Duke of Monmouth. None of the women were strikingly pretty, but all well-dressed in velvet gowns. We had dinner with the Pearses, played cards late with John Creed, were waited on hand and foot. But I was still glad to be back in our own home and I put it to Sam that perhaps it would be possible to have Pall as a waiting woman –

closing my eyes to the possible problems – and Sam was quite keen since he more or less has to provide for Pall anyway. So we had warm conversations in bed about the pleasures we'd had over the turn of the year, and our plans for the future.

On Twelfth Day we dined at brother Tom's with John Creed and then all went to the theatre to see *Twelfth Night* by Shakespeare – a silly play, not relating at all to the name or day, according to Sam, but then he doesn't like Shakespeare's comedies. He thought *A Midsummer's Night's Dream* the most insipid ridiculous play he'd ever seen in his life though I rather enjoyed it. But it was all friendly and kind. Sometimes John Creed is an emollient between us, and sometimes an irritant.

And then things went bad because Tom's maid told Jane that Sarah had met Sam and told him all sorts of untrue things about me which Sam has kept quiet about until now, such as that I gave Balty one of my lace collars for his wife (this is true but I'd already told Sam about it so I don't see that it needs repeating). And that I'd borrowed money from Will Hewer to lend to Balty, which is untrue. Will Hewer always seems to have money – I don't know how, I suspect his father must be more prosperous than we realise – and one day when Balty was here Will offered to lend him a pound and Balty accepted, it was nothing to do with me. Sam said he hadn't believed anything she'd said, apart from the lace collar, and so smoothed things over.

But the next day I woke up at five in the morning – and there's no point in waking up at five in January, it's much too early to get up without a great fuss of candles and fires being made. But if you're awake and can't get back to sleep, there's nothing to do except think sad, silly thoughts, and mine were that I didn't like to be talked about behind my back and that if I had a waiting woman there wouldn't be the familiarity with the servants that enabled Sarah to make her accusations. So when Sam finally woke up – it seemed ages – I was already in a tearful way and I began talking about a waiting woman and he began talking about expense so I asked him to reread the letter I'd sent him about my loneliness. He said he didn't have it any more so I gave Jane the keys to my trunk and asked her to bring my papers.

And then it turned out he'd never read the original letter at all. He'd thrown it on to the fire unopened.

Which made me fiercely glad that I keep the pages of this my journal safely stored at my parents' house. At least I have something to prove that I have my own thoughts and feelings.

So I sat on the side of the bed and read the letter to him, stealing glances at him while I did so, and there seemed to be conflicting feelings running over his face. He grimaced at one point as though to hold back tears but when he looked up at the end it was to desire me to tear it up. Which I desired to be excused. Then he commanded me to tear it and I again desired to be excused, at which he forced it out of my hands and tore it into little pieces which lay all in a mess on the red and blue Turkey carpet. He was mad with rage that I'd written it in English not French so even Jane could read it (though it was locked away from her). And it was in with all my other papers where it would have caused so much dishonour to him if anyone had found it. And then he grabbed all the other papers, our old letters, his will, old accounts from Axe Yard, and stuffed them all in the pockets of his breeches and began dressing himself in a fury. Once he had put on his stockings and his gown (as though he had to be dressed to give this due seriousness) he pulled the papers out one by one and tore them all to bits in front of my face.

I was sitting on the bed in my nightgown, begging him not to do it, crying, but he took no notice. Despite my tears, something inside me went cold at this exhibition, watching this man lose all control of his temper. When he'd done, he picked up most of the pieces and took them into his closet and I believe burnt them. I felt as though in destroying those pieces of paper he'd destroyed the innocent fondness of the early years of our marriage. It seemed there were no memories between us any more and I was plunged into the present with nothing to hold on to from the past.

(The ideal prince is absolute master of his passions.)

He went to the office. He came home to dine. We were cool with each other.

And by the end of the day – he was sorry he'd torn up the old letters and I should have a new moire gown. But why did we have to go through all this? We can afford a new gown. But what's torn up and burnt is gone for ever.

Perhaps it's foolish to expect fondness after so long. One must harden oneself – we don't live in a far-off noble world. Better a new gown than not a new gown.

It was ready in time for a fine dinner we gave. I got up at five o'clock and went to the market in darkness and we had a man-cook in to dress it for us, which took a great deal of strain off me so I could enjoy the day. We had the Pearses and the Clarkes and a couple of Dr Clarke's relatives and we gave them oysters followed by a hash of rabbit and lamb and an excellent chine of beef. Then we had a great dish of roast fowl and a mince tart and finished with fruit and cheese. We can seat ten perfectly well at our table and eight in great comfort.

We talked about the new French custom of requiring servants to have a Certificate from a friend or gentleman of their good behaviour and their abilities. It seems a good idea. And about the German Princess, imprisoned for bigamy – the penalty could be death. She's a fiddler's daughter from Canterbury but she's posed as a German noblewoman compelled to flee marriage to a man of eighty. She's done it so successfully and has such wit and spirit that the people love her, and everyone wants her acquitted.

Afterwards the ladies sat in my closet playing cards and the men were in Sam's closet looking at his books and then we ended with a cold meat supper and I made a sack posset using eggs as well as cream with the wine which was a bit of a risk but it worked perfectly and was declared a triumph. As we sat round the fire drinking it, Sam and I gave each other a secret smile. Hard to believe we were the same couple who had screamed and cried at each other a few days ago.

The leftovers ran out just before the solemn Fast for Charles 1's murder, unfortunately, for we'd both forgotten about it and with everything closed we had to survive all day on bread and milk. We thought for a bit there was another possibility of a wife for Tom but once she'd met him she refused him because of his stammer. And Balty has proposed a new waiting woman, one Mary Ashwell, but I haven't broached Sam yet.

FEBRUARY

Always the worst month of the year. It seems as though winter will never end and nothing will ever bloom again. We all have chilblains and Sam's been ill. For two days he was in a torment of itching and his body swelled up and was red. At first he thought it was a louse but then he put it down to the Danzig gherkins he'd eaten. Whatever it was, his apothecary, Mr Pelling, advised him to have a sound sweat, and two nights of that cured him. We've had to sack Jane Birch for rudeness – she wasn't really experienced enough to be a chambermaid, always standing on her position. Our maid Susan has been ill. I've had desperately bad monthlies. Sam's eyes often hurt him.

It sounds like February.

But trying to be more positive . . . Sam has been surprisingly easy in the matter of Mary Ashwell. We had her father to dine and they left it to me to agree the conditions with her when I met her. So I went to her school at Chelsea with Balty and his wife (who turns out not to have a penny, of course) to see the entertainment the girls were putting on. Mary's a senior girl who teaches the little ones, and they had a pretty show of singing and dancing and a little play. She seeems pleasant enough, and accomplished. We agreed she'll start in a month.

Captain Ferrer visited with the latest Court gossip. It seems that while dancing during a ball one of the ladies dropped a stillborn child but none of them would admit to it and all turned up early for their duties the next morning. The King kept it in his closet for a week and dissected it. He made a great joke that he had the greatest loss by it all because he had lost a subject. I didn't think it was funny, it put a horrible picture in my mind of the King wearing his crown, bent over the tiny body, cutting it up.

The King has given Lady Castlemaine all the silver plate the peers gave him for New Year. Her jewellery is much richer than the Queen's. So she still has the King in thrall despite the fact that he's also besotted with Frances Stuart. Lady C. invited her rival to an entertainment and began the frolic that the two of them must be married and so they were, with Lady C. playing the bridegroom, and they had a ring and ribbons and a sack posset in bed and flinging the stockings. And then Lady C. withdrew and the King took her place as bridegroom. Lord Sandwich lost £50 to the King at cards and said he'd willingly lose it every time so long as the King sent for him to play.

I don't care for their ways but still I find great interest in hearing the details of their lives, and it's a pleasant enough way of spending an hour on a bitterly cold grey day.

Sam was thirty this month.

∞

LENT

I saw Captain Ferrer again when he came to invite me to his child's christening. I took my woman, Mary (what a pleasure to write those words) with me, and Sam and John Creed. Their house is very prettily furnished – perhaps Lady Jane brought some things with her. She was lying-in in some state but as cheerful as ever and it was sweet to see how tender Robert was to her. He's a bit of a rogue but he has a good heart. There were many fine ladies there – I felt so much more their equal having my own woman.

Mary Ashwell is an asset, no doubt of it. She talks merrily and plays the harpsichord well enough that Sam has bought her a book of music. Just before she came I had a terrific row with Lady 'Bad' Batten. I'd asked her maids if Wayneman could go into her house to turn on our water cock (such madness having it located next door) and they said yes but she stood very high on it and told him she would teach his mistress better manners. When he came back and told me, I went into the garden and said very loudly that she hadn't manners enough herself to spare. Since then, silence.

Not that I'm great friends with the Penns either. Our maid Sarah, who left here in such floods of tears claiming she'd never get over it, was working for the Penns within the week. I was miffed, more so as I know she's been talking about me and our household. Sir William has now sent her away to try to improve relations between us. But having Mary as a companion makes things lighter somehow. She had a fearful toothache and I took her to Mr Marsden but just the sight of the chair made her quake and when he put the pliers in her mouth she jumped up and wouldn't by any persuasion let him do anything. We teased her later for being such a baby.

We had an excellent Stone Dinner, ten of us altogether. We had a fricassee of chicken and rabbits, a boiled leg of mutton, three carps, a side of lamb, roasted pigeons, four lobsters, three tarts, a lamprey pie and a dish of anchovies. Our new cook-maid Hannah did it all very neatly. I gave her a lot of help but I still had time to let Mary dress me properly (the moire). It's a great relief to have a cook we can rely on.

Seeing Mary Ashwell dance has made Sam agree that I need lessons. I start after Easter – longing to begin.

∞

SPRING

My dancing master is Mr Pembleton, a man of this parish. He's rather a handsome man, dark-haired, very firm and graceful in the way he moves. He's not tall but his body is very neatly – I might say beautifully – proportioned. Mary plays the virginals for us to dance to. Through the window I can see the apple blossom drifting on the breeze and when he takes my hand to guide me, his firmness makes me feel as light as the petals falling on the grass. He says I have a natural talent for it. He comes every day, quite often staying beyond his hour.

Sam's clearly jealous though he tries not to show it. Instead we had a shouting match about me dancing too much instead of keeping the house clean. He called me a beggar for bringing no dowry and I called him a prick-louse for being the son of a tailor (always makes him mad).

Whether he designs to turn the tables or not I don't know, but I see him taking great pains teaching Mary her music and he always has time to talk to her. The funny thing is he's decided that it's a useful thing for a gentleman to know how to dance, so he is now Mr Pembleton's pupil as well. He's learning a coranto, and the contrast between the two men is sometimes almost comical, Sam not being quite as slim as he once was. It's hard for a man beginning to be portly to look graceful doing a running step.

He came home one day and found me and Mr Pembleton not dancing but walking and talking (about his wife, as it happened) and he was clearly unhappy all night, though he said it was his work which troubled him. In the morning I could see him watching me to see if I put on my drawers which of course I did, as I do every day, and I made some joke about this being a French custom the English ladies would do well to adopt, just to let him know I was aware of him watching.

A couple of days later, a beautiful evening, Mr Pembleton was still here when Sam came home from the office and we all went over the water and walked from Rotherhithe to Halfway House, picking cowslips in the fields on our way. The light was soft and gold, the sky a pale, pale blue. I felt happy and alive. At Halfway House we played ninepins, me and Jack Pembleton against Sam and Mary. And if Jack sometimes took my hand in play, it was only in passing. At least it meant Sam paid scant attention to Mary, he was too busy keeping his eyes on me.

I think he's afraid that the dancing is making everything else go out of his control. There was a moment at dinner the other day when I described a certain shopkeeper as a very devil and Sam told me not to use that word and I said what other word would he have me use of a man who cheated his customers, got his maids with child and threw them out, whipped his children for pleasure and beat his wife to within an inch of her life for no good reason? Now there was a time when I wouldn't have dared answer like that because if it made him mad enough he might well try to hit me. But with Mary Ashwell sitting beside me, he can't do it.

It just happens that I've been to church morning and afternoon for the last two weeks. If I see Mr Pembleton there it's hardly surprising, for he's a parishioner of St Olave's just like we are. I'm leaving for Brampton in a couple of weeks and it's been amazingly easy to get Sam to pay for country clothes, although he pretends to scowl and grudge. I know that he'll pay almost anything for the dancing lessons to be over.

It all culminated in a long tearful night of him reproaching me for my conduct and me crying that it wasn't my conduct it was his jealousy that made the difficulty – I like dancing with Mr Pembleton and I enjoy talking to him, but that's all of it, it's innocent enough. So when he turned up for my lesson next morning I told him he couldn't come in unless Sam was here. I told Sam what I'd done and he looked a bit shamefaced. When Mr Pembleton returned in the afternoon I sent word to the office asking Sam to come home so I could have my lesson with no impropriety and he sent word back that I should begin and he would be over soon. When he did come, it was with his clerk Tom Hayter and they sat in his closet talking over business for a long time before he came up and joined us. Then I paid Mr Pembleton off for the month and we all had an apparently merry supper together. And I can dance quite well now so it hasn't been time or money wasted.

Meanwhile the household runs on. We've been given a blackbird which sings so sweetly that the man who brought it was offered twenty shillings for it on the way. It's lovely to wake to its song, but I think it will have to 'escape' because it makes me too sad when it tries to fly in its little cage.

But it's not all harmony. Sam was deadly mad when he found the cellar door had been left open and half the wine had been drunk. He accused Will Hewer of sitting up late drinking with the maids, which was denied of course. I'm beginning to find Mary irksome – she talks to me sometimes as though I were one of the little girls at her old school. And a couple of yards of new ribbon mysteriously moved from my drawer to hers though of course she denies stealing it. Sam and I seem to argue over every little thing: he thinks Penn's boy is much finer than his own, I have to disagree and support Wayneman. So we argue over things that really don't matter. He doesn't like the worsted cushions I made last year, they're far too small. I point out that a year ago he thought they were excellent.

And his delight in Mary Ashwell's company is becoming a little trying, though innocent enough, I suppose. I didn't take her with me when we went to see Betterton playing Hamlet – and who should be acting in it but Winifred Goswell, my first woman, and looked very good though not a speaking part. We saw Lady Castlemaine, beginning to look a little decayed, I thought, and Sam agreed. As the house became more crowded, the ladies of fashion held up their vizards to their faces and we both thought it was a becoming sight, so as soon as the play was over Sam took me to the New Exchange and bought me one – very pretty in a harlequin pattern.

I don't know when I shall get the chance to wear it because I leave for Brampton tomorrow with Mary Ashwell. Sam sent everyone to church this morning and we stayed home on our own and had a long talk, reckoning our household accounts and discussing our future. We'll part as good friends, I believe.

SUMMER

Thank goodness my Lady is at Hinchingbrooke and we were truly pleased to see each other again. She advised me to ask Sam to buy me one of the new silk-striped petticoats which look particularly appropriate in the country so I mentioned what she'd said in my next letter and lo and behold the following week a very fine petticoat arrived by carrier, much richer and better than I'd expected.

Lord Sandwich hasn't come down himself, which means his men aren't here either – Captain Ferrer for example. My Lady is slightly perplexed that her husband doesn't come, though the weather is certainly not an inducement. It's been raining all summer and I can't remember when we last had a sunny day. This doesn't improve tempers at home. Pall's constantly trying to make mischief between me and Mary and I'm sick of them both. I was reading *Cyrus* as an escape from it all and when it went missing I was distraught – and then furious when it turned up in Mary's room after Pall dropped a hint. Mary lied in her teeth about it and I boxed her ears to teach her a lesson, whereupon she hit me and there was ranting and raving all over the house. Sam's parents seemed to think they must inform my Lady of this incident (so loyal) but all she said to me was something about these young girls being difficult. She said it rather sadly so I wondered if there was a difficulty with Lady Jemima, though I've no reason to think so.

I've done six weeks down here now and return to London on the 12th of August, thank goodness.

∞

SEPTEMBER

I wasn't quite sure how I'd find Sam because of course he'd had news of all the arguments, but he was very loving and tender, didn't want to know the details, agreed that Mary must go, despite missing her accomplishments.

He had much more interesting news, but he made me swear not to say a word of it to my Lady. It seems Captain Ferrer told him that Lord Sandwich was finding great pleasure in his lodgings in the country at Chelsea. Sam wasn't sure whether he meant simply that he was pleased to be staying there or whether he was hinting at something about the daughter of the house. A few days later Will Howe told him that my Lord dotes on this girl, Betty Becke, and spends all his time and money on her. People at Court are taking notice that he hardly attends and neglects his business. The girl herself is an impudent wench with a bad reputation. She's the reason he's not going into the country. I feel so sorry for my Lady.

I told Sam what she'd said about young girls being difficult – did it mean she knew? He was very distressed at the thought that she might. There was some other gossip – the King more than ever besotted with Frances Stuart, Lady Castlemaine being ignored when he's with the Queen, yet the ladies say Lady C.'s hold is as strong as ever. One little swipe the Queen managed to give her: the Queen was having her hair dressed and it was taking a long time and Lady C. came in and said, 'I wonder your Majesty can have the patience to sit so long a-dressing.' 'Oh,' the Queen says, 'I have so much reason to use patience, that I can very well bear with it.' I trust Lady C. blushed, if she knows how.

On a smaller scale our own household has been rather in and out of favour. The first thing when we got home was that Mary Ashwell should go, and Sam has spoken to her father and she will go in a few days. Wayneman ran away once too often and Sam refused to have him back. Then Susan came looking for a lace collar that she'd left and Hannah was wearing it and took it off and tried to hide it. Sam took that as the occasion (he already thought she was dishonest) to charge her with it and in a huff she said she'd be gone that night if we paid her wages, and we said that was good enough. So now I had no woman and no cook-maid. We took Susan on again. Within a day she was up to her old drunken tricks which we'd forgotten but they came to mind again soon enough.

In his capacity as my Lord's faithful steward, Mr Moore has spoken to Sam about my Lord's debauchery and Sam has resolved to speak to Lord Sandwich . . . if he can . . . seasonably . . . The joiners have arrived to relay all the floors in the house, starting with the dining room. Mr Moore warns Sam that speaking to my Lord may do him no good and Sam some harm.

I am forced to let Susan go, leaving the house filthy, wet washing everywhere. I call in the handyman's wife, Goody Taylor, to help out. It's still raining. Will Howe entreats Sam to speak to Lord Sandwich about these matters that are ruining his estate and Sam has resolved to speak, come what may.

A little girl called Jinny, a parish child from St Brides recommended by the church warden, arrived in the morning to be our new servant. I spent three hours delousing her, washing her, and dressing her in clean clothes, and by six o'clock she'd run away. She was brought back the next day by the parish beadle and I took her new clothes back and sent her away. Poor silly girl, she'll end up on the streets sooner than later. But the beadle also brought a new Susan, who might serve well enough as a maid of all work. In all this time of dirt and trouble Mary Ashwell has done nothing whatever to help. There were no tears shed when she left. But at last I have a cook, Jane Gentleman, deaf, but willing enough.

Lady Jane Ferrer came to see me and told me she'd visited Lord Sandwich in Chelsea with Lady Jemima and even in front of his daughter he was doting on his slut. Lady Jem very upset of course. I'm going nearly mad with the dirt and sawdust everywhere. The joiners are doing all the floors as well as moulding and panelling in various rooms and it looks excellent but it seems to be taking for ever. We're constantly emptying one room of furniture and moving it to another. Brother Tom has asked to borrow £20 and Sam's troubled about the state of his business.

And then the joiners had finished and I set to with what servants we had to make the house clean. Sam is determined my closet shall be improved so we've had some lovely times going out buying things. There's something about a husband and wife who have the means and share the taste going together to buy things for their home – it solidifies their life together, as though the physical fabric binds them as much as their vows. So, we went to Cornhill (after dinner with John Creed, who came with us) to choose a 'chintz' for hangings and linings and we looked at dozens and dozens. 'Chintz' is Indian calico, painted with birds and flowers, so many different patterns and so pretty.

Captain Hicks sent me a bag of little shells for my shell work though I'm so busy making hangings I haven't time to do any yet. Sam took me to Bartholomew Fair with Ned Pickering and we watched the monkeys dancing on the tightropes and, very curious, a horse with hoofs all curved, like ram's horns, poor creature couldn't walk very well. Also a cock with three legs and a goose with four. We saw Jacob Hall on the ropes, much the best of all the dancers. Ned Pickering is severely out of favour because he disapproves of my Lord's behaviour even though he hasn't said anything. Lord Sandwich makes him eat with the servants and has mocked him for his small estate. Sam has resolved not to meddle but to let my Lord go on till his conscience and thoughts of his Lady and family put a stop to it

Sam's bought me a pair of globes and is teaching me about the world and astronomy. It seems strange to me that we can see the sun go round our sky every day and yet it seems we are going round the sun instead. I still don't quite understand this but I find it fascinating and Sam loves to teach (and is very good at it). We've been getting on rather well, to the point that the day before he was due to leave for a session of Brampton Court he said to me, with such a plaintive look, 'Well, shall you and I never travel together again?' that I decided at once to accompany him.

We travelled with my Lord's steward, Mr Moore, and Cousin Tom Pepys and it was a long day's riding. When we came to our lodgings for the night I was very hot and drank some cold beer and suddenly felt terribly ill, sick and faint, and almost collapsed. Poor Sam was desperately worried (told me afterwards he thought I was going to die) and called the mistress of the house to bring strong water and attend me. They lay me down and I felt as though I was an icicle slowly melting away, dissolving into the bed, a horrible feeling. But after a few minutes I began to feel better and within half an hour was fully recovered. I'll never forget the look of concern on Sam's face though. It made me realise that this is the nature of fondness after a long time, not so much in acts of tenderness as in dread of what loss of the other would mean.

At the court he managed to sort out most of the detail of who owns what mortgaged lands and then he had to go into the Fens for a couple of days to settle things with the Wisbeech relatives and returned with his lips dry and bleeding from the wind and his face covered in midge bites. He managed to find time for us both to ride out to Brampton Woods (his only hour of pleasure in the whole trip, he said) and I steered us, without really being aware of it, to just the place where Robert Ferrer and I had stopped the year before. Once again the leaves were turning gold and the cobnuts were ripe and the milkmaids were coming home singing. I thought how sad it was that a year ago I still respected Lord Sandwich and was flattered and slightly charmed by his proposition, while now . . . He's finally come down to Hinchingbrooke but he's so ungracious to my Lady it's painful to see, and he makes it plain he doesn't want to be there. My Lady makes no mention of it of course but she is growing thinner and doesn't smile as easily as she used to.

Ah, men are our servants when they woo us, but our masters when they marry us.

The ride back to London was hard. We had two local men leading us on the way to Bigglesworth, for there were deep ditches full of water either side of the road and as it grew dark it was very frightening. The next day Sam decided I should wait for the coach while he rode on ahead and I was more than happy to agree. When at last I arrived back, he'd bought a good fowl and it was roasted and we were both utterly content to be in our own home again.

I went to see my father a few days later and he's had bills printed which show he has a patent on a cure for smoking chimneys, which is such a problem that if he has the solution it might make his fortune. So that was good news. And we've been fitting out my closet and ordering a velvet coat for me and a new suit and cloak for Sam, and he's very pleased with the care I take of our house and the time I spend putting it all in order. And we have a new maid, Bess, and everything in our household seems calm and under control for once.

Autumn turns to winter

There seems to be illness everywhere. For a week Sam was in the most dreadful pain with colic. He had a couple of Mr Hollier's pills put by so he took those and stayed home the next day hoping for results but he was still quite unable to break wind or produce a stool and the pain got worse and worse. He had trouble making water but felt he needed to all the time. Mr Hollier said it was nothing to do with the stone, but he was naturally costive and had taken cold so he must stay very warm and meanwhile there were bottles of foul syrup to drink. Nothing worked very well, and his straining to pass a stool made all his privates hurt. This went on for days, while he did the work he had to do, going out and about, not revealing his pain, and I felt like screaming at the people who were making demands on him, until at last on Mr Hollier's direction I gave him an enema. I mixed it up myself of a pint of strong ale, four ounces of sugar and two ounces of butter. He lay on the bed with it in him for a couple of hours, and then thinking it hadn't worked he got up and started walking round and, very soon, excellent results.

So now he has some Rules for his Health:

1. Always keep warm.

2. Strain as little as possible because it will cause pain later.

3. Take physic forward or an enema backward to maintain ease.

4. Take action as soon as he finds himself costive, don't wait.

Sam's illness, however painful, didn't threaten his life. The Queen's did. She had spotted fever and we heard that she'd told the King that she left the world willingly, apart from leaving him. This affected him greatly, it was said. Her terrible fever continued. Sam postponed the making of his velvet cloak until he knew whether the Queen would live or die. Such a waste to have a cloak he couldn't wear if we were all in mourning. The King was said to be weeping at her bedside – and spending every night with Lady Castlemaine. Surgeon Pearse told us that the Queen thought in her fever that she'd been delivered of a boy and she was troubled that it was an ugly boy but the King was by her and he said no it was a very pretty boy and she said that if it was like him it was pretty enough and she was well pleased.

William Coventry told us that she still raved and fancied that she had three children and the girl was very like the King and the first words she said on waking were, 'How are the children?' I feel so sorry for her, I know that ache.

The Queen slowly recovers. I begin to have my pain in the usual place. They say there's plague in Amsterdam.

NOVEMBER

The periwig-maker came with a wig for Sam and without more ado cut off all his hair, and even though he'd
been expecting it, it seemed a terrible shock to him. I
said he wasn't Samson and think of the time he'd save
not having to comb through for nits, and the servants
all said the periwig looked wonderful, but still it took
a lot of reassurance. Hair is something not entirely
under our control, whether thick or thin, balding or
full, and he always has trouble with things that can't
be sorted out by intelligence and hard work.

Meanwhile Elizabeth Hunt has been teaching me
how to make quince marmalade. We have several
quince bushes in the garden and I was determined
to get the fruit before Ladies Penn or Batten, which
I did. The smell seeps through the house, autumnal,
promise of good food to come, preserves made, the
store cupboard filling up.

The hard thing is that Will Hewer has moved
out of our house to his own lodgings, and I miss
his presence very much. There's quite a confidence
between us now and although he and Sam still have
words sometimes, his behaviour to me is like one
of the ideal Princes in *Cyrus*, always civil, gentle,
submissive. The same day news came that Wayneman
is on a ship bound for Barbados – it's that or the
gallows, Sam says. I see that; it's just that he's such a
very little boy still. And his mischief is only mischief,
it's not malicious.

And it has no repercussions in the way Lord Sandwich's has. Sam tried to talk to him but found him so unapproachable that his nerve failed and he resolved to write instead. And so he did, on the Queen's birthday, when the constables had had to come round and order the bonfires to be lit. Poor creature, such is the unpopularity of the Court, though not at all her fault.

Sam wrote of his great care for my Lord's honour and because of that care he felt bound to report that the world, both City and Court, talked about him to his disgrace. Sam himself didn't believe a word of it but my Lord should know what others said.

While we were waiting in some trepidation for his response, my swelling came back in the old place, very badly, and Mr Hollier came to look at it with Sam. He said there was a hollow three inches long, fortunately running along the skin, not into the body, and he'd have to cut it open the whole length. I couldn't bear the thought of any of our maids attending me during this and it was going to have to be Sam who helped, which he readily agreed to though I know he was quailing inside. Then Mr Hollier came again and said if I was cut I'd have to have a nurse and he thought a fomentation would do as well, so my maid could attend me and we could tell her it was piles. In the end that's what we did.

I got better and visited my parents. Balty had to put his oar in, saying I should look after my own family more, now I was so well-circumstanced. I told him in no uncertain terms to stay out of my business – it's no thanks to him that I'm well-circumstanced, it's my hard work and most of all Sam's. I think Balty must be finding it more expensive to keep a wife than he'd imagined.

Lord Sandwich talked to Sam about his letter, thanked him for his concern, but insisted that the young gentlewoman of the house was beyond reproach. Though he was taking another house, meaning to live in a different manner, that was not because of the talk, it was simply to please himself. He owned his opinion of Sam's good intentions, but his tone was very cool. When Sam came home he was deeply troubled by it all and we talked for a long time. He said my Lord was clearly displeased and he's worried that he's done himself an injury by speaking out; he said if he had the chance again he'd do nothing. I tried to reassure him that my Lord would come to his wits eventually and recognise Sam's faithfulness to him. He agreed, but he still went to bed very gloomy.

Some hard work on the East India Company's accounts put him in a better frame of mind, to the point that he suggested we should make a trip to Calais next year in one of the Navy's yachts, all of us. Bess was wild with joy, mad to go, but Jane said she couldn't, she'd be much too scared, and Bess said if Jane didn't go she'd stay home with her. We all thought this very sweet-tempered of her. I'd love to go of course, the thought of it is like a ray of sunshine in the winter months ahead.

DECEMBER

It's been cold and snowing and I've spent as much time as possible in bed. The cold weather makes Sam take extra care of his health. I've been encouraging him not to strain for a stool but to go often in a leisurely way and he's followed my advice and is now almost back to his natural course. I've been troubled with terrible toothache, first one side then the other then both. Will Hewer came with me to the dentist – I can't go on my own any more because I nearly faint every time I walk into his room, even though Mr Marsden is as gentle as the nature of his task allows. I had the worst one drawn – every bit as painful as I expected (though Will told me I'd been very brave).

Will Howe brought news from the Sandwich household that my Lord had been very displeased by the letter and had spoken slightingly of Sam whenever his name was mentioned. But now he's come to himself and moved out of Chelsea and left the slut, and Will thinks he'll show Sam as much respect as ever. Sam finds my Lord coolly friendly but their former easiness is by no means restored.

Our cousin Edward Pepys died and Sam asked my Lord if his coach could accompany the hearse through the City. He agreed at once so Sam and I rode in it on the day. There were about twenty coaches altogether, some, like my Lord's, with six horses. We agreed he wouldn't have sent it if he intended an open break with Sam. We must wait for time to smooth ruffled feathers.

Our Christmas has been very quiet but with good content. Sam has been teaching me addition and subtraction and multiplication but we're going to leave division until we've done some more work on the globes. After we'd dined on Christmas Day he spent the afternoon reading to me about them, a lovely peaceful time and much nicer than rushing backwards and forwards to the Penns and Battens as we have in the past.

Thank God we all approach the new year in good health. May it last. (And God help the poor souls in Amsterdam and Hamburg where the plague is daily growing worse.)

1664

∞

JANUARY

Sam has taken a vow to see one play a month
(effectively this means me as well) until he has
spent fifty shillings, and then none until next New
Year's Day. (Unless he becomes worth £1,000 before
then, in which case he's free to come to some other
terms with himself.) If he breaks the vow he has to
put money in his poor box. So we have to find our
own entertainment at home and we take pleasure in
him teaching me geography. Which is not to say I
wouldn't like to go to the theatre more often, but
I don't mind so much not going if he's not going
either and he's here at home instead.

I managed to escape the Penns' anniversary dinner
by being ill, though I was well enough for a merry
dinner at home the next day, all masculine company
apart from me, which always makes things a little
more piquant and interesting, I think, as though
one were an honorary man for a few hours, and
privy to male secrets. I was wearing my Indian
blue gown for the first time – many compliments
on how pretty. Surgeon Pearse was there and a

couple of Sam's colleagues from Exchequer days, Llewellyn and Symons. Will Symons' wife had died a few days earlier and he kept changing in a moment from misery to merriment. Enough to make a dog laugh, Sam said, but I wished if I'd died my husband would be quieter. Surgeon Pearse told us that the King hasn't put Lady Castlemaine by, even though he dotes on Frances Stuart. He slights the Queen and she always pauses before going into her dressing room in case she finds the King in there with Mrs Stuart, as has happened before. Poor woman.

I always know that Sam will be out of the house on Monday mornings because that's the time the Navy Board attends the Duke of York, wherever he is, and that always takes all morning and often means dinner out as well. So it's a good time to do things that would be different if he was here. For example I quite often invite Will Hewer over for his breakfast beer so I can know exactly what's going on at the office. And when I heard that Father Fogarty was visiting London it was on a Monday morning that I invited him to call. It's ten years since I last saw him, when I was thirteen and he was a young curate. He still has his lovely manner, straightforward and intelligent, and his eyes warm as ever, though his hair is beginning to grey at the temples. He asked me if I ever thought of becoming a Catholic and I said that I often did, but it was impossible in my circumstances, it would do Sam so much harm. And he understood perfectly and said that a wife's first duty was to her husband and Our Lord knew all our hearts. And he blessed me. I can talk to him so much more easily than to Mr Milles at St Olave's. As it happened Sam came home while he was here and confessed afterwards that he liked the man very much (though I can tell he's frightened of the effect it might have on me, in making me turn more toward the Catholic faith).

A strange thing with Uncle Wight: they came to dinner – a very good roast swan from Hinchingbrooke – and he got me alone in a room and kissed me and said he hoped I was with child, he'd be very glad. From which we assume he has some good intentions toward us.

I went to Aunt Wight's to get a place to see the hanging of 'Colonel' James Turner for robbery. He was in the cart an awful long time, saying many prayers while hoping for a reprieve, but none came. In the end he had to mount the ladder. He'd petitioned for a silk halter – being soft and slippery it closes tighter and kills quicker than a stiff one. When the hangman had put the noose round his neck and flung him off the ladder, his cloak billowed out with a life of its own as his body swung. There was a kind of sigh from all the people there – they say twelve or fourteen thousand watched. He kept his composure to the end.

Uncle Wight made it the occasion to repeat his wish that I was with child, very fond and kind.

Poor Tom is sick, with a consumption, it's feared. Cousin Jane Turner says he won't last two months, though he doesn't look that bad yet. Lord Sandwich continues cool, but to everyone, not just Sam. Sam is beginning to be jealous of Will Hewer, found him coming out of our house and demanded of me what he was doing there, but I'd only been asking him if he knew of a place for Balty. (Who it turns out is going to be a soldier in Holland, which worries me.)

For some reason a ship's surgeon thought a mastiff dog would make the perfect gift for us and it duly arrived, a splendid beast called Towser, but big enough to eat my little Fancy. Or worse. Luckily she didn't become proud until Towser had been safely dispatched to Brampton. When she did, I had Mrs Buggins' dog in to lime her – he has the most beautiful colouring, so finely mixed it looks as though an artist has painted him. Unfortunately he's very small – too short to reach the spot – so the maids and I drew the parlour curtains and tried to help him to it. When Sam came home he clearly didn't like the idea of our witnessing them pleasuring themselves – but oddly enough he himself was provoked to more than usual pleasure with me in bed that night.

FEBRUARY

As he's a fishmonger, I went to Uncle Wight for our Lenten provisions and he's continued his attentions to me and we're convinced that if he dies without children he intends us very well. 'Father' Bowyer, whom I stayed with when Sam was at sea, has drowned in the Thames near his home. A good old man.

But we're more concerned about Tom, whose illness grows worse and worse, though not so bad as to stop Sam ranting at him for the disorder of his business, finding his bills and papers loose on the table, all in the sort of muddle Sam can't abide.

Lord Sandwich remains cool to everyone and we're concerned that he owes Sam £700. It's not a good thing to have a man both angry with you and in debt to you. And if there were to be a war with the Dutch and my Lord were killed at sea . . . We had a long talk about how Sam should handle himself and I advised him to be polite but to keep himself at a distance and he agreed this was the best way.

He's trying to arrange a marriage between our linen draper, young Betty Lane, and John Hawley, an Exchequer clerk. She's a pretty girl and he'd make a good husband. We're also trying to get the recently widowed Captain Grove for Pall. It's too late, alas, to think any more of a wife for Tom.

SPRING

Tom died on the 15th of March, aged twenty-nine.

I'd seen him a few days before and although he was desperately thin and weak from all the coughing, he didn't look as though he was at death's door. But on the 13th the Joyce brothers came to tell us that he was ill enough to need a nurse and of course Sam agreed to arrange it. Just as they were leaving, a message came from Cousin Jane Turner that he was so ill she feared he couldn't last much longer. This in itself was a terrible shock to Sam, made much worse when William Joyce drew him aside and told him that

Tom was actually dying of the pox which he'd had for a long time and never had cured. Uncle Fenner had recommended a doctor to Tom and the doctor had told him this as a secret, so of course he told his sons-in-law.

Tom was in bed, still well enough to know us but beginning to babble. His poor face seemed to have no flesh left on it, his cheekbones sticking out and his nose sharp and thin. We left him once the nurse had arrived but the next morning he was worse and didn't know either of us. Sam had a long talk with Tom's maid and found out that he was in debt to many different people, and whether he lived or died he was a ruined man. Uncle Fenner confirmed this. Sam found this as shameful as the nature of his illness. Later in the day we saw him again and the doctors had given him over and he knew no one and couldn't talk any sense. Cousin Jane Turner knew about the pox now and was talking of it in front of strangers, much to our mortification. And his mother was on her way to London which didn't make us feel any better.

In the middle of all this we were still able to have a fierce argument about me having new lace for my gown, which Sam refused, though he was prepared to spend the same amount on a new, plain one.

The next day, however, Cousin Jane turned up at noon to tell us that she'd had her own doctor in and he could find no trace of the ulcer in Tom's mouth that the other doctor had taken as proof of pox, and Tom had been able to talk sense and denied to the doctor that he'd ever had it. That comforted Sam and he ordered in a barrel of oysters and we all dined quite cheerfully. But after dinner when we went to see Tom he was clearly much worse and didn't know any of us.

The strange thing was that he talked in French, reciting proverbs, and there was not a trace of his stammer, his speech was perfect. About eight o'clock his pain on spitting became much worse and though he still talked, the words were indistinct and we couldn't make them out. It was dreadful to watch him drowning in his phlegm. When the death rattle began, Sam couldn't bear to see any more and left to take Cousin Jane home. I stayed and watched with Tom, holding his hand in mine until he took his last breath and a great flood of phlegm and stuff poured out.

The nurse had cleaned the worst of it up by the time Sam returned fifteen minutes later. She was holding Tom's eyes closed but hadn't had time to bind up his jaw so his chops were fallen open and the sight sent Sam into a transport of grief and crying. He stayed beside Tom until he was nearly cold and then he left the room while I helped the nurse and the neighbour lay him out. And there wasn't a trace of pox, his skin was as white and unblemished as new-fallen snow. Poor man, poor man.

We spent the night at Cousin Jane Turner's and Sam held on to me like a baby, full of grief. He got up very early to start making arrangements. I went to Tom's as soon as I was up to supervise the cleaning and try to put things in order and arrange for an inventory to be taken. We dined at Jane Turner's but my monthlies came on so badly Sam had to rush me home in a coach and help me to bed. The next day he arranged the burial, to be at St Brides, where their little brothers and sisters are buried in the churchyard, but he decided Tom should go inside, in the middle aisle, as near as possible to what had been their mother's pew. It cost an extra twenty shillings but he was determined to do it.

On the morning of the burial he went to his shoemaker to have the soles of his shoes blacked. Then he went to see the gravemaker at St Brides who said the middle aisle was very full but for sixpence he'd jostle them all together enough to make room. What we come to, when we're dead. A hundred and twenty people had been invited at one to two o'clock but people didn't come until four or five o'clock and by then there were about a hundred and fifty of them. There were six funeral biscuits apiece and whatever they wanted of mulled claret. The women sat in some rooms and the men in others. Sam and I were very fully occupied seeing to our guests; at one moment we met on a staircase and raised our eyebrows at our mutual endeavour. At last we went to church and saw poor Tom laid in his grave and then the company broke up.

We went back to Salisbury Court with the Turners and other close family and fell to a barrel of oysters and cake and cheese. It is astonishing how merry we were within an hour of his burial. Not to say his death wasn't keenly felt, it's almost because of the depth of the feeling that afterwards, once he was under the ground, we were so relieved that it broke out as merriment.

Thinking over it later, the whole business made me wish more than ever that I could at least die a Catholic, if not live as one, but I know that can't be.

Looking through Tom's papers, Sam has found that their brother John has been writing treacherous things about Sam not paying enough to their father. Sam was deeply upset and faced him with it but he just made silly, churlish answers. The more things are looked into, the worse it seems Tom's matters were. Apparently he owes £290 and he was so negligent he let the servants do all the cutting for his tailoring business instead of doing it himself, and as they say, the money's made in the cutting.

Meanwhile, life goes on at home. We argue about how much I can spend on clothes and now that Jane Gentleman is leaving we wonder whether to promote little Bess, from a good-natured cook-maid to what might be a proud, bad chambermaid. I've found it hard to think about it clearly. Like everything else, it's been overshadowed by Tom's death.

Sam's eyes hurt whenever he has to work by candle-light (which is most nights). My gown, newly laced with gold thread, has come home and is considered very handsome and well worth the doing – and the terrible argument we had about it the day before Tom died, as though there were nothing more important in the world, now all forgotten. But the next day when Sam came home and I was wearing it, there was an inquisition about where I'd been – which was nowhere. I gave him a short answer and he pulled my nose, and apart from the indignity it hurt and I cried. He apologised and blamed my beauty for inciting his jealousy. I know we're both prone to jealousy – the difference is that mine is usually justified.

We made up. And I was longing to wear the gown

out on Easter Sunday but Sam wasn't well enough to go out himself so I reluctantly stayed home with him. In the end it was a pleasant enough day and we spent it reading in Dr Fuller's book of *Worthies* about my family, the Cliffords, Earls of Cumberland. (The Pepys family isn't mentioned. Ha!)

Then it turns out that Tom has a bastard daughter from a former maid of his, an ugly wench. The baby is being cared for by a couple who want some assurance of money for her future. For a moment I think how it would be if we were to adopt the child – this never even crosses Sam's mind. Then I think, the child of a weak man who stammered, and an ugly maid-servant, and I find that the old pain of being childless is not so terrible that I would seize any chance. And if we're not to have children of our own, it doesn't mean we need to take in any waif that appears, as long as decent provision can be made for her, which I don't doubt Sam arranging.

It was like a time of transition, from feeling the loss of being childless to thinking that God has ordained our lives this way, and there are compensations in the way of a happy life together, our common enjoyment.

The nightingales are singing in the garden. Their song provokes us to joy. We're alive.

Lady Sandwich comes to visit me but I'm out. Sam, in the office, hears she has come and rushes home – to find her using the pot in the dining room, to the embarrassment of them both. They make conversation but she doesn't stay.

The House of Lords has voted its approval of a war with the Dutch and suddenly Sam is so busy with public business that he must do all his private papers at nights or on Sundays. It was a rare moment when we made a trip to Hackney via Whitechapel and Bethnal Green and then to Kingsland, where he and Tom boarded with Goody Lawrence when they were very young. The air was fresh and the country green. Then back to Islington to the King's Head where they used to know the landlord, Mr Pitts, and we ate and drank, a good dish of cream. But Sam was sad with the memory of old times, and the thought that the Pepyses were decaying and nobody in the family looked likely to increase them – although it turned out that Uncle Wight had certain intentions in that direction. He'd continued his great civility to me, so every time I bought our Lent fish from him it was the occasion for him to express his admiration for me, though he said he must be cool in front of his wife who was unreasonably jealous. We still thought he meant us both some good – his wife told me he was worth ten thousand, so I didn't offend him, while offering no encouragement. It all came to a head one day when he visited Sam at the office about some business and then came over to see me, knowing Sam was still at the office and he could talk to me alone.

And what he had to say was that he lacked children with his wife and I lacked children with Sam, and so we should try to have one between us and he would give me £500 beforehand and make the child his heir. Then he got closer and said how lovely my body was, and for all he knew what he proposed was perfectly lawful, as though I'm the village idiot to believe that. I could smell fish on him. I told him very plainly that I'd never dream of agreeing to his proposal. He didn't argue with the rebuff, didn't even try to pretend he'd been joking, but desired me not to tell anyone. As if I'm not going to tell my husband what his uncle's been up to! As soon as he'd gone I sent for Sam and told him what had happened and he agreed that all the man's kindness was simply lust. He's not quite sure how to deal with it yet. I find it slightly comical and slightly disgusting.

There seems to be trouble everywhere. The plague is increasing in Amsterdam and any ships coming from there are quarantined. Sam's had another bout of colic and tried tying his hands together in bed so that they couldn't lie outside the bed and cause him to catch cold, but he couldn't endure it for more than one night. The problem of a husband for Pall is becoming more pressing – if she stays unmarried for much longer then nobody will have her and she'll be completely on Sam's hands. Uncle Fenner has died. Sam was sad because one more of the family has gone, rather than because of any affection for the man himself. But he was half-brother to Sam's father and of course it makes Sam wonder how long his father can last.

∞   •

JUNE

Lord Sandwich has taken up with his Chelsea whore again. He's had his daughters boarding there so he has an excuse to visit and then as soon as he arrives he sends them out to the park while he does his business with Betty Becke. They hated it but thank goodness their mother is back in town now and they're with her. We had such a piquant day with them – they're staying at Dean Hodge's house in Kensington while their lodgings at the Wardrobe are refurbished. We went over after dinner and there was lots of company, including Lady Carteret, but everyone was most interested in Mr Becke of Chelsea and his wife and daughter. Miss Betty Becke hasn't a single outstandingly good feature but a fine figure and a good carriage. Very pleasant, and brains enough to entangle my Lord.

To see my Lady entertain her . . . We went into Sir Henry Finch's garden next door, most beautiful with arbours and orange trees and a splendid fountain, and we sat in the shade and sang and my Lady was most solicitous for Miss Becke's comfort. To one who didn't know the background it would have seemed the most beautiful and innocent of scenes. Truly, civility must be counted a bastion of the virtuous life.

The next day my Lady's daughters came to dine on a venison pasty and roast chicken, peas, lobster and strawberries. Very good. John Creed had invited himself along as well. After dinner we played cards, then at five o'clock took a boat down to Greenwich – the luxury of long summer days – and walked to the top of the hill and sat on the grass and played cards again as the light softened into dusk, and then to the Cherry Garden. Then back by boat, singing, to the bridge where we got off and walked round and took another boat for Somerset House (Lady Paulina's fearfulness being such that she wouldn't even consider going under the bridge by boat).

It was a pleasure to help the girls escape for a few hours the shadows that attend their parents. My Lady is desperately worried about my Lord's debts, particularly with so many children needing provision. She talks of the time six years ago when Sam was in charge of the household while my Lord was at sea, and we all lived in the Whitehall lodgings, how things seemed easier and clearer then. She says nothing of Betty Becke and remains very thin. My Lord and Lady are both thirty-nine but life is harder on a woman that age than on a man.

Oddly enough (or perhaps not) John Creed was with us again on a trip to Halfway House. He'd dined with us and I was dressed to go to a christening when Sam decided he wasn't going which meant I couldn't either – it was the child of one of their office clerks so I was invited as Sam's wife, not in my own right. I'd spent a long time dressing and was looking forward to going out and – something about Mr Creed being there – I talked sharply to Sam about keeping me at home, not wanting me to go out. He managed to keep his temper (because of Mr Creed) and we all went over the river to Halfway House but I felt close to tears and kept thinking of other times when he deprives me of things for no good reason. Someone gave him twenty pieces of new gold for a service he'd done them and he brought them home and showed me and I'd never seen such bright perfect coins before and wanted to hold them in my hand but he refused and kept them in his own hand before putting them away. Why? Why couldn't he allow me that simple pleasure? And other thoughts like that. And there was some trifling difference between us, whether we'd have some cherries, a silly argument, and I began crying and couldn't stop. He kept his temper again (because of Creed) and we made it up that night, though it took some doing.

I don't know what it is about John Creed that draws out of me things I wouldn't say otherwise – perhaps he subtly encourages our disagreements as a way of doing down his rival.

The next day Sam brought some cherries home and we lay together for the first time in two or three weeks because of his illness and mine.

SUMMER

There was a big argument about me buying earrings – beautiful amethyst pendants, cost 25 shillings – of my own accord. He was exceedingly vexed I'd spent his money without his permission. This is a man who has a thousand pounds in coin sitting in the cellar. I regard the money I save by prudent housekeeping as my money. He says every penny in the house is his, earned by his efforts. I say his desire to control every detail of my life is so extreme it verges on lunacy. Round and round we go, screaming and shouting. He says either I take the earrings back and get the money for them or he'll break them, but in any event I'm not having them.

So eventually I send Bess to the Exchange to get

the money for them, promising myself to make his life a misery for the next few days. He follows her and when he sees her going into the shop, he stops her and says that now he can see I've yielded he's content for me to have them.

But he didn't forgive me my words and continued angry with me until a couple of days later when we had the sort of day out that he excels at arranging. He'd decided the day before, on the spur of the moment, to go down to the Hope, where the fleet lay at anchor. The Pearses and the Clarkes were invited. I took great care preparing and packing our provisions, knowing that if he could be proud of my housewifery it would be the end of the coolness between us.

We left by barge at eight in the morning and had our breakfast of beer and calves' tongues and played cards, until we arrived at the Hope about one o'clock. It was a splendid sight, so many big fine ships riding gently on the waves, and as we sailed round them Sam knew each one and took great delight in naming them all. We had the cold collation I'd prepared (gammon, anchovies, etc.) and then set off back, playing cards again and guessing games.

They made good company though Dr Clarke wasn't there himself, having to bleed the King who'd taken a chill by leaving his waistcoat off. But his wife Frances is lively enough, though conceited about her rank as wife of the King's physician and constantly fluttering her clothes to show them off. I could have done with a little less of Sam's admiration of Elizabeth Pearse's complexion (the best he'd ever seen on any woman, young or old, or even a child) but Surgeon Pearse was equally complimentary to me. There's a particular merriment among married couples of the same age and interests. I was glad to be married. I was glad to be married to Sam. As we sailed back up the Thames, bringing night with us, we were both content.

And I was wearing my amethyst pendants.

∞

BRAMPTON 11TH JULY – 5TH AUGUST

Usual stuff.

∞

BACK TO TOWN

Sam and William Joyce rode out to Stevenage to meet me, great joy when my coach arrived. We dined at Welwyn and were home in time for supper. My heart leapt when I walked into the house again, it looked so neat and clean and I was so happy to be back. Next morning we had our traditional long lie-in, caressing each other and talking. My news from Brampton was only of the sluttish, improvident way his mother and father and Pall live down there. For example they buy good meat and then don't serve it until it's rotten. The food was dreadful the whole time.

Sam's news was more positive. He's in charge

of the contracts for the victualling of Tangier and he thinks it must be worth at least £200 or £300 a year from the suppliers he chooses. Mr Gauden has sent him two superb silver wine flagons with the most elaborate tracery I've ever seen. He's been giving serious thought to a woman for me and it seems Will Hewer has suggested a young woman from the family where he lodges, though Sam thinks she might be a bit too young. He's to have a new boy at last, Tom Edwards, who was in the choir of the Chapel Royal but must leave now his voice has broken. He comes highly recommended and Sam's determined to do his best for him. The news from Amsterdam is bad – seven hundred a week are dying of plague there.

So life has resumed and we're doing well together. I've burnt out the silver thread from an old lace collar and sold it to the silversmith so I can buy new silk lace for a petticoat. My little dog Fancy is lame, and it breaks our hearts to see her in that condition. Sam managed to get over his vow of spending no more money on the theatre by lending John Creed the money to take us all to *Henry the Fifth*, but he had no hesitation in paying £5 10s for a microscope. We spent all Sunday after dinner on it but had great difficulty at first in seeing anything at all, then when we managed it we looked at a drop of blood but all I could see was what looked like thousands of tiny red and yellow dots. We had no idea what we were supposed to see and whether this was right or not, but Sam's studying Dr Power's book of *The Microscope* with great delight, so I'm sure he'll master it.

In the Exchange we met Betty Lane, as was, Betty Martin as she is now and she was full of woe about her marriage. She'd rejected John Hawley who would have been a perfectly good husband, able to provide for her securely, if modestly, in favour of some ne'er-do-well. And now her husband hasn't a farthing to his name, she's with child, Sam must find him a place. I don't quite understand why she's so importunate to Sam. I know he thinks her very pretty and she's always charming to him but I've always assumed she's like that with all her customers. I wondered for a moment if there might be something more between them but afterwards he was scathing about her and said he'd offered her Hawley and she wouldn't have him so now she could brew as she'd baked. There didn't seem too much to worry about there.

On the way back from the Exchange we stopped at Charing Cross to see the Dutch giant, who's been measured by doctors and is certified to be nine feet tall. He lifted his arm out and Sam could walk underneath with his hat on and not touch it. And even on tiptoe, stretching his arm up as much as he could, Sam couldn't reach as far as his eyebrows. It's true the giant wears high-heeled shoes and a turban and long flowing clothes, but even so . . . He was a comely man, and his wife, quite small, was a comely woman.

Sam began to suffer baseless jealousy himself again. Young William Penn returned from Turin after two years abroad, in Paris and Saumur as well. He was wearing pantaloon breeches, looked very modish, a fine gentleman, all that a young man of twenty might hope to be. His father has summoned him home because of fear of a war with the Dutch.

We talked in French and he was very astute in his observations. He clearly enjoyed being able to show off to a lady three years older than himself. I in turn enjoyed his youth, his enthusiasm, his vitality. Sam, when he met him, thought him a fop who'd learnt little from his time abroad. (But he was annoyed because his French isn't good enough for the kind of conversation we were having.)

There was an occasion – it was late September and the wind was beginning to rattle the windows and the candles were having to be lit earlier each day – when young William came to visit. He and I sat together in the late afternoon. I ordered the fire to be lit and we talked of what he wanted to do, because he's still openly non-Conformist and that bars him from most opportunities here. And somehow we drifted into talking about his idea of establishing a community of like-minded people, but it couldn't be in this country because of the laws. He was imagining taking ship to America with them – as some have already – and we went through what they would have to take with them on the boat to ensure their survival. We decided on cows (and a bull of course) and sheep and chickens and geese and pigs (all with the requisite males).

Then we did hardware: axes, hammers, knives, nails, horseshoes. (We know there are horses out there already that can be bought from the natives.) Cooking pots, linen, seed-corn, needles, thread, scissors. As to the humans on board, nobody too old to work, young men and women preferred, babies and young children unlikely to survive the voyage and first winter.

I'm fascinated by the idea of living in a very different world. The candles flickered as we moved on to the location. To start with it must be somewhere with woods and rivers for shelter and water and wild food, the berries and beasts of the forest. And what would he call it? I suggested Utopia but he said it would never be that while it was populated by ordinary men, no matter how God-fearing. Arcadia? That took no account of drought and snakes and disease and death. What about Sylvania, simply a wooded country? He liked that. I said if he was taking the people out there he could go further and call it after himself, Penn-Sylvania. He thought that would be too proud, but when I urged that it sounded right he said it might be possible if it was named as a tribute to his father, not himself. This is not sheer fantasy, because Sir George Carteret has been granted land between the Hudson and the Delaware Rivers, and has called it, in honour of his birth place, New Jersey.

And then a message came from Sam for me to join him at supper at the Blands', and we blew out the candles and our dreamy talk drifted away on the smoke.

AUTUMN

I love the low September sun and hearing the wind rustle in the trees and the way the air is fresher after the dog days of August. Bartholomew Fair is always the marker of the change. We went as usual – I was in bed with my monthly and Sam had to persuade me to get up but I enjoyed it. There's something reassuring about the same people appearing year after year – Jacob Hall on the ropes as always, and the men with the dancing monkeys almost look like old friends. We took Sam's new boy, Tom, and it was lovely to see his innocent excitement. It was dark by the time we strolled through the little stalls, very prettily lit up with lanterns and candlelight, and I bought some little combs to give to the maids.

The thing that has most changed my life is that I have a new woman. She's Mary Mercer, whose mother Will Hewer lodges with. She's seventeen but I don't think she's too young, as Sam feared. I'd been married two years by that age, it's not so young. And she certainly knows how to dress hair. She did mine before I attended Mrs Milles's child's christening and she knew it all: the loose curls on the forehead, 'favourites'; the long ringlets over the ears, 'heartbreakers'; and the little ones close to the cheeks, 'confidants'. She did them all perfectly. And looked very neat herself while she attended me at the christening.

The next test was a dinner for the Joyces and various other relatives, eleven of us altogether including Mary, and she took her place at table and was a very natural part of the company. Sam had been out that morning and bought a dozen silver salt cellars and we had our new wine flagons on the table and our silver plate displayed in the cupboard. We could see everyone eyeing it and there was a moment that we briefly, privately, raised our glasses to each other, and it was such a warm feeling, our life together.

After dinner Sam went off to a Tangier committee meeting and our company left, and when he came back we had a cold collation and sat singing and playing the harpsichord with Mary and little Tom until eleven at night. Sam is so joyful to have such pleasure in his house that our small disputes are forgotten and we both thank God for our condition.

This is not to say that there are no thorns at all in this bed of roses.

The nature of Sam's work is such that there'll be times, particularly when the fleet is being prepared to go out, that he'll be immensely busy and I'll hardly see him. I fully accept this and I know that his hard work is the source of all our wealth. So when news came that Captain Robert Holmes − I always knew he'd go far − had taken all the Dutch forts in West Africa on the Guinea coast, it brought the likelihood of war much closer. And when news arrived from America that the Dutch had surrendered New Amsterdam to Richard Nicholls and it's now to be called New York, war with the Dutch looked certain. So Sam had a great deal to do to ensure all the ships were fitted and supplied and manned. All this I understand.

But what I find difficult is that he'll go to church on a Sunday morning and then not come home, but spend all the rest of the day gadding about from church to church, searching out beauties to look at. And when I overhear a neighbour's maid telling Bess that Mr Pepys has been seen ogling a woman and making such persistent advances to her that in the end she pulled out a pin and made as though to stab him with it, while I've been at home all day on my own, wondering where he is and when he'll return, then I have plenty of time to get angry about it.

Which I told him very plainly as soon as he walked through the door and he said he thought I'd been ill and didn't want to be disturbed, but he let me rant on because he knew he was in the wrong. Then he offered me lots of sweet words and we were at peace again. Except that every time the cog of trust moves back a notch.

A few days later it was his turn to rant at me – quite unjustly – in bed in the morning and we even came to blows. I hit him because he was so unreasonable and sometimes I know that a good smack in the mouth will make him realise the case more than any number of words. It was over the way dinner had been served the day before. We'd had the Pearses and Frances Clarke and her niece to dine with us by invitation, and we had oysters and a good chine of beef and various pies and tarts, and cheese and fruit – the usual thing. And we sat over it very pleasantly all afternoon, it seemed to me.

But there's something about Elizabeth and Frances. Sometimes we three ladies dine together and then go to the theatre and some of our merriment involves the mockery of men. But these same ladies, who mock in private, fawn in public. As soon as a man apears they have to put themselves to flattering and beguiling him. And Sam is of course delighted to be the object of their attentions but I think it makes him unduly critical, as though everything must be more than perfect for them. So he thinks the beef was undercooked. It wasn't and if it had been we could easily have cooked it some more. To come to blows about it the next morning seemed ridiculous.

On the 10th October it was our ninth wedding anniversary but Sam was too busy for us to keep it in any extraordinary way. The leaves are falling and there's a chill in the air.

∞

EARLY WINTER

Bonfire time of year. Our gardeners are burning leaves, sweet smell. On Gunpowder Plot Day we went to see *Macbeth*, a pretty good play but best for the acting and amazing spectacle – witches flying and a cave that sank into the floor. On our way home we had to go all the way round by London Wall because of the number of bonfires in our path. I wonder sometimes with the sparks flying around in the streets that the houses don't catch fire but it never seems to happen that way, it always seems to start from the inside. A couple of months ago there was a bad fire at the dockyard in Deptford, and if the wind had been blowing in a different direction they would have lost all their stores, at a time when they were trying to get the fleet out. But no harm done this night, except taking so long to get home.

November has been quite a quiet month, Sam working hard. We have dined with my Lady a few times while my Lord is away with the fleet. She says that Lady Castlemaine's beauty is so decayed one wouldn't know her. She's very calm about my Lord going to sea, presumably because at least it means he isn't with the woman from Chelsea. Sam thinks our own dinners are every bit as good quality as my Lady's (when Lord Sandwich is away). I'll take that as a testament to my housekeeping. Our estate continues to grow – I'm sent a pair of good silver candlesticks by a purser who wants a favour from Sam, who finds himself worth about £1,300 now. A heavy iron chest has arrived to keep the money in.

Our little Tom has been ill and Mr Hollier has diagnosed the stone. Please God it doesn't get as bad as Sam's did, I don't think I could bear to witness another of those operations. Sometimes he wakes very early and stays in bed and plays his lute until it's time to get up, so we're woken by music floating through the house, lovely. Quite often Thomas Hill, Sam's old friend, comes in the evenings and then there's much playing and singing – Mary Mercer can also sing well.

I went to the burial of a little boy of William Joyce's. Even he was quiet for a few hours.

The Dutch fleet has withdrawn into its own harbours and everyone claims it as our victory. But it's merely the weather that has driven them off, and we shall certainly see them again next spring. Meanwhile Christmas is coming and the goose is getting fat . . .

Sam has ordered fruit to be sent down to his parents for Christmas and, great luxury, we've changed to wax candles instead of tallow to see if they'll be easier on his eyes when he has to work by candlelight. He doesn't mind the extra expense if it means they'll smoke less and not irritate his eyes so much. They certainly burn more steadily but we still use tallow for the servants and kitchen.

Someone gave us an eagle (Thank you) which lived for a few days mainly in the house of office because I couldn't stand it fouling everywhere else. We managed to pass it on to Cousin Jane Turner who was mighty pleased with it, though she has no more suitable space for it at Salisbury Court than we have here. I think it would be better to just let the poor creature fly away except I think its wings have been clipped, so it must make its life where it can. As must we all.

We don't lie together as husband and wife nearly as often as we used to. Sometimes that's a relief but sometimes I long for more physical tenderness. I think of the eagle tethered to her perch. We live our lives the best we can.

A week before Christmas we went to bed early and so woke up early, and calling for the servants to come and light the candles, they had no light and had to go out and beg one from the house next door. Sam was furious I didn't keep the command of the servants that I should have. It was just too early in the morning for this and I snapped at him and he hit me a very painful blow over my eye and drove me into a fury so I scratched and bit him, mad with having to live like this.

Then he wheedled me into not crying and sent for butter and parsley to put on my eye but it was black and I had to lie with a poultice on it all day. He was vexed to the heart when he saw what he'd done, but too late, a black eye takes two weeks to come and go and it meant my Christmas would be spent indoors at home. I used my good eye to read *Cyrus* . . . the ideal prince is tender and gentle . . . But it was almost worth it, to see the guilt on his face every time he looked at me.

News came that de Ruyter and his Dutch fleet had retaken all the Guinea coast, completely undoing Captain Holmes's work, and that our Royal Guinea company was ruined. Even more certainty of a spring campaign.

And a comet has appeared in the sky. It's low in the sky and difficult to see for all the buildings and smoke in London, but I saw it, large and fuzzy, with the ghost of a tail, and of course everyone wonders what it portends, whether it's the Dutch business or something we don't know yet. I don't really believe in those superstitions and yet it does seem significant that it comes at the end of the year when we all naturally wonder what the future will bring. Time will tell.

Meanwhile I'm grown close to my servants who are unspokenly sympathetic about my black eye and we concentrate on having the house clean and stocked with food and we all eat dinner together on Christmas Day. Sam goes to church again in the afternoon then spends his time setting his books and papers in order while I go to bed with a new volume of *Cyrus*. The next day Sam goes to a grand dinner at the Battens, which I have no heartache at missing. His manner very kind to me – it could hardly be otherwise.

I stayed up with Will Hewer and Mary Mercer and little Tom and Bess and Susan playing cards and blindman's bluff until four in the morning. Sam left us to it when he came back from the Battens and went to bed. He was up at seven in the morning to go to

Woolwich. We all slept very late and consequently the next night stayed up even later and I didn't go to bed until eight o'clock, meeting Sam on his way down as I went up. He raised an eyebrow but didn't say anything.

On the last night of the year we each put our accounts in order and then as the clock struck one and the New Year began he kissed me in the kitchen and we wished each other a merry New Year and went to bed in health and happiness.

1 6 6 5

∞

WINTER

Cold, cold, cold. No coaches in the streets because of
the ice and snow. Cosy afternoons in my closet with
little Tom, telling him stories from *Cyrus*: how as a
newborn baby Cyrus was exposed on a mountainside
by his jealous grandfather and rescued by a shepherd
who substituted his own dead baby, which was torn
to pieces by savage animals, so the grandfather was
convinced it was Cyrus's body; how every time
he comes near rescuing Mandane, some trick or
treachery plucks her from under his nose; how noble,
beautiful men and women sit in forest glades telling
of The Absent Lover, or The Jealous Lover, or The
Lover Whose Mistress Is Dead. There's so much and
I love retelling it as much as reading it. Tom sits
on a low stool with his chin cupped in his hands as
darkness falls and the fire is our only light, flickering
on his face.

   An innocent enough pleasure, and there's nothing
much for him to do while Sam's at the office, but the
other servants don't like it of course. Our cook Jane
has turned out to be a cunning wench and when I

warned her about her poor work she took the chance to tell Sam I favoured Tom above everyone and always defended him and blamed the rest of them. If I defend him it's because he's young and does his best, he's not deliberately lazy and if he oversleeps it's because he's very tired, not that he can't be bothered to get out of bed. The end of it was that Jane left and as always Sam blamed me – but he doesn't spend the time with these people that I do, he has a world beyond this house. I shrugged it off. We can get another cook and until then I'll do it myself rather than have someone who makes me uncomfortable in my own home.

There's been trouble with Bess as well. She brought a vagrant woman, known to be a thief, into the house to help her with the washing. Sam was furious and ordered Bess to be locked in the cellar for the night, which I did, although I also gave her a blanket and a candle, unknown to him. But I can see she won't last much longer.

Mary Mercer is still a loyal member of the family, though. We have pleasant domestic evenings in the kitchen sometimes, when Tom plays his viol while she combs through Sam's hair for nits or perhaps washes his ears or feet.

She and I had a visit to the hot-house together. First you're rubbed with oil and salves to allow the heat of the steam to penetrate into the body while stopping the water getting in, and after sitting in the steam for a long time you immerse yourself completely in a tub of hot water. When you get out you're wrapped in cloths soaked in myrrh and pomander and saffron and you lie still until the cloths are removed and then your skin feels wonderfully soft and smooth and you vow that you will come regularly because the sensation is so pleasant, despite taking five hours. I made Sam wash himself in hot water so he would know how it felt to be really clean and he agreed it was pleasant enough, though not something he'd want to do every day.

He's much more excited by the fact that he's been elected a member of the new 'Royal Society' where learned men gather to talk about all sorts of things in nature. He's been asked to enquire of my old admirer Captain Holmes about using a pendulum clock to determine longitude. (I understand latitude but despite our work on the globes I don't quite understand longitude yet.) Enquiring of Captain Holmes meant going to the Tower where he was imprisoned as soon as he returned from Guinea (simply to appease the Dutch, he isn't charged with anything). The conclusion was that pendulum clocks were no better than vulgar reckoning.

A terrible story came home from the Exchange, that de Ruyter, the Dutch commander, when he re-took the forts in Guinea had thrown all the people, men, women and children, into the sea, tied back to back. There was the most intense feeling of outrage at this, but two days later the man who'd brought the news, a Swede, confessed it was a lie and the judges ordered him to be whipped round the Exchange and to choose between having his ears cut off or having his nose slit. He chose to lose his ears. Whatever false stories may be spread, the fact remains that the Dutch are better at many things than we are. It takes us sixty men to plait rope where it takes them twenty. And while our dockyards are untidy and dirty, theirs are neat, and everything safely stowed. And they pay their men with money, not tickets. God help us if it comes to war.

But everyday life goes on. We had a fine Shrove Tuesday dinner of fritters, which I made. The streets were full of boys playing football and for the first time I saw the customary game of flinging at cocks. The boys stand in a circle and throw sticks at a tethered bird and whoever knocks it down and catches it before it gets up again wins it. Great merriment at all its squawking.

On Valentine's Day, Dick Penn, William's younger brother, came very early to our bedside to claim me as his Valentine. Sam was claimed at the front door by Mrs Bagwell, the carpenter's wife, who seems to have to visit Sam rather a lot about work for her husband. A pretty woman, too. We heard the same day that Mr Barlow had died, saving us the £100 a year Sam paid him for giving up his claim on the clerkship. It seems such a long time ago, all that struggle to get his position, and now it's almost impossible to imagine Sam not being a man of importance and influence.

On the last day of February we had a terrible falling out because my kitchen accounts were 7 shillings short (I'd given it to my mother but I couldn't admit to that) and he immediately flew into a rage and called me a beggar and reproached me for my family, so I called him the son of a prick-louse and a washerwoman and it went on and on, both of us very angry. But to have such a reaction to the loss of 7 shillings is absurd. However, I had to make it up with him the next day because he'd promised a long while ago to give me £20 for Easter clothes on March

1st and I was determined he wouldn't wriggle out of it. And how he boggled at having to hand it over, but he did, eventually.

I went straight out and collected Elizabeth Pearse. There are times, particularly when I have money and feel more her equal, when she can be an excellent companion. We went to Unthank's (she originally recommended him to me as a tailor) and I chose an ash-coloured flowery silk which will make a noble suit, I think. Then we went to the New Exchange and bought two lace collars and some ribbons and some rosewater, and rode home in a very good humour. On the way she pointed out a new shop. On one side of the street Mr Farr's shop has a sign saying 'The best tobacco by Farr' and now a rival has opened opposite him with a sign saying 'Far better tobacco than the best tobacco by Farr'. It tickled us all the way home.

The new suit was ready by the time we dined with my Lord and Lady. All differences seem to have been forgotten and Lord Sandwich showed us both the greatest respect, carving for us himself. Afterwards my Lady talked of getting Sir George Carteret's son for Lady Jemima. (Nobody mentioned that she has a crooked neck and he has a gammy leg.) She told us about the looseness of the Maids of Honour at Court and what mad pranks they get up to — one of them dressed up like an orange wench and went about crying oranges until she fell over in the mud and showed her fine shoes, and she was put to a great deal of shame by the people. Few men want to venture on them for wives.

The cold caused Sam another attack of colic and

he passed two stones. He bought a hare so he could have a hare's foot with the joint attached to carry about — his old one didn't have the joint so it didn't work properly, and strange to say, as soon as he handled the new one he broke wind and felt much better. Who knows if it's the hare's foot or the turpentine pills? Winter's nearly over and he's always better in warmth.

∞

APRIL

There's plague in St Giles's parish, a few dying every week, but people say the true figures are higher — the unfortunate families are too terrified to report it because of fear of being shut up in their houses. But it seems to be staying there and hasn't spread much beyond. St Giles is a poor place, there's always a lot of sickness there. There's no trace of it in our life in the City, with Sam very busy still on supplies for the fleet and even more work now he's Treasurer of the Tangier Committee as well, which he finds time-consuming and not yet very profitable. But on the Fast Day against the Dutch war there was time to go to Hackney with John Creed and Mary Mercer and we all enjoyed taking the air and stopping at an inn to eat a bit and play shuffleboard.

We were both taken aback, though, when my Lady told us Mr Creed wished to be the servant of Betty Pickering, her niece. My Lady had sung her praises to him quite innocently, and she didn't think she'd been severe enough in her reply to his presumption. Sam can't bear the thought of his rival (though Sam has far outstripped him in office and income) aiming so near my Lord's family. He advises my Lady not to let Mr Creed come as often as he has in the past.

It appears that the King knows Sam by name now, for when he was walking in Whitehall the King called him over and asked him about the ships still sitting in the river for want of supplies. It's an honour, of course, to be known personally, although it means he can be called to account at any moment. The same day he was angry with me for acknowledging the receipt of a watch from a solicitor by opening the box and giving the messenger 5 shillings for bringing it. But it was only a little anger and the watch turns out to be worth £14. I understand his concern: it's a subtle business, gifts.

The trees are in blossom in our garden and all over the town. The fleet is out and nearing Holland, over a hundred ships. And the plague is growing in the western parishes of London.

SUMMER

Early May and the weather gets warmer and fear begins to grow of what the summer will bring. All we can do is trust in God. More immediately, poor Aunt James came up to town to have her breast cut off for cancer. And Sam, having grown his hair long again, had it all cut off for the convenience of wearing a periwig once more. So, great things and small, we live our lives.

Sam's mother came to visit (and is here still). As long as it's at my home I'm as patient as I know how with her in her dotage. I took her and Mary Mercer to the christening of Thos. Pepys's child, which she seemed to enjoy. Sam naturally finds he has to be busy all the time she's here, which is sad for her because she'd much rather have him beside her than me. At least I had a lovely new hood for Whitsun, of yellow silk with tiny black bird's-eye dots. And Mary and I went to Mr Langford, the tailor who's taken over Tom's business, and ordered two new silk suits for Sam – an expense he says he can least afford but can best bear with.

The Dutch fleet is out, about a hundred men-of-war, and fireships etc. In the third week of May plague deaths are said to be about fifty a week. I took my mother some calf's tongue and brain (and the most recent pages of my journal). My parents live in Long Acre – a wretched part of the town, I'm ashamed and sorry for them that they've come to this and can hardly bear admitting it to Sam – and on my way back I saw the terrible sight of a red cross painted on the door of a boarded-up house and the words 'God have mercy on us' written over it. There were cries coming from inside but nobody could go to them and the house was being watched so they couldn't get out. I walked as distant from it as I could. I didn't even tell Sam I'd seen it in case he wouldn't let me visit my parents again.

We took his mother on a tour of the old haunts,

out through Whitechapel and Bethnal Green to Hackney, finishing at the King's Head in Islington as usual. This was his mother's native region and she talked incessantly as each familiar sight brought out more stories. At least from a coach one can look out at the view instead of being trapped in a room with her, and gazing at the trees and the green fields I even had a certain sympathy. She had to gabble about it to hold it close. This was part of her early, happy life and it was possible she might never see it again, being the age she was – we never know when is the last time we'll do something, only looking back afterwards, if we live to do so.

I didn't know when I went to the theatre in the middle of April that it would be my last visit for a long time, now the Lord Chamberlain has ordered all the theatres to be closed until the plague is over. And the strange thing is that the play we saw was called *The Ghosts*. Not just the theatres are closed either, but all the public places: the gaming tables, dancing rooms and music houses, puppet shows, rope dancers, anything that causes people to gather together. (Except for church and business.)

The fleet has sailed to engage with the Dutch, who've taken eight of our merchant ships bringing supplies from Hamburg – a serious loss. On the 3rd of June we could hear the distant gunfire of the battle off Lowestoft. In the streets the apprentices outside the shops stopped shouting 'What do you lack? What do you lack?' and stood quietly, straining their ears to listen to the dull booms from a hundred miles away. Lord Sandwich is in the battle, and Mr Coventry with him, and they're much in our thoughts. We dined with my Lady and she was neither confident nor fearful but calmly trusting in God. The days dragged by, waiting for news. We expected to hear on the 7th, but nothing. There were rumours that Lord Sandwich was dead.

And then on the 8th came the news of a great English victory – we have taken or sunk twenty-four of their best ships and killed or taken six thousand of their men, while not losing more than six hundred ourselves. The Duke of York, Lord Sandwich, Mr Coventry and Sir William Penn all safe and done well. That night we had a great bonfire at the gate and all gathered to celebrate, our enmities forgotten for the moment.

But we and the Dutch have a common enemy which has not forgotten us.

On the 10th of June we heard that the plague had come for the first time inside the City walls, to Fenchurch Street where Dr Burnet, our good friend and physician, lives. The next day his door was shut up. He'd found his serving man stricken with it and voluntarily shut himself up in the house with him, earning great good will from his neighbours.

The weather is very hot. A bad thing for disease, and it looks set to get hotter.

But still we live our lives. We dine well at home, the Joyces with us, one minute they're all honey to each other, the next all turd. We sing late with Thomas Hill and Thomas Andrews. I'm learning to paint. We walk in the garden in the cool of the evening. We buy me a lace collar from Mary Batelier, our pretty sempstress in the Old Exchange, but business is slack, she says, people are leaving town. I take Sam's mother to supper at Will

Hewer's. He treats us nobly, but talk always comes round to the plague. One hundred and twelve dead of it last week. Tobacco the best preventative, it's said. I believe in the power of tobacco because I've seen it for myself. We were in a coach when the horse suddenly got a terrible fit of the staggers. The coachman cut its tongue to make it bleed but the horse was desperately ill and looked as though it would drop down dead. Then the coachman blew some tobacco in its nose and the horse sneezed and within a few minutes was well enough to draw us home. But I won't smoke a pipe and chewing it is very loathsome. There are other ways to escape.

Sam has been to see William Sheldon, the Clerk of the Cheque at Woolwich, to ask if I can go to stay for a month or two if necessary. The Inns of Court are leaving town. It's beginning to be noticeable that there are fewer people in the streets. The poor people flock to astrologers and fortune-tellers and doctors who promise infallible remedies. Toad amulets, unicorn horn, pure gold are all certain to cure it. I urge Sam to make his mother return to Brampton, for her health's sake. (And mine.) She is reluctant because she has much better care and entertainment here than she will have at her own home, but Sam persuades her it's best, and says that I'll be moving soon as well.

It was when I took her to the Cross-Keys at Cripplegate to board the coach to Brampton that I fully realised how bad things were becoming. There was an atmosphere of fearful hurry, waggons and coaches driving off fully loaded with people leaving London to get out into the country where there was no plague. Sam's mother still didn't want to go, although she didn't say so, and put off getting into the coach so long that she lost her place and had to travel in the open part behind. They set off at last and after I'd waved her out of sight my attention was caught by a poor servant girl running after another coach crying, 'Mistress, don't leave me, don't leave me to be starved and undone.' But her mistress turned her face away and wouldn't look at her and soon they left her behind. She saw me watching and asked if I needed a servant and I said I didn't because I was leaving myself and she said, 'So are they all. Then I shall starve if I don't die of pestilence first.' I gave her 3 shillings, all I had on me.

In the third week of June there were 267 plague deaths. The following week there were 470. The King and the Court left for Syon House, and the Queen Mother left for France. On July 1st the Lord Mayor issued his orders. There will be an examiner in every parish to enquire which people are sick and if he finds they have the plague the constable will be ordered to lock up the house. Two watchmen, one for day and one for night, will make sure that nobody comes in or out. There are to be searchers, poor women of the parish who'll examine every body to find out the cause of death, and they must carry a rod across their body at least three feet long to keep people away on either side. They may not go into any uninfected houses or have any other employment. The burial of the dead must be at night and the graves must be at least six feet deep. No children are allowed to attend a burial. A hackney coach that has carried an infected person must be aired for five days before being used again. All dogs and cats are to be killed.

It's time to go. I leave for Woolwich tomorrow with Mary, and I'm taking Fancy as well, I'm not going to let them kill her. I'll make a last trip (for the moment) to my parents and leave these pages with them.

∞

PLAGUE SUMMER, WOOLWICH 1665

Mary Mercer and Mary the maid and Fancy and I are settled in William Sheldon's pretty house near the dock and we hope that being six miles down river from London, and the air being fresher, we'll escape, if it's God's will that we should.

Sam came down very late on the first Saturday night and stayed so we could go the next day to dine with Sir George Carteret and his family. There's to be a marriage between his son Philip and my Lord's daughter Lady Jemima. (So she hasn't ended up as a pedlar with a pack on her back after all.) Philip is very modest and good-natured, but even so my Lady Sandwich, who was there as well, wondered privately to us if her daughter would like the match. We assured her she would. Lady Carteret showed us the most hearty kindness – they're all greatly content at the prospect.

∞

THE WEEK ENDING 11TH JULY, 700 DIED OF
PLAGUE.

I worry of course about Sam still being in the city.
We parted very fondly when I first came here, yet
when I went to the Carterets again for dinner, with
Will Hewer escorting me, and met him there, we
were like strangers with each other. I suppose not
being in our own home and being on public view
made us shy of being fond to each other.

Sam volunteered to go with Philip to Dagnams in
Essex where he'd meet Lady Jem for the first time.
They were nobly received but Philip was too shy to
say anything or take any notice of her though when
Sam asked him he said he liked her mightily. Sam
told him he must take her by the hand and lead her
to church, and he told him the compliments he should
pay. But still at church that morning he did nothing, so
Sam urged him again and after dinner they were left
alone in the room, everyone slipping away quietly,
and a little girl coming last and innocently shutting the
door on them, which made everyone laugh. After an
hour they emerged for church again with him leading
her by the hand. So that was that.

Before they left, Sam told him he must tip the
servants and he recommended £10 to the chief
man-servant to share out. It's strange that the young
man's own father hasn't taught him any of this. No
wonder they're all so grateful to Sam.

The weather continues very hot and airless. We

walk down to the dock most nights but even there no breeze comes. Cooler than being in the city though. Sam stayed one night and we were very merry but I'm beginning to wonder how long it will all last. It should finish with the cool weather in September, but that's six weeks away.

∞

18TH JULY — 1,089 DIED LAST WEEK OF PLAGUE.

Over a thousand last week. It's got to King Street and I fear for our old neighbours there in Axe Yard. The churchyards are running out of space for burials but the poor people beg to be buried there, not in the plague pits where the bodies are just tumbled in from the carts. Everyone knows the figures are false. When the consequences of the sickness being known are so terrible, the whole family locked in with the sick one for forty days, which means they all die one by one, then it's worth any money to bribe the searchers to find another cause of death. But over a thousand, admitted, is bad enough. It's so hot and there are thunder and lightning storms but never a drop of rain. Even here in Woolwich the drains are stinking, with no water to wash them clear.

I haven't seen Sam at all this week, though he sends frequent messages. He's been to Hampton Court where the King and Court have moved to be further away, and he's been to Dagnams again on the marriage business. He's also trying to do something for Balty but he's not keen to see too much of him because he lives in one of the western out-parishes where the plague is worst. I miss him. Although my drawing master, Alexander Brown, is good company – and a good teacher, of course.

∞

25TH JULY – 1,840 DIED LAST WEEK OF PLAGUE.

Sam managed one night here this week – greatly admired my drawings. The Court is moving to Salisbury. The Carteret marriage is done, in a hurry, because of the times. Apparently in the morning they were both red in the face and looked well enough pleased with their night's lodgings.

The plague is come to St Olave's, our own parish. Dear Mr Milles saw fit to be one of the first to leave, so he's not there in the hour of his parishioners' greatest need. I'm sure Father Fogarty would never leave his flock like that. I wish Sam would leave but he says it's impossible for him to live at Woolwich while the office is still in Seething Lane. May God preserve us all.

∞

1ST AUGUST — 2,010 DIED OF THE PLAGUE.

A thousand a week seemed shocking enough and now it's double. And we still have all of August to get through and the sky remains cloudless and the sun, instead of being welcome, is like a malevolent presence, burning us up. Sam travelled all the way from Seething Lane to Whitehall, and there and back he saw only two carts and two coaches. Everyone with the means to go has gone, except those who stay to do their duty, a very few physicians, a very few ministers. The Lord Mayor and the Fathers of the City have stayed, and outside the City walls Lord Albermarle has taken charge of Westminster and the other out-parishes.

Sam arrived late one night when Mary and I were at the quay listening to a fellow in a barge fiddling, the music carrying over the water, and we saw Sam's boat approaching and his weary smile and I felt very grateful to have a husband who made provision for me. He had to leave early in the morning, but not before he looked at my pictures and some of Peg Penn's which were there (Mr Brown teaches us both). He found hers very short of mine, which pleased us both. Troubling, though, was the news that de Ruyter and his Dutch fleet have slipped past our English fleet and got safely home. This will be some dishonour to Lord Sandwich.

∞

8TH AUGUST – 2,800 DIED OF THE PLAGUE.

They have to bury the dead in daylight now, there aren't enough hours of darkness to bury them all. The country people won't let anyone from London through their villages; I often wonder what happened to the little serving wench I saw abandoned at Cripplegate, whether she tried to escape by walking out of London and met her fate, like so many others, dying of starvation in a hedge or ditch. At the Court in Salisbury a groom's wife has died of it, and a man on one of our ships at Deptford, and a man near the rope yard here in Woolwich. The poorest parishes are the most grievously afflicted. The sufferings of women in labour, shut up with no midwife or woman friend to attend them, are past imagining.

I heard of a tradesman in Smithfield whose wife had the plague on her and fell into labour with their first child. He ran distracted from house to house but couldn't get a midwife or a nurse to attend her and his two servants both fled from her. The only help he could get was that a watch-man promised to send a nurse in the morning. The man went back broken-hearted and assisted his wife as best he could, delivering a dead child and his wife dying within the hour in his arms. He held her body fast until the morning when a nurse came at last and found him sitting with his dead wife in his arms. He was so overwhelmed with sorrow he died himself in a few hours, with

no sign of the infection but sunk under the weight
of his grief.

∞

15TH AUGUST — 3,880 DIED OF THE PLAGUE.

At last the Navy Office is to move, to Greenwich
Palace. There was no point in the office being in town
because no merchants would come to see them there,
whereas they're willing to venture to Greenwich. The
offices are being made ready but it will take a week,
and God knows how many more will be dead by then.
The tolling of bells for the dead is ceaseless in town.
As one church stops, the next one begins. That and
the night cries of 'Bring out your dead' are the only
sounds, save the wailing of the dying and bereaved.

But life here still follows more or less the usual
course with only one or two houses shut, though
outside in the country on the way to Greenwich
there's Combe Farm with thirty people shut up in
it and the only way they come out is in a coffin.

I continue with my painting. Sam spends a night
and a pleasant morning with us, sitting in the shade
in the garden, though there's little enough grass left
because of the drought. He says my pictures please
him beyond anything in the world. Mary and I talk of a
pearl necklace for me and he promises one worth £60
within two years, or sooner if my painting continues
so well. God please we may all live to see the day.

22ND AUGUST — 4,230 DIED OF PLAGUE.

Sad news that good Dr Burnet who disclosed his servant's infection and shut up his house of his own free will has died of plague. The sadness is that he had been through the forty days and his house was open again, but he bravely assisted another doctor in opening a dead body to examine the organs and in doing so he caught the infection and died.

The Navy Board are now meeting at Greenwich but still Sam chooses to sleep at Seething Lane, I don't quite know why. 'Lady' Brouncker has been to visit me, the mistress of Lord Brouncker, one of the new Navy Commissioners. She's not in the least interested in me, simply wants to establish her position, I think. And I've had trouble with Mary Mercer, having to restrain her from gadding abroad with some Frenchmen we met in the town, which occasioned high words on both sides.

The plague is established now in Greenwich and Deptford and Woolwich. It seems we won't escape it so easily.

∽

29TH AUGUST — 6,000 DIED OF THE PLAGUE
LAST WEEK.

The Clerk of St Olave's told Sam nine died in the
parish last week of plague but he only returned six,
ascribing the remainder to other causes. This happens
all over the town, and everyone knows a truer figure
for last week is near ten thousand. So many souls.

But at last Sam has come to lodge at Mr Sheldon's
house here, and despite the thought of death all
around, our time is livelier because he always brings
visitors in his wake and life is more social. So Captain
Cocke came to dine and we visited the Penns who
are lodging near the rope yard (Peg Penn's nose well
out of joint that my pictures are so much better than
hers) and young William Penn came to visit me and
we talked of France and had a merry supper when
Sam returned, and for a couple of hours forgot our
situation.

Sam and the other officers met the Justices to
try to find a way to stop the townspeople coming in
crowds to burials — it's forbidden but there's a kind
of madness abroad. There was a complaint against a
man in the town for bringing a child from an infected
house in London. It was the youngest child of a saddler
in Gracious Street who'd buried all his other children
of the plague and he and his wife were shut up and
despaired of escaping. So they prevailed on a friend,
and handed the child stark naked through the window
into his arms and he put it in fresh clothes and brought

it to Greenwich. When the officers heard this story they agreed that the child could be received and kept in the town.

Twenty-one people are dead so far at Combe Farm. The Lord Mayor has ordered bonfires to burn throughout the City to clear the air. There's no Bartholomew Fair this year.

∞

7TH SEPTEMBER—7,000 DIED LAST WEEK.

I had a letter from Balty that our father is desperately ill, though not of the plague, and I asked Sam to send them something and he gave me 20 shillings. These are odd and melancholy times. Sam went to Sir Robert Viner's house to get a promise of him lending money to the Navy, and it was a very fine house as might be expected, but what stays in my mind is that he'd had a blackamoor boy, as the fashion is, and when the boy died of a consumption Sir Robert had his body dried in an oven and now the blackamoor lies there, entire, on display in a box in the hall. Amid all these plague deaths I still find that unbearably sad. It's as well, I think, that none of us knows what our end will be, or how should we endure it?

We walk in the fields in the evening. At home we sing or play backgammon. It has poured with rain, putting out all the bonfires, but what a welcome freshness afterwards. It must get cooler now, we must be near the end.

But still, people have guests and dinners must be

eaten. Captain Cocke took me to join Sam at the Brounckers', where I met his friend John Evelyn, a charming, cultivated man. A good venison pasty and merry enough. But our fleet is returning in shame having let the Dutch escape, and there's no money to pay the sailors off when they get here. Great rejoicing then when news comes that Lord Sandwich met with part of the Dutch fleet and took two of their East India ships and four men-of-war. A very good prize (which may help him pay off some of his debts).

Captain Cocke took me and Mary to see his son at school in the country at Bromley. We weren't allowed to alight at any village on the way but it was refreshing to be out of a town even though the fields, despite the recent rain, were hard and brown. We returned to supper at the Penns' — Sam hadn't known where I was and was rather anxious. I sang a French song and he and William Penn had a long, heated argument about the exact meaning of it. I knew William was right but I've learnt better than to contradict my husband in public on such things.

We're all waiting impatiently for the next Bill of Mortality, hoping that the cooler weather will have done its work.

1 2TH SEPTEMBER — 6,540 DIED OF PLAGUE.

'Only' six and a half thousand last week. But the first time the figure has gone down since it began. Among those thousands were the fathers of Will Hewer and our little Tom Edwards, both in St Sepulchre's parish. Will came to me and put his head in my lap and cried like a baby. Sam and I told Tom together and he screamed that it wasn't true, over and over, before he would accept it and give way to his grief. A very melancholy time.

There's prize from the Dutch ships Lord Sandwich took. If Sam puts up £500 he'll get £1,000 worth of goods: mace, cinnamon, nutmegs and cloves. Life goes on.

But above all we hope and pray the plague figure will be down again.

∞

19TH SEPTEMBER — 7,150 DIED OF PLAGUE.

It isn't.

No doubt any more what the comet presaged.

No boats on the river. Grass growing in the streets. Barely enough living left to bury the dead. No sextons left to toll the bells. Too many of the poor to count. The Quakers not registering their deaths. The true number ten, twelve, fourteen thousand last week?

The sick breathing out of their window to infect the healthy. The 'nurse' infecting the rest of the family with soiled dressings so she can steal what little they have. The searcher rudely poking at living and dead alike. The bearers, the very basest of men, pulling out the bodies with hooks.

One of them, when there are children in his cart-load of corpses, holds up the dead child by its leg, shouting, 'Faggots, faggots, five for sixpence.' At the edge of the plague pit he takes frenzied delight in exposing the naked bodies of young women. He at least is punished, taken to the pest house and whipped in front of the people and whipped round the fields and sent to prison for a year.

No man will pass close to another. In what shops are left, the money is put into a bowl of vinegar to cleanse it of infection. The streets are piled with rotting rubbish, nobody spare to clear them.

At first the victim feels merely a little unwell but then a chill comes on him and shivering and a feeling of unspeakable horror. There is profuse vomiting and an intolerable headache. The buboes appear and there is dreadful burning pain as they rise. If they break, there is a little hope, if not, none. The pain drives men into a frenzy, they may break open the door and run into the street, naked and wild-eyed, and run this way and that until they drop down dead. Or the high, high fever leads to delirium and convulsions and death. Or sometimes it's very quick and a person feels quite well until they see spots on their body – the tokens of death – and then they know they have only hours left. A man may wake to find his wife, healthy the night before, dead beside him.

This is the disease that killed Will's father, and Tom's, and Sam's waterman and Dr Burnet and is killing thousands more even as I write. I don't understand how a merciful God can let this happen.

26TH SEPTEMBER — 5,500 DIED OF PLAGUE.

A good drop. The weather is cooler. The clapper has
fallen out of the Great Bell of Westminster — this
happened before when the previous plague was ending. And the jackdaws are returning to Westminster
Palace and the Abbey, another sign that it's ending.
Please God it may be so.

There's trouble about the prize goods. It seems
that Lord Sandwich allowed his commanders and men
to take their traditional share of all the goods that lay
between decks before it was legally judged to be prize,
and the King takes a very poor view of it. So when
Captain Cocke turned up at the office with the first
wagon-load of goods, they didn't dare keep them at
the office, that being the King's house, and they stored
them instead with a friend of Captain Cocke's. A few
days later Lord Sandwich assured Sam that he had the
King's approval and he gave Sam his certificate that
he'd bought the goods and could dispose of them as
he liked once he'd paid the duty. It was a great relief
for it to be above board and legal.

Mary Mercer and I have been too much in each
other's company and we fall out over silly things.
She thinks she needs a maid of her own which is
quite ridiculous. Someone mistook her for the lady
of the house and that turned her head so I took her
down a bit and she threatened to tell Sam that I had
a particular affection for my drawing master, which
is untrue, I'm fond of his company but no more than

that. But it's all made up now – life is hard enough, better to be friends.

Meanwhile the office has no money to feed the Dutch prisoners or to pay our own sailors who've been sick and are now recovered, but not allowed back on their ships in case they're infected with plague. They stand outside the office, pleading, but there's no money in the pot.

∞

3RD OCTOBER – 4,900 DIED OF PLAGUE.

Down again, thank God, though still increasing in St Olave's parish. Sometimes it seems we'll never return. Mr Sheldon is very kind to us but it's not like being in your own home. I measure out my time, hour by hour, day by day.

But we've had some merry dinners and suppers at the King's Head in Greenwich, Mary and I, John Creed, Elizabeth Pearse. Sam's decided to give Pall £400 as her marriage portion, but we can't send for her until the plague is over.

More prize goods arrived from Captain Cocke – followed by two customs officers who attempted to seize them but Sam showed them his warrant from Lord Sandwich and persuaded them to let the goods be locked up at Mr Tooker's and the constable to have the key until Monday morning. A few days later more goods arrived, again with customs officers in pursuit, and this time the goods were locked up in a barn. Captain Cocke managed to get a possession order for them, and didn't doubt he could sweeten the customs men with a few drinks and a bribe. But the whole business is muddier than Lord Sandwich allowed. In private Sam strikes his head, says, 'Why? Why didn't he wait until the prize was officially his? Why did he rush in like that?' To which there seems to be no answer.

∞

10TH OCTOBER — 4,300 DIED OF PLAGUE.

The tenth day of the tenth month and our tenth wedding anniversary. My husband spent the day trying to sort out more problems about the prize goods — and arranging a lodging for himself at Greenwich. To be nearer the office, he says. To take me to in case the plague worsens in Woolwich, he says. And he's ready to pay for the convenience: £5 10s a month for three rooms and a dining room, with beer and bread and butter nights and mornings. I can see that the journey from Greenwich to Woolwich is difficult in winter, but it still gave me a sad feeling that on our tenth anniversary he should be arranging separate lodgings. I know that Mr Sheldon's house is more practical for me and all our maids, but even so . . .

Oh, even so we had a merry enough evening here with Mr Sheldon's niece Barbara, a lively young lady, and Captain Cocke who brought a neighbour's daughter, Frances Tooker, and Mary Mercer and a daughter and cousin of Commissioner Petts, and Will and Tom, and we had a fiddler to play and a good supper and forgot all the troubles of the world outside for a few hours. Sam went to bed after a while and left us to our dancing. (Rather different from the night ten years ago.)

The King is taking a very severe view on the prize goods, notwithstanding what he may have said before, and it will all be examined without respect to Lord Sandwich's rank. It all sounds to me more trouble than it's worth, but it's not my business.

∞

17TH OCTOBER — 2,600 DIED OF PLAGUE.

It seems an age ago, the beginning of August, when 2,000 dead in one week was shocking and terrible. And now we say only 2,600 and are cheered and encouraged by the figure. In the same way we pass a coffin or a shroud being carried in the street, or women weeping, and it hardly means anything, we've all seen too much.

Sam is happily ensconced in his Greenwich lodgings. I took Mary with me and went there one evening, just to remind him, 'I'm your wife,' and he was not particularly pleased to see us, being very busy on his Tangier accounts. But we spent the night together and the next morning he suddenly had more time to talk and be pleasant. And bless him, he's asked the Duke of Albemarle if Balty can be a member of his guard, and the Duke's agreed.

∞

24TH OCTOBER — 1,400 DEAD OF THE PLAGUE.

People are beginning to return to London, Sam says, quite a few at the Exchange, but the City is a dismal sight. All the buildings show signs of months of neglect and the streets are still empty but for swarms of beggars with plague sores. Most shops are still shut, their signs swinging in the wind, signifying nothing.

Mary Mercer and Barbara Sheldon and I went on another uninvited evening visit to Sam at Greenwich, and again he was busy at the office and not overjoyed to see us at first, but he came round to it. It happened that the Ferrers were staying at his lodgings as well. They hadn't seen each other for fifteen weeks while he was at sea so they were in a merry mood, and little Fran Tooker and her mother came in to see us and we all danced until midnight. Pleasant talk in bed the next morning — Lord Albemarle has proposed (on Mr Coventry's advice) that Sam should be Surveyor General of Victualling. This will be worth at least £300 a year. It's strange how we prosper in the middle of this plague.

~∞~

31ST OCTOBER — 1,000 DEAD.

Captain Cocke's blackamoor boy is dead though the searcher said not of the plague. But still nobody wants Captain Cocke in the office for fear of infection and they fall over themselves trying to make excuses to keep him out.

I stayed at Greenwich for a couple of nights and we had a very merry evening dancing with Eliz Pearse and Mr Hill and Fran Tooker and then Mrs Coleman sang for us from *The Siege of Rhodes*. She sings on stage so she was very good, had a sweet voice. The Ferrers were there as well, and other company.

A very different condition from the seamen who grow mutinous outside the office. They set on Mingo, Sir W. Batten's blackamoor servant, and tore his cloak from him and beat him, and they've broken the windows and swear to pull the building down. All the officers are in despair that the men go unpaid while the King lavishes riches on his mistresses and isn't interested in the least in the business of governing the country. More bad news is that the plague is beginning to increase again, having gone mainly to the eastern parishes, but now it's growing inside the City walls. A little boy at Sam's lodgings is ill and Sam feared the plague and sent Will Hewer to talk to the boy's mother but she said it wasn't that, and the little boy offered to be searched for buboes. Even so, Sam's staying away for a few days, lodging with Mr Glanville, John Evelyn's brother-in-law.

꧁

7TH NOVEMBER — 1,400 DEAD.

The rise in the figure reflects what everybody feared, but perhaps it's not so surprising since there are now more people in town. Our cook-maid Mary is leaving, by mutual consent, and I took her to Seething Lane to collect her things (without telling Sam who would certainly have forbidden it, but I haven't seen him for days). The house was so still and quiet, only the mice scuttering away when I opened the door. People may be coming back but I don't know where they are, only beggars in the streets. And so quiet, nobody shouting their wares, no coaches rattling on the cobbles. They say there's not a physician left alive in the whole of Westminster, and only one apothecary. I found out that one of our neighbours is dead of the plague at Epsom, and another died in the country of falling from his horse — his foot caught in the stirrup and his brains were beaten out. Death finds all sorts of ways . . .

They say people are foolish to have come back after all this time in the country and gone straight into houses that are full of dead people's infected goods and bedding and not waited to air or fume them, so it's no wonder the number was up last week.

∞

There are gales and without any question it's cold. It doesn't seem false hope now to think we are coming to the end.

A lovely story about our 'friend' and neighbour, Lady Batten. The officers of the Navy Board were dining with the officers of Trinity House at the King's Head to choose a new Master for the river men. After dinner, who should come in but Lady Batten with a troop of a dozen or so women, demanding to be made much of, as though she had a divine right to male attention, but nobody took any notice of them. (I've noticed before that when men are with their peers discussing serious men's business they don't want to be distracted by female company, and woe betide the woman who barges in.) So when she saw they were not regarded, she marched out in a pet. It was foul weather and she had to walk through the dirty lane in her galoshes and one of them got stuck in the dirt so she was forced to go home through the mud in her spick and span new white shoes. All my sympathy.

Sam came just once this week, and finding me in bed with my monthlies and no wine in the house left pretty soon for Greenwich. He's sold his share in the prize goods to Captain Cocke, so he's no longer involved in any way.

We heard that our old friend Llewellyn, from Exchequer days, was dead of the plague in St Martin's Lane.

21ST NOVEMBER — 600 DEAD.

A very hard frost, excellent. Will Howe has been arrested for his part in the prize goods business. Captain Ferrer has been sent away for cutting another of Lord Sandwich's servants with a sword. The Exchange is pretty full again. There is the hope of ordinary life.

But the plague is growing in Woolwich. Time to move to Greenwich. I make preparations for a farewell dinner but there's plague in the house behind us. Sam arrives and sees the sickbeds being carried out to be burnt and decides we must cancel the dinner and all leave first thing in the morning, which is what we do.

28TH NOVEMBER — 350 DEAD.

After a night at Woolwich we decided to send our maids home, and I was determined to go myself as soon as possible. Sam agreed so I went back to Greenwich to pack up our things and give Mr Sheldon £10 for my entertainment while I've been there. And then back to Seething Lane and my own house at last, after five months away. Oh, the joy of walking through my own rooms, seeing pictures I'd forgotten, seeing how neat, though dusty, the hangings were, of setting the maids to work, and setting to myself to make it a living house again. Beginning to stock the larder (a few stalls open at the market), even our old milkmaid coming to the door with her cow. It seemed once that this might never happen again.

Sam came home for dinner and we had to make the fire of faggots, there was no coal to be had. And Balty came to tell us that not only is he to be admitted into the Duke of Albemarle's guard, he is to be his right-hand man. I hardly dared to believe that at last all was coming to rights after these terrible months.

∞

5TH DECEMBER — 150 DEAD.

The numbers may go up or down a little as more people return but I think the worst is over and we've survived. And everyone else believes so too, so when we meet at Greenwich at Elizabeth Pearse's we're ready for a merry evening and the dancing is more graceful than it has ever been, and the singing sweeter. The Colemans were there, Mr Lanier and Mrs Worship and her singing daughter. And Surgeon Pearse arrived unexpectedly from Oxford, and there was a Mrs Elizabeth Knepp, a very pretty, mad-humoured actress. Sam was in an ecstasy, didn't know whether to praise more the beauty of the music or the ladies. He invited everyone to his lodgings in two days and exactly the same company turned up and again it was as though we were all making up for lost time and we danced the harder for the ghosts that lay around our lives.

We dined at Captain Cocke's with John Evelyn and Thomas Hill, good food and good company, went home to sing and play music until late. Mr Gauden, the Navy victualler, has given Sam £500 for his help in getting his accounts passed, far more than he was expecting.

31ST DECEMBER

It's been bitter cold and snowing. The plague figures went up a bit as more people returned but they're down again now. Sam stayed at Greenwich so I asked Barbara Sheldon to come here for Christmas and we've been merrry enough. But to walk through the churchyard on Christmas morning and see the plague graves piled high on either side, so many, was a sad and awesome thing. Whatever happens in the year ahead I pray to God that we don't see anything as terrible as we have seen in the year past.

1666

January 1666, the Year of the Beast – but surely we had him last year, in the form of the plague?

At this time of year there's never much business done until after Twelfth Day, so I couldn't understand why Sam claimed he still had to be near the office and stay in Greenwich rather than come home to Seething Lane. I went over to his Greenwich lodgings, to prepare a supper for the Colemans, Mr Lanier and the Knepps (she has a surly husband, a horse trader). So strange that a beautiful woman can throw herself away on a base man like that. Mrs Coleman sang Sam's setting of 'Beauty Retire' – he's very proud of it and it sounds very fine. And Mrs Knepp sang 'Barbara Allen' and when she came to the words 'Oh Mother, Mother, make my bed/For Mother I am dying', her voice was so sweet and poignant it brought tears to my eyes.

And then she sang 'Dapper Dicky' which I hadn't heard before – another song of lost love – and afterward there was enough joking of the 'my little Barbary Allen', 'My Dapper Dicky' sort between her and Sam to make me wonder if her presence in Greenwich was what stopped him from coming home. But I couldn't see anything more than great good humour between them, nothing I could fix on.

Then Captain Rolt came in with terrible pain from toothache and rather dampened our merriment, and I soon found I had toothache myself and went to bed, and so the party broke up.

I went to Sam's lodgings again, uninvited, on Twelfth Day, having packed up all our things in Woolwich and brought them to Greenwich. He was out playing cards with Lord Brouncker, but Captain Ferrer was there, hoping for a bed for the night. And we had a fiddler in and merry dancing with Mary and Will and little Tom. Sam looked in when he came home and then left us to it. The next day he came home to Seething Lane at last. Could this have anything to do with the fact that Mrs Knepp is to return to London as well? But he seemed pleased enough to be here and we walked over the house and made plans to fit new hangings in our closet.

The Navy Board moved back shortly afterwards and life has begun to resume its regular course. Lots of the City shops have reopened although Covent Garden and Westminster are still deserted, no Court or gentry willing to return yet. So we've been out to buy damask for the windows and the bed and I've worked like a horse making them up – to Sam's great admiration. The truth is that when I have something to do from start to finish, where I can see the result of my work in that something has been created which wasn't there before, then it's absorbing and satisfying. What I'm not so good at is the endless day to day cleaning and tidying. The maids do it, but they don't do it properly unless I take a close interest and sometimes I don't have that interest and then things get into a mess. But not very often these days, despite being short of a chambermaid.

Mary Batelier came to visit me with her sister, a friend of Mary Mercer's. She's ready to resume her linen draper business now. Sam was there and greatly enjoyed her company which was no surprise but also no pain because she's pretty and modest, unlike Mrs Knepp, who's pretty and free.

It was quite comical to see Sam's disappointment the next evening when we were invited to Mr Boreman's at Greenwich to come and be merry, dancing and singing with Mrs Knepp. We took the Pearses with us and went by water and there was plenty of company and a good supper but no Mrs Knepp. So messages were sent to her and the whole evening spent wondering whether she would or would not turn up – not that I cared, but Sam did, and she managed to ruin the evening by her absence. When she did turn up it was very late, after supper, and she was undressed, just wearing a loose gown, so in the end there was no singing or dancing. And it was all pray excuse her . . . and she couldn't venture out . . . and there are times everything is so difficult . . .

No excuse at all except her whim. But men will put up with that if the woman's pretty enough. She managed to appear a few days later though, at Elizabeth P.'s – she hadn't much choice since she was staying there. Captain Cocke was there as well and we danced till late and were merry enough.

Kate Joyce came on family business to talk about her husband Anthony giving up his tallow chandler business and becoming an innkeeper. Sam's gloomy about their prospects whatever they decide to do. He's thinking of Mr Harman, our upholsterer for Pall; he's a decent enough man.

There's been a furious storm, no boats out in the river except those that have cut loose and are thrashing about all over. Bricks and tiles falling off houses, sometimes whole chimneys coming down. Thank God our house is solid and can endure it. The next day news came that King Louis of France has allied himself with the Dutch and declared war against us. And Sam had a long talk with me and warned me that Lord Sandwich is out of favour (and is to be sent as Ambassador to Spain to get him out of the way) and also Sir George Carteret, who's connected to him by the marriage of their children. The Board is under attack for not having the fleet supplied in time to go out (though want of money is hardly their fault). In short, there could be rough weather ahead.

WINTER

We in turn have declared war against France, not that it matters a great deal at the moment because no fleets go out in winter.

Meanwhile we've been enjoying the fruits of Sam's labours – the Tangier victualling is proving lucrative, and he's now worth over £4,000. So we've been buying silver dishes and changing some of the silver plate we've been given for more useful pieces and our cupboard looks very handsome. There've been plenty of occasions for it to be admired. John Evelyn came to dine with us, very knowledgeable and interesting on every subject. And all five Houblon brothers and Thomas Hill came for supper. The brothers are remarkable for their great love of each other. They're all successful merchants and Thomas is to go to Portugal as their agent, which is good for him but we'll miss him very much.

On Sam's thirty-third birthday we somehow managed to entertain only – Mrs Knepp. Sam spent the evening teaching her his setting of 'Beauty Retire' and she acted various speeches for us and told stories about what goes on at the playhouse. I have to admit that when she bothers to make the effort she is excellent company. I can see why Sam finds her attractive, but that doesn't make it any easier to tolerate their fulsomeness with each other.

This year my Valentine was Thomas Hill. Elizabeth Pearse claimed Sam. I've had some merry times with her and Mary, and indeed Mrs Knepp, while having my portrait painted by Mr Hales. I take Mary with me and then Elizabeth and Mrs Knepp visit and perhaps Sam and Thomas Hill and they all sing while I sit still and then we have cakes and ale. Sitting there in the middle of the room with sweet singing all around me I feel ridiculously happy and loved.

More and more people are returning as the plague figures fall. It's about sixty cases a week now, nearly all in the east parishes. The King came back on the 1st of February and even Mr Milles has thought it safe to venture back. He made no apology for being away from his parish in its hour of need. The Hunts are back and a great pleasure to see them again, but

Elizabeth has grown very fat. She told me she was so frightened of the plague the only thing that assuaged her fear was eating sweetmeats.

We ended the month with a trip to Cranborne to say farewell to Lord Sandwich before his Embassy to Spain. All his family were there and the Carterets. He had a long private talk with Sam, telling him who was trustworthy and who not.

Among we ladies the talk was of Lady Castlemaine making the King neglect his business, and the sluttishness of the Duchess of Albemarle. She was the Duke's laundress when as plain George Monck he was imprisoned in the Tower during the Civil War, and she was kind to him in various capacities. Strange how laundresses are often filthy and sluttish themselves. In complaining that the Duke of Albemarle will have to go to sea next year she said if he was a coward he could be excused and be made an Ambassador — clearly referring to Lord Sandwich. I heard that the Queen had suffered a miscarriage but Dr Clarke had examined the membranes and said they were perfect and no reason she shouldn't bear a child.

After a noble dinner we walked in the park and then the young people sang and played guitar. After supper this turned into a mad game of cushion throwing, all over the house. Lord Sandwich left very early the next morning and we left later to go to Windsor, Sam very pleased with the fact of our travelling in the coach and four he'd hired, with servants and a woman, and so well received everywhere. At Windsor we were greeted by Dr Childe, the organist of St George's Chapel, and we heard an anthem specially sung for us and were then shown round the castle. We had a fine dinner at our inn and then Sam went round the college at Eton (I stayed in the coach and had a nap). Home late and very tired.

Mary and I had a most pleasant day in an unexpected way. Sam has been trying to reorganise the way the pursers keep their accounts and to that end he needed a great quantity of paper to be ruled to make up into books for them. So he called us into the office and we sat at a large table in the middle, carefully ruling lines across and columns down, all day. It was very satisfying to see the pile of finished paper growing, but even nicer was to be working among all the clerks who of course made much of us, and there were jokes about them being done out of their jobs. It's strange how working somewhere else, not in the house, doesn't seem so much like work. I'd be more than happy to do it every day (and listening to the clerks talk we thought we could have made some sort of fist at their work too) but of course this was an exceptional occasion.

Lord Brouncker and his doxy, Mrs Williams, also known as Lady Brouncker, insisted on an uninvited visit one evening to see our house, along with Captain Cocke and Mrs Carcasse. We gave them wine and oranges (very rare since the Dutch war) and they were all much pleased. Sam remarked afterwards how fortunate it was that the house 'happened to be' mighty clean and I retorted that it was like that most of the time and it didn't just happen to be clean, it was clean because I supervise my maids and make them attend to their business. He hadn't much to say to that.

We had our last supper with Thomas Hill who was leaving for Portugal in the morning, and it was sad to say our farewells and wonder if we would ever see him again. A single man friend is a great asset to a married couple when all parties are fond of each other, and Sam and I were always friendly together during his visits, as though we saw our better selves reflected in his good humour. And he in turn enjoyed the permanence of our establishment, and the certainty of good food on the table. Before he left he gave me gloves and silk stockings for my Valentine present.

Sam couldn't avoid any more laying out on his Valentine so Elizabeth and Mrs Knepp came to dine and then we all went out to the New Exchange. He bought Elizabeth a dozen pairs of gloves and a pair of silk stockings, and Mrs Knepp, to keep her company, six pairs of gloves. A few days before he had given me 20 shillings to lay out on her when we went shopping. I couldn't help but reflect that this was the amount he'd given me for the relief of my parents at the height of the plague. But his stance is that he'll take his pleasure while he can; too many men postpone it until death or ill health prevents their ever having the joy of their wealth.

There was a supper and dancing at Elizabeth's, the usual people, me, Mary, Mrs Worship and her daughter, Mrs Knepp, Barbara Sheldon, and a couple of men I didn't know who were mighty taken with Mrs Knepp. One might wish for more equal numbers of men and women, but better dance with another woman than not dance. I think it's the lack of the theatres being open that makes us have such entertainments so frequently.

Pall has been much in our thoughts. Sam offered £500 to Mr Harman, the upholsterer, to marry her and at first he said it was too much, his business wasn't worth that much, but within a few days he'd changed his tune and was asking for £800 which is quite ridiculous. Now there's news of a possible suitor in the country and I'll probably go down to Brampton to look the gentleman over. Sam has the offer of muster master for Balty which would be a good preferment for him though it would mean going to sea. And the great news for our household is that Jane Birch is back. I managed to lure her away from her other place though her mistress used every stratagem she could think of to keep hold of her. As soon as she arrived, Alice the cook left but that's no great loss and Jane will be cook for the moment. Most uncharacteristically, Sam has let his personal and business accounts get into a frightful muddle and doesn't see that he'll ever get them clear again. For once I could be very smug about my kitchen accounts – correct to the penny.

Spring

April comes in like a lamb. The weather is getting warmer but the plague figures stay down, about forty a week. I decided on the spur of the moment (when the sun was shining) to leave for Brampton the next day to have a look at Pall's suitor. I took no one with me but Will Hewer rode beside me to my first night's lodging. I stayed as little time as possible, just a few days, but long enough to make enquiries concerning Mr Ensum. He lives with his uncle, a lawyer, has an income of £150 a year from rents, and expects £1,000 on the death of an old aunt. He has no family dependent on him. Not particularly well-bred and drinks a bit too much, but if they'll have each other she could do worse. He asks for £600 down and a further £100 on the birth of the first child. I agreed on Sam's behalf, knowing he'll think it cheap at the price to have Pall finally settled and off his hands.

When I returned, we had our usual long time in bed the next morning. I told him his father needed money because his rents were coming in so slowly, and his mother was very impatient and troublesome, and both of them infirm. This makes him thoughtful, though he perks up a bit when he tells me Mrs Clarke, the doctor's wife, has been seen entering a bawdy house with a man not her husband. While I was away he had railings fitted to the leads outside my closet and a bench put there, so now we have another place to sit outside. We tried it out one mild evening when the garden was turning green and just beginning to be fragrant, and very pleasant it was until a terrible stink began which drove us indoors, and it turned out they were emptying the shit pot in the Penns' house of office. The two sides of nature.

Balty came to take leave of us to go to sea as muster master. It's worth £100 a year to him, and he keeps his pay in the guard as well. I'm very pleased of course, but worried for his safety if it comes to a battle again, which it almost certainly will. Sam has given me lots of ruling work to give my father so he can earn something. Needless to say the plan for curing smoking chimneys had come to nothing. I can't believe how much I still have faith in him – and how much I still have the capacity to be disappointed. But Sam also decided I should have my pearls, up to £80, and I found a beautiful three-strand necklace for exactly that amount. There's something about a set of pearls, so much quieter than diamonds, something in their subtle sheen and the way they're so perfectly matched that speaks of order and permanence, that the wearer is established in life and knows true worth.

We had some pleasant days until at the beginning of May Mr Brown reappeared to continue my drawing lessons. Our maid Susan had been so ill that we had to send her away with a nurse, so we were very short of servants and when Sam came home for dinner on the morning of my first lesson the house wasn't as perfect as he would wish (though not the complete mess he claimed). So there were words about that and the next day when I invited Mr Brown to stay for lunch, there were very loud words after he'd left, to the effect that Sam wanted his house to himself without some stranger, and a mechanic at that, being privy to all his business. I pointed out that a drawing master was hardly a mechanic and he'd invited his music teachers in the past – were they mechanics too? It ended that he would have his will done without dispute, be the reason whatever it may. So Mr Brown doesn't dine with us – for the moment.

But the next night we were all friends again. Sam came home from the office at eleven o'clock, and being very warm we both and Mary and Tom walked in the garden and sang with great pleasure. Our neighbours opened their casement windows to hear us, and the stars were bright in the sky and the scent of lilac in the air made, for an hour, a world of perfect harmony.

Within two days I had an abscess in my cheek, awful throbbing pain and looking a fright because my face was so swollen. Balty's wife Esther (seven months with child) had come to dine and later Elizabeth Pearse and Lady Jane Ferrer came to visit but I found it hard to entertain them in my condition. The next day we had dinner and supper alone together, just Sam and me, quietly, which was much easier for me.

The following morning he's up at five o'clock to go down the river to Deptford dockyard and doing various business all morning. He's home at twelve for dinner and then says he has to go to the Lord Treasurer's, which doesn't usually take long. He's out all afternoon, until six, and I'm in a lot of pain from the abscess and spend the whole afternoon wondering where he is or, more important, who he's with. The hours pass very slowly. So when he walks in with Elizabeth P. and Mrs Knepp I'm ready to explode. It turns out they've been to Mr Hales's house and sat around there admiring their portraits and then they must go to Cornhill to choose a picture for Elizabeth's chimneypiece. This has taken nearly four hours.

Knepp and Pearse exchange glances when they see the expression on my face and decide they'll visit our neighbour, Betty Turner. When they've gone I call Knepp a whore while Sam protests it was an utterly innocent afternoon. This time, perhaps, but I've seen how they are to each other when they're together. So he leaves the house and goes round to Betty Turner's and I find it impossible to go there myself so I send Sam a note asking him to come home. As soon as he walks in I can't help but carry on with the argument, I feel like a watch spring that's wound too far. I need some air and ask him to take me abroad in a coach.

So we drive out to Bow and we drive back and he doesn't speak a word either way. I ask if we can't be friends and he doesn't reply. As soon as we get home he goes straight to bed.

This (victory?) is hardly worth having. I'm stricken with colic, doubled over with pain from that and the abscess in my cheek. I stagger up to our chamber and call to him and he gets up and holds me and I cry and say I'm sorry. Then he and Jane help me undress and put me to bed and in a little while the pain ceases on all fronts and I feel much better and we sit up in bed together and eat asparagus for our supper.

Very hot for mid-May. My abscess broke inward into my mouth. Great relief. Lightning in the sky at night but no thunder or rain. We take Elizabeth Pearse on the Islington tour and I'm told off for telling too many stories from *Cyrus*. I complain that I can't do anything right when he's in the company of women he likes, he forgets my worth.

But we make up. We have to. How else could we live?

Balty came home from the fleet for a day or two so he and Esther dined with us and we did the

Islington tour. Sam's very pleased with the reports he's had of him. A week later Esther was brought to bed of a child — too early — and it was born dead. It was very sad but in my heart I couldn't help feeling it will probably be better for them both to be without a child for a little longer.

Mary Mercer has brought up a fledgeling sparrow so tame that it flies up and down the table and alights and pecks wherever it chooses and we're all mighty pleased with it.

We hear that the French fleet is out and our fleet is divided.

∞

SUMMER: WAR WITH THE DUTCH

2nd June. The Duke of Albemarle sends a message to the King that he's about to engage the Dutch fleet. The sound of distant gunfire is heard in Greenwich Park. Sam sends off two hundred soldiers to the fleet from Blackwall, drunk, kissing their wives, letting off guns. It seems that we have losses, because the message to Prince Rupert to rejoin the fleet took too long to get to him and he was then so tardy in acting on it that his ships weren't there when most needed. On the 4th June people are standing at the gravel pits near St James's Park listening to gunfire from the Essex coast. For some reason the gravel pits make the sound louder. No news at all on the 5th. On the 6th comes news that the Dutch have retreated and out of their 100 ships barely 50 got home.

Bonfires are joyfully lit all over the town. We go to Will Hewer's lodgings at Mary Mercer's mother's house and he gives us an excellent supper. Then we have a bonfire at the gate and Mary's little brother Will sets off serpentine fireworks. There are people there with muskets and when Sam gives them a crown for drink they fire a volley. Great joy all over the City.

And then the next day we hear that, on the contrary, we've taken nothing from the Dutch, instead they have burnt the *Royal Prince*, the best ship in our Navy. On the 8th, Balty appears, safe, thank God, despite being on the quarterdeck of *The Henry* the whole time they were under fierce attack. The Duke of Albemarle's conduct is condemned both in the fighting of the battle and in so many ships running aground in retreat. Prince Rupert's first words to the King on his return were to complain about the Commissioners' delay in getting the fleet out, which should have been three or four days earlier.

So Sam is hard at work drafting an answer to the King against this complaint. Meanwhile Mary and I fell out about her acting as though she was the lady of the house and she went home to her mother's. Her mother came to see me the next day but I said I wouldn't speak to her, I would speak to Mary, and in the evening (after some words from Will Hewer) she came back. We were good enough friends to drive out to Hackney a couple of evenings later with Lady Penn in her coach. Sam overtook us and we visited two beautiful gardens, with orange trees in fruit and several labyrinths and aviaries.

The next day we hear the Dutch fleet is out. Sam

is very busy trying to get ours out, and doing so much close work that his eyes are desperately sore. There is talk of a French invasion in the north. Sam intends to have all his money in his own hands. News comes that the Dutch fleet is off the French coast and there are six thousand armed Frenchmen ready to go aboard. And there's no money to pay the pressed men being held at Bridewell.

The press of men for the Navy is a terrible thing. Stepney, where so many of the seamen lived, was so badly afflicted in the plague that few survived and the numbers must be made up of any able-bodied men in the street. (Which is why suddenly no able-bodied men are seen in the streets.) Mary and I walked down to Tower Pier after supper to watch them going and there were women and children on the quayside looking at every group of men who were brought out, to see if their husband or father were there, leaving them destitute through no fault of their own. And how they wept over each vessel that sailed in case their loved one was in it, and how they gazed at each boat sailing into the moonlight until it was lost from view round the bend in the river.

The plague is growing in the country – I'm not surprised, it's so hot. Thank God our figure stays down in London. Sam has brought home £1,000 in gold, though it cost him £70 to change it up, but it takes less space, can be moved more quickly if need be. At Mr Unthank's I hear that the Court lie in bed all day, knowing it's not seemly to play at their sports and games in time of war, but not knowing how else to occupy themselves. At home we walk in the garden on a hot, thundery evening and later there is lightning and then heavy rain. And the garden is like a little enclave against the world, where we walk and talk while plague or war rages outside.

And the world raged fiercely enough a few days later when there were upward of three hundred women in the yard outside the office clamouring for the money due for their husbands who are prisoners in Holland. There was none to give them. They eventually broke up, on promises, and we were able to send our venison pasty out to be cooked without fear of the cook being set upon.

On the 20th July the fleet went out again. Mr Simpson the joiner came to fit our new bookcases, and not before time – books have been lying in heaps on chairs and tables for weeks. Guns are heard in the park.

Elizabeth Pearse's baby has died, aged one month. Mrs Knepp's baby has died, aged one month.

The bells ring out for an English victory on St James's Day, but Sam says we have held the sea, that's all, no great gain. I notice that he takes far more pains teaching Mary Mercer to sing than he ever has with me. He admits it but says she takes it more readily than I do. I don't feel any happier knowing this is true.

Sometimes, when he says he's going out on business, he puts on a poor suit instead of a good one. Why? Because he's going somewhere he doesn't want to be noticed? Some mean inn where he doesn't want to be known as Mr Pepys because he's with a woman not his wife? If I question him there's always an excuse: he doesn't want to wear out his good clothes unncessarily; it's too warm to wear his best clothes. When you suspect a man is lying, but he's lying in his teeth, there's not a lot you can do – unless you have proof, and he's too clever for that.

Hot summer Sunday afternoons. We take a barge upriver to Mortlake, stop and walk under the trees at Barn Elms, land at Wandsworth to eat and drink, buy a melon at Chelsea, and so to the Old Swan where Betty Mitchell and her husband make much of us in their strong-water house. We walk home (staggering a bit, having drunk strong water) and very late we walk in the garden, just us two, and Sam warns me that Parliament may find fault enough with the office to turn them all out. But if that happens we have enough to retire on now and for the first time I begin to think that living in the country together might be quite pleasant after this London life.

I had a falling out with Elizabeth Pearse. Mrs Knepp had come, supposedly to visit me, though she knows I have no love for her. Of course Sam rushed home from the office as soon as he heard she was here. Then Elizabeth arrived, fawning over Sam, and it annoyed me more than usual. I'd heard she'd said I was growing into a gallant – me, who has fewer clothes than any other lady I know. I challenged her on this. She said I shouldn't trouble myself about such discourse because people at this end of town (i.e. me) had equally bad things to say about others, particularly herself, who had been called crooked, which was quite false. I denied saying any such thing (God forgive me, I've called her a hunchback twenty times to Sam). Mary Mercer had taken it upon herself to tell our former maid Mary, now with Elizabeth, about this. We had words.

I enjoy myself more freely when those two ladies are not around. We had a wonderful night on the Thanksgiving Day for our victory over the Dutch. Sam spent the morning on business and then after we'd dined he and I and Mary Mercer went to the Bear Garden and watched the bulls tossing the dogs, and one of them was tossed into a box where people sat, right into a lady's lap. There were a great many hectoring fellows in our box, and they drank a health to Mary which Sam answered with his hat off. We all agreed it was a rude and nasty pleasure. Back at home Sam went to his chamber while Mary and I prepared for our guests for the evening.

Mary Batelier and her brother William came, and Mrs Mercer and her other daughter Anne, and Mr le Brun and Will Hewer. So we supped very merrily on a venison pasty and then at about nine o'clock went over to Mrs Mercer's where there was a huge bonfire in the street and her son had provided serpentine fireworks and rockets. So there we made merry, flinging fireworks at each other (and Lady Penn and daughter Peg had joined us), and smutting each other with candle grease and soot until we looked like devils. Then we went back to our house and drank some more and danced, and Sam and Will Hewer dressed up like women and Mary Mercer put on a suit of Tom's, and Peg and I put on Sam's periwigs and so we were mad until three or four in the morning.

News comes that Captain Holmes has burnt 160 Dutch ships and the town on the island of Terschelling – the Dutch are calling it Holmes's bonfire. More bonfires in London to celebrate. Unfortunately, it turns out that Terschelling is inhabited by a group of Mennonite Christians who don't believe in killing their fellow men. Not a very worthy target.

Very hot, and a dry east wind.

The Fire

I keep thinking of that time we danced round the bonfire on Thanksgiving for Victory Day. We were fire-virgins then, with an innocence that's gone for ever now.

I have to set it all down, to comprehend it in my own mind. Some of the things I saw for myself, and some of it was told to me by other people. I need to put it all down together, to master it all, to understand it.

Sunday, 2nd September

The maids are sitting up late preparing things for dinner the next day. At three in the morning Jane wakes us to say there's a big fire burning in the City. We go up to her room at the top of the house and through the window we can see that indeed it is a big fire but far enough away not to worry about, and not much bigger than we've seen before. We go back to bed and to sleep.

When Sam gets up at seven he thinks the fire is smaller and further off than it had been earlier and he sets to ordering his closet after its cleaning the day before. Jane has been out and runs in to tell us that three hundred houses have burned down in the night and the fire is burning all the way down Fish Street by London Bridge.

Sam decides this needs attention and walks up the hill to the Tower where he climbs to the highest point and sees all the houses at this end of London Bridge burning. The Lieutenant of the Tower tells him it started in a baker's in Pudding Lane, one Thomas Faryner. Because it was the middle of the night – and a Saturday night at that, when people went to bed late and tired, and having taken drink – and there was a strong wind blowing, it wasn't controlled quickly enough and houses weren't pulled down, which would have been the only way of stopping it. On either side of Pudding Lane, in Thames Street, are warehouses full of oil, pitch, tar, wine, brandy, coal, timber. Whatever will feed a fire is there, in quantity. And it's been hot and dry for months, and all the houses are wood, their overhanging roofs nearly meeting in the middle of the street. The fire leaps from side to side.

Sam gets a boat through London Bridge and finds the fire burning its way all along the wharf. Already Betty Mitchell's strong-water house at the Old Swan is burnt to the ground. There is fire all along the river for about a third of a mile. People are trying to remove their goods into boats in the river. Nobody is trying to fight the fire. Sam watches as it begins to rage into the City.

He goes to Whitehall, to the King's chapel, and everyone wants to know what he has seen. The King summons him to his closet and Sam tells him and the Duke of York how bad it is. (In the middle of it all I feel so proud that it is my husband who has informed the King of the situation.) Sam tells the King that unless houses are pulled down nothing will stop it and the King orders him to command the Lord Mayor to pull them down wherever needed.

He comes back by coach with Captain Cocke and Mr Creed and finds the Lord Mayor in Canning Street. He's been up all night, and they've been pulling down houses as fast as they can but the fire always runs faster. The streets are full of people fleeing with their goods. Sam passes Isaac Houblon's house and sees him receiving goods from his brothers that have already been moved twice. The churches are filling with people's goods when it should be themselves quietly there.

It doesn't feel like a Sunday. It feels like a day of the week that was never known before, that has no name. At home I supervise the preparation of dinner for our guests – Barbara Sheldon, now Mrs Wood, and her new husband, and Lord Belayse's secretary, Mr Moon, and his wife. All morning Jane has been running in and out and I don't reprimand her because we need to know what is happening. At twelve noon Sam returns and our guests arrive, and we eat a very good dinner, only everyone has an ear cocked to the outside. Sam abandons his plan of showing Mr Moon all the books in his closet, nobody can think of anything except the fire. Strange how we keep up these forms of serving and eating when all around us is falling into dust. Mary Batelier rushes in to ask if we have seen two of her relatives whose house is burned down, and rushes off again.

Sam goes to have another look from the river, and we take a coach round by the Wall and meet him in St James's Park. His boat is waiting at Whitehall and we go up and down on the water, as close as the smoke will allow us. Facing the wind we're almost burnt with showers of fire drops, blowing in the wind like infernal snowflakes, landing on untouched houses and starting new fires to join, soon enough, the great one. The river is packed with craft carrying goods away, and things fallen off and bobbing in the water. When we can stand no more we stop at a little alehouse on the south side, opposite Three Cranes Wharf where earlier there was hope the fire might break. That hope is now gone.

We watch the fire grow. As darkness falls, the river looks like a sea of gold and even the smoke in the sky looks golden from the flames. They're leaping up in grotesque shapes, like devils' tongues. They make a terrible roar and we can hear the houses cracking. We can feel the heat, hear the cries of people across the water. As we watch, church steeples burst into flame, and the fire burns its way up the hill towards the heart of the City. We watch mostly in silence. It's too awful a sight to talk about. By the time we leave, there's a solid arch of fire running for a mile along the waterfront.

Back at home we find that Tom Hayter has arrived with some goods he saved from his house which is burnt down in Fish-Street Hill. Sam invites him to lie at our house and thinks of going to bed, but I think the fire sounds as though it's getting much closer.

We begin to pack. We pack all night.

We take a lot of our goods out into the garden, and Sam and Mr Hayter carry his iron chests of money into the cellar. He puts his bags of gold and his main accounts in the office, to take if we leave. At four o'clock in the morning Lady Batten sends a cart for Sam to take our best things – the money and plate – to Sir William Rider's house in Bethnal Green. Sam rides with it in his nightgown.

The fire has levelled Cannon Street to the ground and is heading for Cheapside. There's a very strong wind.

∞

Monday, 3rd September

In the middle of all this Mary Mercer ups and goes home to her mother and I tell her to stay there, I can't be doing with her tantrums at such a moment. Meanwhile the maids and I pack pictures and books and hangings and linen and clothes into bundles and boxes, and Sam has managed to get a boat from Mr Tooker (and that would have been impossible without the Naval connection, every craft on the river spoken for). There's a great shortage of hands to help, so the maids and little Tom and Will Hewer and I spend hours going up and down Tower Hill to the quay to fill the boat. All over the hill people who've been burnt out and have

nowehere else to go are camping in the open with
their goods.

At home there's a moment when I'm running
out of holders to put things in, and in one hand I
have Sam's silk suit and in the other a fine damask
tablecloth and I wonder, if it comes to it, and I can
only save one, which one it will be. And I decide it
will be the damask cloth, because it will still be in
use in twenty years' time, while the suit will be out
of fashion in two. But there's time to save both.

In the streets every person who is fit to carry
anything is bowed under a burden, hurrying. At
night the streets are as light as a bright noon day.
It's forty hours since any of us has slept. We eat
yesterday's leftovers cold, nothing remains in the
house to cook with. Sam sleeps in the office on a
quilt of Will Hewer's and after a while I join him
there. The servants sleep at the kitchen table.

The fire has got up beyond Cornhill, burnt the
Royal Exchange to the ground (they say once it got
into the galleries there the whole building went in a
matter of minutes). Lombard Street and Fenchurch
Street have gone. All through the night we hear the
terrible sound of houses crashing to the ground. The
wind persists. There is timber lying in the streets
from houses pulled down, no time, no people to clear
it. The fire accepts the invitation, dances across the
street to the next row of houses. There's a terrible
procession from the advancing flames of women from
their childbed, children from their sickbeds, lying in
carts, never expecting to see their homes again, the
flames so close. All the booksellers have brought their
books to the crypt of St Paul's, to the Church of St

Faith's which lies under the main church. Every book in the City that is not in a private library which has been removed lies there.

The fire is two miles long and one mile deep. Cheapside is almost gone.

TUESDAY, 4TH SEPTEMBER

The fire advances west and north and east. West of Cheapside and north of Blackfriars it begins to circle St Paul's. St Paul's is a tall stone building. There are no small buildings nearby. It could escape. Unfortunately it's being repaired and there's scaffolding round it. The scaffolding catches, and then the roof. The lead melts and runs down like snow before the sun. Stones fly off the building like grenades. The roof collapses into the crypt and every book in the City is burnt to a cinder.

The fire roars on down Ludgate Hill and jumps the Fleet River to make its way down Fleet Street. In the north it reaches Cripplegate, in the east, almost to the Tower. They say the Guildhall stood for several hours after it was burned through, like a single brilliant coal, before it crumbled into dust. Smoke darkens the sky. The sun, if it's seen at all, is blood red.

Sam and Sir William Penn dig two pits in the garden for their wine and our parmesan cheese and some office papers. The rest of us spend the day toiling backwards and forwards over Tower Hill again, loading another lighter. Sam suggests calling up all their men from the Woolwich and Deptford yards to pull down houses here so they can save the office. We sup in the office with the Turners on a shoulder of mutton from the cook's. We're all filthy with dirt. (That time we smutted each other round the bonfire . . .)

We walk in the garden now and then. It frightens us. The whole sky seems to be on fire. Sam takes my arm, looks at our house, says they've been the best years of his life. I lean my head on his shoulder. Will Hewer arrives from resettling his mother after she was burned out of Pye Corner. He says it's reached the Temple in the west and they're going to try to stop it at Somerset House. They're pulling down all they can between there and Charing Cross. At that moment comes the noise of explosions more terrible than anything we've heard before – houses being blown up in Tower Street, at the bottom of our lane. The noise and the flames together make a vision of Hell.

∞

WEDNESDAY, 5TH SEPTEMBER

Sam is dozing on Will Hewer's quilt in the office. I'm sitting in the kitchen, not daring to fall asleep. At two o'clock I hear new cries of 'Fire!' and looking out of the door see Barking Church burning at the end of our lane.

I run to wake Sam and he decides that this is the moment. It's time to go. We must all leave at once. So we two and Jane Birch and Will Hewer and Tom Edwards leave our home and walk up Seething Lane wondering if this is the last time we'll ever see our house. Our eyes are weeping, not just from the smoke.

A boat waits for us at Iron Gate Stairs. It's a terrible, sad feeling, pulling away from the smoke and the flames and the explosions, abandoning our home to them. We sail downriver to Woolwich, watching in silence as London burns. And all the way the fire lights the sky.

We're carrying over £2,000 in gold and as soon as we arrive at Mr Sheldon's, Sam finds a room that can be locked and warns Will to stay with it at all times. Jane and I wash as best we can and share a bed, exhausted. Sam goes straight back to Seething Lane, on the way seeing our goods are well guarded at Deptford. When he arrives at Seething Lane at seven in the morning he finds that the office is safe and the fire has stopped four houses from our door (thanks in large part to the workmen he summoned from the yards, who have been blowing up and pulling down since they arrived).

The main thing was, the wind dropped. Or, if you like, the Lord had pity on us, and let the wind abate. I had trouble enough thinking of a merciful God during the plague . . . What have we done that's so terrible, worse than other people, other times?

Once the citizens saw that their efforts to quench the fire might meet with success, they made the effort, and even aldermen who'd refused to pull down their houses before now joined in the common fight. The King and the Duke of York themselves threw buckets of water on the fire as it burned towards Moorfields, and encouraged the people. By Wednesday night, apart from Holborn and Cripplegate, the flames had no new material to consume and were burning in on themselves.

But now a different fear arises – rumours have swept the city as fast as the fire itself that it was started deliberately by the French and the papists. They say 50,000 French and Dutch have landed. The poor people lying in the fields hourly expect to have their throats cut and be robbed of what little they've saved. The militia is armed.

∞

THURSDAY, 6TH SEPTEMBER

Yesterday was all washing and sleeping. Today is the first time I can begin to take in all of what's happened. I can hardly believe that it's only five days since last Sunday night – it seems an age away now, a distant time that we've left for ever.

The rumours of invasion were false and things are a bit calmer. All sorts of regulations are made, about where new markets may be held, all public buildings to be open to receive goods, the country people to bring in provisions for the homeless in the fields.

They say 13,000 houses have been lost and near a hundred churches, and St Paul's, the Guildhall, the Exchange, all the Company Halls.

Thank God for our good fortune that our house

escaped. It's filthy from smoke and every window-pane is cracked, but it stands.

I moved back as soon as I could, after the house had had its first clean. The sky was still full of thick black smoke – the books in St Paul's burnt for a week, cellars everywhere smouldered on, emitting noxious, greasy smoke. Sam took me out in a coach to see the ruins. There was just about a way through the City, though most streets were impassable, being full of rubble. St Paul's was a terrible sight to see in ruins, the greatest church we had, the embodiment of our trust in God. The stones, where they remained, were white from the heat. They say six acres of lead melted from the roof; it has run into the streets all round and is still too warm to walk on.

The stones of those few buildings still standing are white and calcified, like ghosts of themselves. People walking about looked like the lost souls of a once-great city suddenly laid waste, seeking to find some fragment that they could call their own. We could hardly tell where we were but by the odd church tower or spire that had miraculously survived. I saw what had been Salisbury Court, where Sam's parents and Tom had lived and had their business, where Tom had died, where Cousin Jane Turner had lived, where Sam had been cut of the stone. All burned to the ground.

But life must continue. Our goods were returned from Deptford and we had carpenters in to set up the bedsteads and hangings. Everything scattered all over the house, strange workmen walking round, the glaziers taking weeks to mend the windows, and constant cleaning against the smoke. Lots of cellars are still smouldering. Sam moved his wine from the pit in the garden to the cellar, terribly worried that the porters would see his money chests. Balty and Esther are staying with us, very helpful in setting the house in order again. We all have bad dreams of fire and houses falling down.

Kate Joyce came to ask Sam for a place for her husband Anthony. Their house was burnt and he's lost £140 a year in rents. The Mitchells have lost their strong-water house. Mr Kirton, Sam's bookseller, is utterly ruined. The moment St Paul's roof fell in he went from being worth £8,000 to owing £2,000. They say the High Master of St Paul's School is dying of grief at the loss of his library.

Everyone thinks the City, a smoking ruin, will never rise again, that it will be abandoned and everything will move west. Indeed it's hard to see how it will ever recover. We're all numb from it, but the usual things go on remarkably soon. And for those whose houses survived there's easy money to be made. A neighbour who used to let his house for £40 a year can get £150 now. A penny loaf is twopence, a shilling eel is three shillings.

Our books and pictures came home after everything else, most of the picture frames chipped and some books missing which really upset Sam. Balty and Esther have moved to my parents' house and there's trouble between my mother and Esther — who is said to stay out and paint her face when Balty is away — and Balty isn't giving them any money out of the position that Sam has helped him to get. As though there isn't enough difficulty already.

Sam wants me to have Mary Mercer back but I'm reluctant. I like her as a person but she's got too confident, too above herself for either of us to be happy with her as a waiting woman. Sam doesn't really understand this, just misses her singing and dancing. I'm looking for someone else as life returns to something like its usual course.

Autumn

I have a new woman, Nell Barker, who is doing well enough, though Sam finds her singing voice a little furred from want of practice. I took her to Unthank's to order a gown for her (and she looks a great deal better in it). Mr Unthank tells me the Duke of York is wholly given up to Lady Denham and doesn't care about anything else – though he did well in the Fire when the Duke of Albemarle was away at sea. And the King has decided he and the Court will wear a new fashion. It's like a long Persian vest, or cassock, close to the body, with white silk pinking showing through, and then a coat over it, and black ribbon ruffling the legs. It's meant to curb profligacy of dress in the Court and is a deliberate snub to French fashion. Mr Unthank isn't grumbling if it means everyone must have new clothes.

So all the Court duly appeared in the new fashion – and the King said the pinking made them look like magpies and has bespoken one of plain velvet, which means they'll all have to get new ones of plain velvet.

This seems to be the limit of the King's care for his kingdom. Mr Unthank is delighted.

Sam and Sir William Coventry have been at great pains to make clear to the Duke of York that they can't do anything for the fleet without money, and both have threatened to resign if no money is forthcoming, because they don't see how they can serve the King. But Sam's troubled that it's always he who has to explain these things to the King, as with the Tangier accounts, always he who has to tell them what they least want to hear – that there's not enough money.

Alongside this we hear that Thomas Killigrew is banished from Court because he said that even when she was young, Lady Castlemaine was a lecherous little girl and used to rub her thing with her fingers or against the corner of a bench. He was the Duke of York's servant and the King commanded the Duke to send him away, which he has done, but it's made bad blood between the Duke and Lady Castlemaine.

23RD OCTOBER – MY 26TH BIRTHDAY

My hair is falling out, I think from the strain of the fire and the plague before it. One of those things we can't affect, however much we'd like to.

Sam's been trying to get me to make up with Elizabeth Pearse which I don't mind doing as long as he minds his conduct. I think he misses terribly not having anyone like Mary Mercer around to sing with.

So we visited Elizabeth P. at home and I was received with great respect, and of course it meant that a few days later she (and what a surprise, Mrs Knepp) came to dine at home with us. It went off very well, Mrs Knepp in very good form, great mirth all round, and afterwards Sam took us to the New Exchange and bought us all gloves. They joined us again when we all went to the first play since the theatres were closed because of the plague. All the Court was there, and I wore my new fair hair, which Sam disapproves of, but God knows I have reason to wear false now. The play was nothing, *Love in a Tub*, a silly comedy.

I'm having singing lessons from Mr Goodgroome – Sam is so impatient with me I'm afraid to open my mouth in case I sing a wrong note. He knows this doesn't help and has apologised.

He's worth over £6,000 now, so in ourselves we're secure. His great worry is the state of the Navy, that its business is at standstill because there's no money and no credit. Parliament is reluctant to vote the King money for the Navy because of his profligacy and not attending to his business but giving himself to pleasure. The seamen are starving and mutinous. We've lost more ships than ever before, fleeing from the first sign of fight, running aground on the sands. There's no doubt that unless the King takes control, the Dutch will beat us next year.

It's a strange autumn – the sky still full of smoke instead of clear gold light, and the leaves that should be falling now have already shrivelled on the bough in the heat of the fire so that when they fall they are dark, wizened things. Gunpowder Plot Day this year was kept, needless to say, without any bonfires.

Sam has had a suit made in the new fashion, and it looks very good. It's an excellent shape for a man beginning to be more ample in his girth. He brought me home a couple of prints to copy for my drawing – am I unfair to see these little gestures as evidence of guilt? I have no proof of anything, it's just a feeling. Meanwhile I take a noble cake we've been sent and some wine and go to house-warm Betty Mitchell at their new strong-water house in Shadwell. Balty falls sick. Mr Batelier sends me an exquisitely coloured new puppy.

We went to Elizabeth P.'s house by invitation for supper and dancing – we two and the Bateliers and Mary Mercer (and Mrs Knepp) and various other ladies and gentlemen and all very merry until word comes that Whitehall is on fire. We all look out of the window and see that indeed it is, and one lady faints and one weeps and the men look round in shock and fear at the possibility of another great fire. And there is news of fire in Southwark and one in Westminster, fuelling the fear that foreigners are setting them deliberately. So all the drums are beating and the trumpets sounding to call the militia who are running up and down the streets, and there is the noise of buildings being blown up, and pretty soon the fires are put out. But it's sad to see how apprehensive everyone is, how quick we all are to take alarm. And the fire dreams go on night after night.

With nobody knowing what the future holds, Sam has changed more of his silver into gold, despite the price of it going up. He's written a letter for all the office to sign explaining to the Duke of York in the simplest terms that the Board must either have more money for the Navy or make peace with the Dutch on any terms they demand. Everyone dreads what will happen with them next year.

Meanwhile, we have a row because I'm showing too much breast, having cut away my neckerchief according to fashion. It's not too serious — perhaps things are more in perspective between us these days. But a ridiculous note of fashion: the King of France, hearing of our King's new anti-French gown, has ordered it to be worn at his own Court — by his footmen.

We had a very grand dinner at home for young Lord Hinchingbrooke, my Lord's heir, now aged eighteen and beginning to be a young man of the world, though in no way dissolute. Most attentive to me. And to be eating off our silver plate, in our own house, with everything else that had been saved, I gave great thanks.

And then we're dining with the Joyce brothers and Kate and Anthony are complaining of their life as innkeepers at Clerkenwell and William is crowing about how trade has come to his end of the town since the fire. And later I hear that he goes to their inn and mocks them, calls them host and hostess, and I'm sad that people should behave so to their own kin.

CHRISTMAS . . . COMING . . . GOING . . .

He walks in and considers the cloth crumpled and throws trenchers all over the room. The next day, when the Pearses come to dine, everything is to his satisfaction. Surgeon Pearse tells us that Thomas Killigrew publicly told the King that there was one good, honest, able man who could see all things well executed, and that man's name was Charles Stuart – who now spends his time employing his lips and his prick about Court. But the King takes no notice of it. Mr Unthank tells me that the King has paid £30,000 to clear Lady Castlemaine's debts.

And in a much smaller world, Pall's suitor Mr Ensum has died, so that was a lot for nothing. Mary Mercer and I went to the theatre and came home quite late and Sam was so worried (because I was wearing my pearls) that it was touching to see. Captain Batters was there talking to him when we arrived, and then he left and the next day came news that he'd drowned in the Thames on the way back to his boat. And I felt angry because there have been too many deaths.

We dined quietly but well on Christmas Day. I'd been up till four o'clock the night before making mince pies so I slept while Sam went to church. He complains that the glare of the snow hurts his eyes. The next day we had company: the Bateliers, the Andrews, John Creed, Mary Mercer, all to a good dinner, then to a theatre in the afternoon then all back for supper and dancing. I'd invited Mr Pendleton the dancing master and got a fiddler in. Will Hewer came over and Nan Wright and old Mr Batelier. We danced until midnight and then sat round the table picking at fruit and cheese and sweetmeats, and plenty of good wine, playing question and answer games with silly forfeits.

There was a moment when I caught Sam's eye and I knew we were both thanking God that we had not only survived plague and fire but in such condition that we could entertain our friends, their faces glowing in the candlelight, our table abundant. So this year ends, but we know that outside the door lies a black and ruined City, and the almost certain prospect of defeat by the Dutch next summer. We're all in God's hands.

1667

∞

JANUARY

It was bitter cold at the start of the year. Peg Penn and I walked out to the fields to frost-bite our faces. It's important for her complexion to look good because she's getting married soon (aged fifteen and good luck to her). I think she's more forward than I was then, so perhaps she'll be happy enough. Her father invited all the Navy Board officers and their wives to dine, but what a mean dinner, and meanly served, no laying out the food on the best plate for them, they don't have any. It's astonishing that people of quite considerable means can be so slack when it comes to providing for their guests.

Our dinner the next day was a model of how it should be done: the tablecloth immaculate, perfectly folded napkins, gleaming silver wine flagons, fresh greenery, the food beautifully displayed, enough silver dining plates (30) to use nothing else throughout the meal. Plenty of good wine and plenty of well-dressed food. A warm and gracious dining room. Our guests were Lord Brouncker, the Penns, with Peg's suitor, Mr Lowther, Lady Batten and the Turners.

Sam made it his business to be merry and there could be no question that people were having a much nicer time than they'd had the day before.

After dinner we fell to cards and singing and talking. Then supper and more cards and a flagon of ale and roast spiced apples. We all shared the big wooden cup to drink it as a Christmas draught and everyone went home merrily. We went to bed well pleased with our guests' pleasure.

We've been to the theatre, to see *Macbeth*, where all the gossip was that the Duke of York's mistress, Lady Denham, was dead and the Duchess was suspected of poisoning her. And we saw *The Humorous Lieutenant*, a silly play although Elizabeth Knepp was in it and her singing was very pleasing (I have to admit). The main part was played by Nell Gwyn, the first time I've seen her and she is every bit as pretty as people say, and an excellent actress. Elizabeth Pearse was in a box above us and called us to her on the way out and Mrs Knepp took us all into the back. We saw Nell and kissed her – the softest skin I've ever touched.

Elizabeth had already invited herself and Mrs Knepp and other actors to dine with us the next day and Sam decided to make an occasion of it and have supper and dancing. (And it's easier for me to be with them if there are other people present too, and something to do rather than just sit round a table getting waspish.) So we cleared the office and had a good fire made and many candles lit. As well as the actors, we had our favourite dancing friends, Mary Mercer and her mother, the Bateliers, Mr Pendleton, Captain Rolt, and we danced and sang and supped until three in the morning. Mrs Knepp felt unwell and I put her to bed. When everyone had gone, Sam spent a deal of time in her bedroom saying goodnight to her. Elizabeth and I shared the bed in the best chamber, while Sam slept in the blue chamber.

It seems we're all hungry for entertainment after the two years we've just lived through. The plague and the fire showed clearly enough that nothing in this life is certain and we may as well take our pleasure while we can.

FEBRUARY

Both the shortest and the longest month of the winter, the ground hard as iron and no buds yet. Perhaps it was the wrong time of year to broach Will Hewer on the notion of Pall being a wife to him. Sam had asked me to try this though I wasn't sure I wished Pall on Will, but it would have been welcome if he'd been connected by marriage to our family rather than some stranger's. But in any event he said he received the honour with great acknowledgement but he had no intention of altering his condition yet. At which I was secretly relieved because I'd hate to lose him to a wife. At twenty-five he has grown into a man of good sense and good humour, always obliging to me and I can trust him, knowing that what I say to him won't be repeated elsewhere. I even told him about the proposition from Lord Sandwich. He was shocked, but pleased at my response. He eases things between me and Sam, explaining us to each other.

Trepanning is the subject of the moment. It seems that Prince Rupert got the pox twelve years ago and now (according to Dr Clarke) it has eaten through his skull so it must be opened and there's great fear for him. Others have claimed it's an old war wound. Whatever, Mr Mullins, the surgeon at Bart's, has done it with great success. Some unkind souls say it lets cool air in where there was hot air before, and it should become a fashion.

An example of meanness without parallel: a City merchant had thirty men helping to clear his house during the Fire and after all their labour he gave them half-a-crown between them – a penny each. And in a smaller way, Dr Clarke invited us for dinner, with the Pearses and Captain Cocke, and it was so mean, a dirty cloth and dishes, and poor food. This man is the Royal physician yet he can't even provide a decent dinner. And it was served so late that we had great trouble in getting a coach to take us home in the dark through the ruins. All the time we were terrified that the coach would fall into a cellar or we'd be held up by the ruffians who are the only ones to frequent this area now. Sam had his sword drawn the whole way.

But when we went to the Mitchells' for their wedding anniversary and a Shrove Tuesday dinner, how different. They haven't the money yet for silver plate, but their pewter is polished and shines with its own lustre. They had all their four parents there, all good friends, and it was sweet to see Betty big with child and so proud of her neat house. The boys in the street were playing football, and flinging at cocks, and there was the beginning of a feeling that we're all picking ourselves up after the late events.

The Penn/Lowther marriage was a predictably mean business. Very private, just a few family. Because it was just before Lent it wasn't considered worthwhile to buy new clothes because the fashions will change at Easter. All day their maids were knocking at our door to borrow things to cook and serve the dinner. The couple were put to bed but there was no music the next morning to call them up. 'As if they'd married like dog and bitch,' Sam said.

My Valentine this year was young Will Mercer, Mary's brother, and he came up to my chamber with my name written on blue paper in gold letters, very pretty. And a good start to the day to have a charming sixteen-year-old at one's bedside. A day or two later (Valentine's Day seems to last for a week now) we were at the Pearses' and it seems that the custom has come in of drawing mottoes as well as names, and Surgeon Pearse drew my name and then the motto 'Most virtuous and most fair', which all the company applauded, and I felt absurdly happy.

Reputation is a delicate thing and Mary Mercer is beginning to be spoken of as keeping too much company. She needs to be married, she's already twenty, but she has very little portion. I'm concerned for her – now she's no longer my woman we're better friends and I don't want her to damage her chances. I heard from the same source (Barbara Sheldon) that little Fran Tooker, the daughter of Sam's neighbour at Greenwich, has the clap, being brought up loosely by her mother and lying in the same bed as her when she had a man in it. I can't imagine a world in which my own mother would have done that; it perturbs me occasionally that we know people who are so loose.

Sometimes I have my doubts about Sam and think that being the man he is, he must be liable to temptation when he's out and about, though he's never had the pox – not that that proves anything either way. There was a day when he came home in the middle of the afternoon in such a sweaty state of panic about who had called, what messages there had been, that I couldn't help but think he was in fear of me finding out something. I couldn't discover anything – I don't like to question the servants too closely because it makes my fears too obvious to them. But I did mention to Will Hewer that sometimes I was concerned about Sam's absences and Will said he was sure there was nothing to worry about, which was what I expected him to say. And as though to reassure me, Sam and I lay long in bed and he talked about the times when we were in our little room in the turret at Lord Sandwich's lodgings in Whitehall Palace, and how I used to make the fires and wash the clothes myself and how he would for ever love and admire me for having done that. And I felt, more or less, reassured.

It didn't stop him making me sing to him and being very critical, though he apologised quickly enough. He admits I'm only trying to please him and it's not my fault if I have no ear. I've started learning the flageolet with Mr Greeting – he's a lovely music master, very encouraging and cheerful, and at least Sam seems happy with my progress on that. We've had some pleasant evenings alone together by the fire with a bitter cold wind outside rattling the windows. It's a refuge at the moment because everyone at the office has fallen out with each other and Sam tries to steer a middle course, but sometimes he says he and I can only trust to each other and let the world go hang, there's too much falseness in it.

We even reached an agreement – without having a fight first – that whatever he spent on gifts for other women, he should spend the same on me. This was after he'd spent 32 shillings on things for Mrs Knepp, who'd claimed him as her Valentine.

We dined with the Carterets, and Lady Carteret told me how she was in Windsor Forest and there were lots of fragments of burnt paper, blown from the Fire, and she picked a little piece up and it had printed on it no more and no less than the words, 'Time is; it is done.' In the City a few cellars are still smoking but great new streets are being marked out with piles driven into the ground and it will be handsome when the new buildings are made – they must all be of brick and all the same height. The streets are being widened and some little alleys lost completely.

Our two families have been cause for concern. Sam got Balty a place as muster master on a voyage to the West Indies but Balty was concerned about Esther in the meantime, as regards his and her honour (I think there's been some jealousy). He would obviously have been very happy if we'd offered to have her while he was away, but Sam told me he wouldn't do that in case anything miscarried at sea and we were stuck with her. I brought them both over here so Sam could have a serious talk with them about the importance of saving money while Balty was away, and that her living with his parents was the most reasonable thing to do but she was dead set against it and wouldn't be moved. And much as I love my parents I can understand her feeling. So Balty's found some respectable lodgings for his wife at Leigh, and at least we don't have to worry about that any more.

And in Sam's family, something much greater – his mother has died. It was hardly a surprise because she'd been ill for a long time, but the exact moment is always a shock, that sudden knowledge that they've gone for ever and whatever their faults or failings, there can be no more complaining of them, and in that way, if no other, we who are left are impoverished. John wrote that she had the death rattle in her throat and that night Sam dreamed he was laying his head over his mother's bedside and crying over her. That was the night she died, and when the news reached us two days later I opened the letter and had Sam called home from the office and brought up to my closet, where I told him. Her last words, two days before, had been 'God bless my poor Sam'. We both wept, but then Sam thought how much better she should go now rather than outlive his father, or even himself, and busied himself in bespeaking mourning. He's resolved to put both of us, Nell Barker, Jane Birch, Will Hewer, and Tom into full mourning, and to give the undermaids hoods, scarves and gloves. And will send mourning clothes into the country as well. A bitter-sweet spring.

APRIL

With its sweet showers. Plants grow all over the ruins in the most precarious places. An abundance of wild flowers blooming next to the digging and hammering which sounds the reconstruction of the City. Moorfields is being built on – paved streets instead of cobbles and all the houses two storeys high.

But the finer weather doesn't seem to make for sweeter tempers. John Unthank told me the King was furious at Frances Stuart's marriage to the Duke of Richmond and Elizabeth P. confirmed it and added that she'd sent all the King's jewels back. If this is true it makes her a jewel among women herself. On a humbler scale Sam declared himself displeased on three counts: my watch, which cost £12 (his idea), has stopped keeping time; the cost of mourning for his mother (£50 so far); and the fact that there is no money to do business at the office and the whole kingdom is in an ill state. Add to this that when Jervas the barber brought his new periwig it was full of nits and he refused to have it.

Even when I went to the Maundy Thursday ceremony with Mary Mercer there was a disappointment because the King didn't wash the poor people's feet himself, it was done by the Bishop of London. Sam took us up afterwards and we went out to Hackney, to eat and drink and take the air, very pleasant. We said goodbye to Balty a few days later. Sam has arranged for Balty to be Paymaster to the Fleet as well, and all the profits will come to me to be paid out as I think fit for our parents' comfort. And what a relief to me to think that I will finally have some money set aside for them, without having to beg Sam.

Ominous signs of his bad temper resuming now we're through the worry of the last two years: Sam kicked Luce our cook-maid for leaving the door open and he beat Tom for staying out at Mary Mercer's (not on the same day). But we begin to enjoy the pleasures of warmer weather. We went over the water to the Jamaica-house where we'd never been before, and took Nell, Jane, and Mary Mercer and her sister, and the younger ones all ran races on the bowling green for wagers between me and Sam. Sweet weather. Spring is advancing, fragrance in the garden, buds opening.

The Duke of York and Sir William Coventry are both gone down to Portsmouth so Sam feels free to go to plays as often as he likes. We've been to several, but Will Hewer told me that the servants and his clerks at the office observe Sam taking more pleasure than usual and it's commented on. I told Sam (after we'd been to see the musical version of *Macbeth*) and he resolved on no more theatre until Whit Sunday, although in fact we went again the next day. But after that nothing for a while.

I've been living very domestically: bought linen and made shirts and smocks, delivered a baby . . . Not by myself, of course. Betty Mitchell sent for me to come to her labour, and when I arrived, there was a midwife and that was all, no other neighbours. Poor Betty was in great straits but the midwife said she was doing very well. I soothed her as best I could and when the time came for her to bear down, the midwife and I stood either side of her and she put her feet on our hips and pushed against us. It was a most moving and frightening sight to see the baby's head emerge, the midwife's hands cupping it and then after another gasp or two delivering the shoulders, and then in a slither the whole baby out, a little girl. And we washed her and swaddled her and put her in her mother's arms, and I think there cannot have been three happier women in all of London.

Two days later I was godmother to the Unthanks' new baby. I still feel a pang when I hold a little one in my arms but I don't dwell on it any more, as I used to. I'm twenty-six and I've been married for nearly twelve years and since it hasn't happened yet I must assume it never will. I must take consolation, I suppose, in the notion that my figure's better than it would have been otherwise. And considering what my monthlies are like, God knows what childbirth would have meant for me.

MAY

I've tried to make it a merry month but there have been difficulties. It started well enough on May Day, watching the milkmaids dancing along to collect their tips, a fiddler leading them, garlands of flowers on their pails. And I took Will Hewer and Jane down to Woolwich to stay with Barbara for the night and gather May dew in the morning. Betty Turner says it's the only thing in the world to wash your face with. So we rose very early and went out into the fields under a pale blue sky and bathed our faces in the dew – but it's quite difficult to gather enough to take home for even one wash. Never mind, it was lovely to be out with no one else around, as though the world belonged to us, to smell the freshness of the earth and hear the larks sing.

Sam has other thoughts on his mind. There comes a time in every man's life when he finds himself in urgent need of his own coach and pair. This moment has come to Sam. He has talked to someone about securing land at the back to make a coach-house. He can't bear to be seen in a hackney any more. A natural progress, I suppose, from our early days when we walked everywhere, to the years when we took a coach if it was raining, to the present time when we always take a coach whatever the weather, and so to the future where we maintain our own. He's incensed by the fineness of Peg and Mr Lowther's coach, to make such show abroad while they live in such squalor at home. I'd love it, to be able to go abroad in my own coach whenever I pleased. I suspect, though, that actually bringing himself to come up with the money may take some time.

I was godmother again at the christening of Betty's baby, called, in my honour, Elizabeth. We had a pair of gloves each, and wine and wafers, and it was very innocent company, and merry. Afterwards Sam and I and Nell went up on the tide as far as Barn Elms and came back through the bridge at ten o'clock when the river was at standing-water and it was calm enough to sail through without fear. I remember that, the feeling of luxury that we didn't have to disembark one side of the bridge and walk round, that we could go straight to our nearest quay and be home the sooner, because there are times when, however pleasant the occasion, after it is over one simply wants to be at home having supper and going to bed.

Life hasn't been as calm again. Sam was furiously displeased with me for wearing white locks, wouldn't say anything, kept silent and then suddenly came out with it – they were unnatural, only whores wore them. I was surprised, I didn't think he'd be so vehement. I thought it best to say nothing. He went to bed without any supper, in silence. The next morning I approached him. I began calmly: if I could have the money to put lace on my half-mourning, I wouldn't wear white locks again. He flew into a completely unreasonable frenzy and that made me mad and I went on at him about keeping company with Mrs Knepp. And then I said I wouldn't wear white locks again if he didn't see her again and that shut him up. And eventually he agreed that I could have money for lace if I didn't wear white locks again. (Exactly what I had proposed half an hour and several screaming fits before.)

So then we're 'friends' and we go to visit the Carterets but they're already dining and we don't wish to intrude so we think of going to a French house for dinner. Sam's periwig-maker, Monsieur Robins, has an ordinary in a very mean street in Covent Garden, but within a moment of walking in, the table is covered and laid and there are fresh glasses, and it's all served in the French manner, one dish at a time, soup and then stewed pigeons and then *boeuf à la mode*. And afterwards we're truly friends, and drive out to Islington and Sam recalls being a boy there, with his bow and arrows.

So that one passed off. Meanwhile both the infant sons of the Duke of York die, leaving him once again the only heir and pointing up the Queen's barrenness. Sir William Batten claims that the young groom Mr Lowther has been to bathe and sweat himself in the hot tub, and his young lady Peg as well, because he has the pox and has given it to her and sweating is the easiest treatment. Our cook-maid Luce was drunk more and more often and on being reprimanded for it she left us, thank goodness. My woman Nell Barker has also gone, having lied to me once too often.

I've had a bad cold and spent a couple of days in bed. It was like a dream floating above all the usual domestic cares. Payne, Sam's waterman, had found us two new maids so the servant problem was taken care of. Sam sat beside my bed and read to me from *Cyrus*, the description of the beautiful Princess Cléomire, with her modesty and calmness and generous spirit, the order and cleanliness of her apartments, sweet-smelling and full of flowers so it is always spring.

Ah well, I try my best. Elizabeth P. came to see me wearing her own hair colour which looks much better than white locks on her. (Sam delighted that I agreed.)

I was up by the time his father arrived from Brampton to seek treatment from Mr Hollier for his rupture which is causing him great pain. The first day he was here we all dined together very pleasantly and then Mrs Daniel appeared to ask Sam to get a place for her husband. Now I never know with these young, comely women – Mrs Bagwell is another – why it is that they have to ask on their husbands' behalf. Why don't the husbands ask for themselves? So Sam has to take her to the parlour while his father and I sit upstairs and then they must go to the office and when he comes back he's flushed and full of animation and I'm suspicious and ask him why he has such a full colour and he says it's the heat of the season. (It's warm but not hot.) I can't say any more, his father is present, but I'm – oh, I feel suspended, as though I don't know where anything true lies, like a navigator who's lost his way.

And then there was a Sunday when Sam, called to account at the end of it, admitted that after we both went to church in the morning and then dined at home with the Mitchells he went off to Westminster Church (why?) and then sailed up to Barn Elms reading Mr Evelyn's book on *Solitude*, and on the way back reading Mr Boyle's book of *Colours*, as though he hadn't a care in the world. And all this time his father was in such a dreadful fit of pain at home that we thought he would die, and I sent for Mr Hollier and sent messages all over Whitehall trying to find Sam. Eventually Will Hewer managed to push the bowel that had fallen down back into his body and that relieved the poor man greatly. Mr Hollier recommends a steel truss for more permanent relief.

I was angry that Sam had been out all day but it wasn't the moment to say so. A couple of days later we were to go to the Pearses' for supper and dancing, with the usual people, Mrs Knepp, the Clarkes and so on. I was wearing the new silver lace on my half-mourning that we'd had the row about a few days before and when he saw it he was furious and said it looked base (which it didn't) and I had lace at my sleeves and it was too soon for that (a matter of opinion, being just over two months since his mother died). So he stormed out to the office and stayed there although it was time to go, and I sent messages over via Will asking what I might wear and he said my plain cloth gown and I said anything but that, but he stuck fast, so in the end neither of us went. He spent the evening in his closet doing his accounts and I went to bed with *Cyrus*.

The stupid thing was that he was cutting off his nose to spite his face, for he was far more vexed at not seeing Mrs Knepp than I was. The next day at dinner we were 'friends' again, by making no reference to it, which was as near an apology as he could bring himself to, I suppose. And in the evening we sang in the garden, roses scenting the air, and all seemed to be at peace.

But it was festering with me, why he should have so much control over what I wear, and he was out on business so much that there was plenty of time to think about it. And it came out one night when he came home for supper and afterwards he and I sang and played our flageolets. Suddenly I found my lip trembling and burst out with why should his humours determine what clothes I wear, and he asks who's paying for them? There are high words on both sides and then he goes and sits in his chamber and reads Boyle's *Hydrostatics* – out loud, so he won't have to listen to me. And I give up, and cry, and he comes and puts his arms round me and we go to bed together (for the first time in a week, because of my cold).

∞

JUNE: WAR WITH THE DUTCH

All the speculation that the Dutch would not come out this year proves false. On the 8th June we hear that there are eighty Dutch ships off Harwich and gunfire has been heard in Bethnal Green. Barges have been sent up to the Hope, to make a bridge across the Thames for horses and soldiers to cross the river if need be. Sam manages to spend the whole of Sunday on his own pleasure, coming home to supper to find orders to set out some fireships to harass the Dutch. Sir William Batten and Sir William Penn have arrived from their country houses and together they issue the orders.

By the next day the Dutch are at the mouth of the Thames, at the Nore, and Sam's desperately busy getting every available ship out. People at Gravesend are moving their goods away for fear of the Dutch arriving. On the 11th comes news that the Dutch are at the mouth of the Medway and they've taken Sheerness. The drums are beating all over town for the trained bands to appear the next morning, armed and supplied with enough victuals for a fortnight. Sam comes home late and tells me how serious the situation is. All the militia are sent to Chatham, there's nothing left to guard London.

The next day we hear that the Dutch have

made no advance and the chain across the River Medway, behind which our great ships shelter, has been reinforced, so they're safe enough. Or so we thought. A few hours later came the terrible news that the Dutch had broken through the chain, and de Ruyter had sailed all the way up the Medway and burned the *Royal Charles*, one of our principal ships, the pride of the fleet. They say it was revenge for Holmes's bonfire. (The Dutch say the Fire of London was divine retribution for Holmes's bonfire.) The easterly gales and the spring tide conspired to bring them so far up the river.

That night Sam took me and his father up to my chamber and closed the door and told us that he feared the office would be blamed for the Dutch success and it could be attacked either by the Dutch or the English and he was very worried about his money. When we went to bed he was still unsure of what to do, frightened and wakeful all night.

Then comes news of a second Dutch fleet in the Hope and the Duke of York commands the sinking of ships in Barking Creek to stop them coming any higher up the Thames. This puts Sam into such a fright that he gives me and his father two hours to leave for Brampton on the coach, carrying £1,300 in gold with us. He can't change any more money into gold – the bankers have none left. What is terrible is that the Dutch ships are full of English sailors who fight for the Dutch because they're paid in dollars not tickets, and the women are out in Wapping, screaming that this is what they've come to, our brave Englishmen forced to fight for the Dutch to earn an honest living because our kingdom can't afford to pay them.

The City is like it was in the Fire, nobody knowing which way to turn. The Navy is in chaos for lack of supplies. The ships that were sunk to block the Thames were the ones that had just been fully fitted out. There's an attack on the Lord Chancellor's house, breaking windows, and a gibbet set up. There's a run on the banks and nobody can get any money. The Court is as mad as ever: the night the *Royal Charles* was burned the King supped with Lady Castlemaine and they spent the evening in great merriment — chasing a moth.

Sam's gold isn't buried as he'd wish. When his father and I arrived at Brampton it seemed very difficult to find a moment to do it when there were not people about to see where it was put. In the end we waited until Sunday morning when everyone was at church, but because it was daylight we could have been observed, and Pall in particular was nosing around. We dug a pit as best we could, near the vegetables, and buried the bags of money and notes, but afterwards it stood out very plainly that the earth had been disturbed.

When I got back to London and told Sam, he was so angry he wouldn't speak to me or sup with me, went straight to bed on his own. I was too tired from my travelling to argue with him. It wasn't as though we'd ridden across country flinging gold coins to all and sundry. We'd done our best. But when it comes to money – his money – his fear of losing it is so great it sometimes verges on lunacy. I must take him as the man he is, because I know I can't change him.

By dinner time the next day he'd come round to the view that it was as much our concern as his, so we wouldn't have acted with no care. And then he took a nap (as is more and more his habit after dinner these days) and woke up in much better temper about it, though determined to retrieve it as soon as he could, now that the immediate threat of invasion was over.

And now the recriminations about the war begin. Why was the fleet not ready to go out and attack the Dutch rather than cowering at home behind our defences? The Navy Commissioner at Chatham is arrested and put in the Tower. Sam even fears the same may happen to him and begins to prepare the Board's defence.

And the little baby Elizabeth Mitchell whom I helped into the world has left us already, dead of a fever at eight weeks old.

SUMMER

The baby's burial was a sad business, just her family and me. Later Betty and I sat in our garden talking over the baby's little life, how good she'd been and never sickly until the end. It seemed so cruel that all around us were flowers blooming and honeysuckle and jasmine twining vigorously and Elizabeth lay cold under the earth. And then it seems Betty's marriage is not as contented as it looks to outsiders; she says Michael's not kind to her, and my heart sank, knowing how much a woman's happiness depends on her marriage – far more than a man's does – and that if he's being unkind to her now it doesn't bode well for the future.

But we must do as we can. My dear apothecary, Mr Pelling, has taught me how to make tea — very simple, put the leaves in a pot and pour on boiling water, leave for a few minutes to infuse and then strain and drink it. He says it will be very good for the cold I have had for weeks now, and also for my discharges. So that takes care of me for the moment.

News comes of peace between us and the Dutch, through a meeting at Breda, though nothing confirmed yet. Meanwhile we go and see the great boy and girl who are recently come out of Limerick in Ireland: the girl is eight years old and six foot tall, the boy is four years old and nearly five foot tall, and both with thickness matching their height. Sam tried to weigh them in his arms but they were both too heavy for him. They've been presented to the King and their age is testified to.

Sam's been out all day, day after day, and I know there's a lot happening at the moment, but it gets too much for me, left alone all the time. When I complained he flew into a rage and pulled my nose and then escaped to the office. I was in such a temper that I followed him there and he was forced to take me out in the garden to stop anyone hearing, and by degrees we calmed down and I went back home. Each time it takes me longer to recover from these arguments. There seem to be more and more things in his life that need his attention away from home. Sometimes I feel like driftwood washed up on the beach while the tide turns without me.

But at other times I feel as though I'm swimming with the current. I went to Unthank's to have a bodice altered and heard the gossip that Nell Gwyn has been seduced away from the Theatre Royal by Lord Buckhurst, who has her as his whore at £100 a year, so she's given up acting, which is all our loss.

A Sunday trip to Epsom.

We leave at five in the morning with Betty Turner and Will Hewer in a coach and four that Sam hired the day before. We have wine, beer and cold fowl to sustain us until dinner time. Clouds of dust fly up from the road but the country beyond is green and fine. On the way we chat about our acquaintances, in particular the pride of Peg Lowther who at Walthamstow insisted on her train being held up by her page – ridiculous behaviour in the country. We get to the Well at Epsom by eight o'clock, much company there, and while Sam drinks the water, Betty and I talk to various ladies we know. The sun grows too hot for us to be outside so we drive into town to the King's Head where we get the last room they have left and have drinks sent in and order dinner. Sam goes to church where he sees the Houblon brothers, then back and we dine in our room, very merry, and Mr Pembleton, who happens to be taking the waters, joins us. We hear that Lord Buckhurst and Nell Gwyn are staying in the house next door, also very merry.

It's hot and after dinner we all lie down for a nap and rise again to take the air in the coach, a lovely breeze now. We go to see a Cousin Pepys's empty house and Sam tells us how pleasant the walks in the woods are. He tries to lead us to one of them but he can't find his way and we get tangled in the thickets.

It's hot and prickly. He tells us often how pleasant the walks are, if he can just find them. We assure him we'll take his word for it but in the meantime we'd just like to find a way out. At last we emerge from it, and Sam manages to twist his ankle jumping down a bank. But after a rest he can walk again and we wander on the Downs, where there's a flock of sheep and a most innocent sight – a shepherd reading the Bible to his little boy. We get the boy to read to us and he does it in a sweet, high voice and Sam gives him a coin. The old man looks after eighteen score sheep for 4 shillings a week and he values his dog mightily. His shoes are shod with iron because the Downs are so full of stones.

We leave him, and Betty and I gather nosegays in the fields, so many different flowers in the grass it makes me think of the colour Heaven must be. We stop a poor woman with her milk pail and Sam produces a tumbler and we drink deep. Then back to our inn where we have a dish of cream. And so home by sunset, in the cool of the evening, well pleased with our day's work. As it grew dark, we saw glow-worms, very pretty. By the time we were home, Sam's foot was so painful he couldn't walk unaided so we got him to bed and wrapped his foot in a waxed cloth to help the swelling. Betty came in the next day and dressed it again.

It was while he was resting in bed that the sad news came that Jane Birch's brother had died, leaving a wife and two children. Sam immediately gave Jane 20 shillings for the widow and offered whatever wine they needed for burying him. Poor Jane, poor widow, poor children.

Esther came up from Leigh-on-Sea and told us how she'd seen the *Royal Charles*, not burnt but towed away by the Dutch, which is even more humiliating, and when they got her out of Chatham River they sounded the great guns on her, it was enough to make any Englishman fall silent. And she had heard Englishmen, soldiers and sailors, say they'd rather serve the Dutch than the King because they'd be better used.

News comes of the Dutch fleet moving all over the place, Harwich, Portsmouth, Plymouth, Dartmouth. Sir William Batten shouts out, 'By God, I think the devil shits Dutchmen.' But then news arrives from Breda of a peace between us. The merchants don't like it, they see this kingdom's trade sacrificed to the King's pleasure.

Lady Castlemaine and the King are quite broken off – he's furious that she's in love with Henry Jermyn, Master of Horse to the Duke of York (strange how these Masters of Horse are so attractive to the ladies – Captain Ferrer comes to mind). And she's with child and swears the King will own it as his or she'll bring it into Whitehall and dash its brains out before his face. Such is the nature of love at Court.

We dined at the Penns' on a venison pasty that stank like a devil. Then out to the theatre and then abroad with Mrs Knepp, and as always Sam had to make a great thing of handing her into the coach and then we were so squashed that he 'had' to have his arm round her waist as we drove through the market gardens on the way to Chelsea. And we sat in an arbour and ate and drank, and as always when she's around I fell into a bad humour. By the time we went home it was so late that the City gates were shut and we had to go through Newgate. There was trouble at the gaol from some prisoners breaking out, and then the coach driver said he could see some rogues, and all in all it was a hard drive back. The evening seemed to have lasted for ever. There wasn't much talk as we went to bed.

It all came out the next morning, before we'd even risen. It filled my mind from the moment I awoke and lots of other things with it, like the way his father behaved at Brampton when I went riding with Captain Coleman, a gentleman I'd met on the coach. Sam's father seemed to regard it as adultery when all I was doing was getting out of that family for a couple of hours, but doubtless he couldn't understand that need. Sam didn't say much. He found it expedient to spend the rest of the day in the office, apart from bringing Will Hayter and Will Hewer home for dinner – good company and such an excellent way of ensuring no difficult subjects are raised.

We have not lain together for – it seems like six months. When I walk by the shops and the prentices cry out, 'What do you lack, lady, what do you lack?' I think, alas, what I lack doesn't lie on your shelves. And sometimes, from the look in their eyes, I think they know exactly what it is.

Sam's eyes are bad. Sometimes I wonder if they're bad so he can't see things that would trouble him – but that's fanciful, I've seen the pain on his face after working by candlelight. It's very hot and we walk in the garden at night and sing with Mary Merer and Barbara Sheldon, or listen to the nightingales as honeysuckle wafts sweetly on the air. Sir William Batten brings out melon. He's been very ill but seems much better.

A Sunday trip to Barnet.

We're up by four o'clock and leave before five, with Betty Turner in the coach with us. We're at the Wells by seven, but it's very cold. Sam drinks the water while we chat with Joseph Batelier, and Will Hewer is there with his uncle and rides beside us to the Red Lion in Barnet, where we drink and have excellent cheese cakes. Then on to Hatfield and the Salisbury Arms, next door to Lord Salisbury's house. Here we have drinks and order dinner, then off to church where many fine people, and back to dine. Then a walk in the park to a stall where Betty and I buy straw hats which are much worn in Hertfordshire. Mine is mighty becoming, I'm told. A rest and then back to Barnet where Will Hewer treats us most handsomely with cheese cakes and tarts and cream. As always Sam and I get on particularly well when he's present as a cushion between us. A walk in the garden among the hazel trees, picking filberts. Home with great content and not too late.

The next morning I call the maids up early for washing and go back to bed. It's chilly now in the early mornings. Sam shivers and cuddles me and we do what we haven't done for a long time. The world seems a happier place.

I take the maids and our linen over the water to Lambeth Marshes to the whitesters. There the women paddle our clothes in their huge tubs of bleach and hang them out on lines to dry and they flap in the wind. When they're dry and we fold them neatly, we bury our noses in them — there is a freshness that only comes from being dried in the full open air, and for a moment there is victory over dirt and disorder, such a satisfying feeling of contentment from a simple smell. By the time we're home it's dark and late and Sam's worried, but we walk in with such virtue, and sweet linen, and he's so pleased to see us.

I want new cuffs to go to see the dancing at little Betty Turner's school. He cannot allow them. An argument. Continues the next morning. End of argument equals new cuffs. Why not just say yes in the first place?

In the larger world, Lord Clarendon, the Chancellor, has fallen prey to his enemies and been deprived of his office. His great town house has a hundred hearths, all paid for by his profits as Chancellor, and it's said the stone used to build it was meant for the rebuilding of St Paul's, and the timber used was intended for the Navy. In addition he's blamed for selling Dunkirk and taking on the worthless Tangier. And the people hate him most of all for ensuring the King married a barren Queen, so his own daughter, as Duchess of York, will inherit the throne.

According to Lord Anglesey, the King sent the Duke of Albemarle to collect his seal from him, at which the Chancellor replied, very civilly, that he had received it from the King and he would deliver it himself to the King's own hand. And so the next day he did, saying he would gladly pay with his head if any wrongdoing could be found. As he left the King at noon and walked through Whitehall garden, Lady Castlemaine, his enemy, ran out on to her balcony in her night clothes, screaming with laughter and showing great joy at his going. And Clarendon paused for a moment and looked up at her and said, 'O Madam, is it you? Pray remember that if you live you will grow old.'

Another one who's taken a tumble is Nell Gwyn. Lord Buckhurst has already left her and her previous lover hates her so she's back at the theatre, poor and friendless. Such are the ways of the world.

Autumn

As the hours of daylight get shorter and he must work more by candlelight, Sam's eyes get worse. Often now I read to him in the evenings. Thank goodness I can at least read out loud very well, even if I can't sing.

He has to save his eyes for preparing the Board's defence of their conduct in the late war. On this account he went to a Privy Council meeting and while business was discussed the King did nothing but play alternately with his dog and his codpiece. This is a man whose idea of retrenchment of Court expenses is to cut down on his falconry. He owes his linen draper £5,000 and is almost run out of clean handkerchiefs and neckbands because the grooms take them at the end of their quarter's service in place of their fees which won't be paid. They say the King is going to make his bastard the Duke of Monmouth legitimate and make him his heir instead of the Duke of York, whose esteem has fallen along with his father-in-law Clarendon.

Bartholomew Fair time again. We went with Will Hewer and ate the traditional pork and watched Jacob Hall dancing on the ropes. There was a poor man who danced on his hands with his legs tied above his head and then danced on his crutches with his feet never touching the ground, but he was so clearly in pain. We gave him money. And we saw a very clever clockwork show of the seven ages of man and we joked about which of them was the same age as us. And also there was a show of the sea rolling and Neptune and Venus and mermaids on a dolphin. Here we met Peg Lowther, with a sore on her nose – from her husband's pox?

For some reason Sam is pleased with me these days. I'm doing much better at the flageolet than he could ever have imagined, but even so I wonder at it. Is he guilty about something, somebody? He and John Creed took me to a prize fight at the Bear Garden where a shoemaker and a butcher fought each other until the shoemaker had so much blood on him he had to give up. I had my vizard up and Sam hid his face in his cloak – the crowd was mostly of rough seamen and he didn't want to be known there.

He bought me a book on heraldry so I could look at my Clifford family arms, and we've been often to the theatre together. And when I suggested that it was time I had a woman again, he didn't object. William Batelier brought a very pretty girl from the school at Bow for me to see, and when I told Sam he said it was entirely in my hands as to having her or not. When she came again I sent for him to come and meet her and he seemed well enough pleased with her but again said it was up to me. She has excellent deportment and talks more gravely than her age would suggest – she is just seventeen. The thing about having a pretty girl is that it does keep Sam in good humour so he takes more pleasure in being at home. I think it's harmless enough because I'm sure he wouldn't try with my woman in our house what he might try abroad with his sempstresses or booksellers or any of those women who have shops in the Exchange, who like to look after their men customers in all sorts of ways.

So I decided to have her and her name is Deborah Willet. Our first journey out, all three of us, was to see Shirley's tragedy *The Traitor*, very good, and then a drink at the Cock before home by the Wall to avoid the City ruins. Deb was very composed, even when two days later Mrs Knepp took us behind the stage and up into the tiring rooms where Nell Gwyn was half dressed and very pretty but so heavily painted. She gave us fruit, and actors walked in and out, only half dressed themselves and talking lewdly.

The very surprising thing is that Sir William Batten has died and none of us even knew he was that ill. We had to leave for Brampton the next day so we missed his burial but apparently there were two hundred coaches following him to Walthamstow.

We stopped at Cambridge on our way to Brampton for Sam to show us some of his old haunts, and he was mighty pleased to be in a condition after all these years to have two pretty women in their neat morning dresses, and a coach to himself, and whatever we wanted that an inn could provide. Both nights of the journey we all three slept in the same room, the first night him and me together, the second night me and Deb. When we got to Brampton we found the building work finished and well done, only the walls needed a little more greenery but that will come with time.

We visited Lady Sandwich at Hinchingbrooke and she was as dear a lady as ever, but she has been forced to sell her best plate, worth nearly £1,000, to help with the Earl's debts. Being Ambassador to Spain brings him no money and great expense (she doesn't mention the English debts that have been growing for years). At least she's happy with the bride proposed for Lord Hinchingbrooke, which is a comfort we don't have with Pall who's looking older and uglier by the minute. She's twenty-seven now, not much time left. We don't say much to each other because she's still smarting from last time I was here when Captain Coleman came to visit and she thought he was interested in her. Only a fool wouldn't know him as a man happy to flirt with married ladies but not in the least interested in marriage himself, and certainly not to a plain woman with a modest dowry.

The purpose of our visit was to recover the gold which we'd buried in June. We weren't allowed to go out and start digging until it was pitch dark in case any neighbours saw or heard anything. It was difficult to find the exact spot in the dark, even by the one candle Sam allowed. And the fact that his father is very deaf didn't make our arguing about where it was any quieter. Sam was in a terrible toss but, by and by, poking with a stick, we found it and began to dig it up. Then he found that each action of the spade was scattering gold coins among the grass and earth because the bags were all rotten and water had got into the notes so he couldn't tell what he had and what he didn't have. He was nearly out of his wits with worry. In the end we gathered up everything we could see and took it all to his brother's room and locked it in while we had supper. Then the rest of us went to bed while he and Will Hewer washed every coin and note and Sam reckoned himself 100 pieces of gold short. He was worried that the neighbours would come in the night and take it so he and Will went out again and found another 45.

First thing in the morning he had Will out again and they sifted through all the surrounding earth and made the 45 up to 79, so he was only twenty or so short and with that even he was well enough pleased, reflecting that sometimes it's as hard to keep money as to get it. So we left by coach, with four men beside us on horseback, safe enough, and the money stowed under the seat where Sam could check every few minutes that it hadn't vanished into thin air. We stayed the night at Stevenage (gold under the bed, never left unattended) and were home the next day by five o'clock and everything safe at last under lock and key.

We've been to the theatre a great many times lately — I wonder whether it's because there have been a lot of good plays or because Sam so enjoys taking Deb abroad.

WINTER

Dark, foggy days. Poor Sam has to work most of the time by candlelight. More and more I read to him in the evenings. Sometimes we all sit in the kitchen, which is the warmest room in the house, and Deb combs his nits out on to a white cloth and we joke about which one can run fastest. Sam tells us the story he heard at the Royal Society about Dr Caius of Cambridge who, when he was an old man, lived only on women's milk, and when he fed on the milk of an angry fretful woman he was so himself, but when he fed on a good-natured woman's milk he became good-natured too. So the Society have hired a man for 20 shillings to have some blood of a sheep let into his body. His brain is a little frantic and they think the sheep's blood will cool it.

Jane and Tom listen to this agog, thinking no one knows they're holding hands under the table. We make Sam promise to tell us what happens to the frantic man. Sweet domestic times. And news comes of a match proposed for Pall with her former suitor's executor and Sam replies post haste that he's still willing to put up £500. So our family is happy and often Sam brings all his clerks home for dinner and the house is warm and full and alive. And I thank God for my good fortune, more so when we hear that Mr Kirton, who lost all his books in the Fire, is dead of grief.

At least he didn't leave behind him the disarray of

Sir William Batten's estate. Betty Turner came round with all the gossip that Lady Batten had made him disinherit his eldest son by his first wife, leaving him just £10. He left Mingo his blackamoor that much, plus £20 a year. But Sam says son and father were equally rogues.

Mr Moore came to Sam to beg him to lend Lord Sandwich £200, without which his credit would collapse. Sam had already refused Lord Hinchingbrooke's request but this time, hearing that John Creed had promised the same amount, he agreed, very reluctantly, as he sees no prospect of it ever being repaid. On the other hand when Kate Joyce asked to borrow £300 so she and Anthony can rebuild their house he was very happy to consider having some money out of his hands on good security.

He was also happy to hear from Captain Cocke that Sir Robert Brooke, who is chairing the Commons committee on the war, is very satisfied with his conduct and says he'll make him the darling of the House. Just a couple of weeks before, Sir Robert and I had both been godparents to Mr Milles's child and I'd taken the opportunity to be as charming to him as I knew how, which has clearly done no harm. Sam's certainly in better condition than our former Chancellor, who's fled to France to avoid imprisonment. He petitioned Parliament in his defence and they ordered the paper to be publicly burnt by the hangman.

I've been ill with various things for weeks – a monthly that was more like a flood, then a severe flux of my bowels. And my poor little Fancy is having fits, from old age, we think. Deb has been very helpful, although I find her a bit forward when she's out with me and Sam. But I think she has a good heart. Her aunt came to visit and proved to be a fine woman, a widow, well-informed on fashion and plays and Court, so much so that Sam spent the whole afternoon at home in her company. She took notice that since she has been with us Deb's breasts have begun to swell – she was beginning to fear she wouldn't have any. It seemed an odd thing to remark on at first meeting, in front of a man at least.

I'd barely recovered from the flux which had left me feeling thin and weak when I developed a terrible toothache and my cheek started swelling. For five days before Christmas it swelled bigger and bigger until from my eye to the base of my neck was the shape of half a football. Mr Hollier came and said it could spoil my face for ever if it didn't break, and laid poultices to it. He gave me medicine for the pain but it did no more than sometimes take the edge off it while I lay for hour after hour with a throbbing pain so bad I wanted to die. One night when Sam came home I saw the fear in his eyes when he looked at my face, which was so swollen we thought it would burst open. I hadn't realised how bad it was until I saw that look, all I knew was the pain from the inside.

He was very good about coming and talking and reading to me. Deb was attentive and took a load from my shoulders in terms of bespeaking Sam's supper, things like that. Men must eat, that's the first rule, they can't be generous when they're hungry. I couldn't eat at all of course, so they ate together. At last, two days before Christmas, the abscess broke into my cheek and my face was saved and gradually

I was relieved of pain. I wasn't well enough to make mince pies, I left that to Jane, but by Christmas Day I was well enough to read to Sam in the afternoon – a ghost story of a phantom drummer. And two days later we were able, for the first time in several weeks, to lie together as husband and wife.

So our year ends with no plague or fire. God grant us all continued health and happiness.

(And to the poor man who had sheep's blood let in to his body. He's well, it seems, but his brain is as frantic as ever.)

1668

A NEW YEAR.

And soon enough a death. Anthony Joyce had come twice to enquire about the loan to rebuild his house which Sam was quite prepared to make him, but he had to have time to consider it (the usual thing — can't bear to pay out at the first time of asking). A few days later the message comes from Kate Joyce that Sam must come at once if he wants to see Anthony alive and Sam goes and finds that five days earlier he'd tried to drown himself in the pond at Islington, early in the morning, sober and quiet. He was found and rescued but did enough damage that now he had the death rattle and in desperation they'd laid pigeons to his feet but he was clearly dying. He confessed to their vicar that it was his great sense of loss by the Fire and not serving God as he should have done that had brought him to it.

Kate was desperately worried that his death would be found to be self-murder, in which case all his property would be forfeit to the Crown. She'd already sent all their plate away, and begged Sam to take their wine flagons, even though the poor man wasn't dead yet. He died a few hours later and Sam went to William Coventry who took him to the King, and the Duke of York was there as well, and he told his story and the King said without more ado that if it was found to be self-murder the estate was to go to the widow and children. The family were all very grateful to Sam, quite rightly. The burial was three days later, a rabble of four or five hundred people of mean condition. I didn't go, and Sam left as soon as he could, although not before hearing the vicar refer to Anthony's death as killing himself, which hardly helped the family's defence that his death had nothing to do with the attempted drowning almost a week before. Sam was furious at these foolish Protestant divines, where Catholic priests are bound by vows of secrecy. An inquest was ordered with the coroner. We visited Kate to sit with her, quietly, not saying much, the way you do.

Elsewhere, Pall's marriage plans with Mr Jackson are going on and we want her to be married here, with Will Hewer and Joseph Batelier as bridemen and Mary Mercer and Deb as bridesmaids. And I think about who else we should invite and what food and wine we should have. It's such a great pleasure to take paper and pen and make lists for this sort of occasion. I'm a great list-maker, I love the order of it, as though writing things down is a talisman against accident and improvidence.

Will Hewer has been very helpful in the matter of Anthony Joyce, and many other things in our life. He gave me a locket of diamonds, worth £40, out of gratitude for our kindness to him, which I tried to refuse, but he left it with me and when Sam saw it he insisted I refuse, because it wouldn't be honourable for me to accept it when Will only earns £30 a year. A little later, Will came to me very concerned that Sam wasn't pleased with him and his work. I talked to Sam who said that he couldn't copy out a letter properly with sense and true spelling, and it drove him mad. So then I told Will but added how pleased Sam was with him in other ways and found him invaluable apart from his copying. I couldn't bear it if he left Sam's service. He and Mary Mercer are the only people I can talk to with absolute trust.

Cousin Roger bought Pall's suitor, Mr Jackson, to dine and he seems pleasant enough though he didn't say much, but John Creed was there as well and once he and Sam are in conversation it's hard for anyone else to get a word in. All this talk of weddings has prompted Jane to confess her love for Tom, and in floods of tears she told me how first he'd blown hot, asking her to love and marry him, and now he was blowing cold, claiming it would displease Sam. So I told Tom it wouldn't displease Sam at all and he should go on with his love for Jane and be true to her. At such times I feel like a mother to them both. I don't feel like that toward Deb yet, partly because she hasn't been one of our family for so long, and also her forwardness vexes me sometimes.

Our Valentines this year were Mary Mercer for Sam and Cousin Roger for me. Sam gave Mary a golden guinea but I am his Valentine too, as he agreed I would be every year, and it will cost him £5 for a ring I have my eye on, a very neat turquoise set with diamonds. I went through all my jewels and I reckon I have above £150 worth, which pleases Sam immensely because only a small part of that has actually been laid out by him.

After all my plans, news arrived that Pall had married Mr Jackson in Brampton. How typical of her to do things in an impatient twopenny-halfpenny way. Sam couldn't care less as long as the business was done and she was safely off his hands. He'd been far too worried and busy because Parliament had called the Navy Board to the Bar of the House to defend their conduct in the late war, and although all the Commissioners were called to account it was Sam who actually had to make the speech.

He spent all of the day before closeted with his clerks, working like a dog, and then late at night read out the heads of his argument to the other Commissioners, who were incompetent to do it themselves but showed no gratitude for his efforts. He came home feeling weary and vexed and sick and we both had a restless night. At dawn he begged me to wake up properly so we could talk and he poured his heart out as to his fears for himself, his discontent with the office. I told him that if it was troubling him so much he should quit as soon as he could get clear of it. He has enough put by now for us to live comfortably enough at Brampton. Whatever the outcome of the day, I promised him my love and support, and I think he found the comfort he was seeking, although still greatly troubled.

So he went to the office and huddled with his clerks, making more notes until at nine o'clock he took boat with Will Hewer for Westminster. They were early so they went into the Hall and had a dram of brandy with Mrs Howlett. Thus fortified they were called in to the House and told of the Members' dissatisfaction and Sam began their defence. For three hours he spoke as smoothly and calmly as if he had been at his own table. It was a triumph: Parliament overwhelmingly supported him, his fellow Commissioners were heartfelt in their thanks. I'd been pacing the house all day wondering what was happening and when Will Hewer raced in with the news, I was overjoyed and we danced round the kitchen together.

Sam went very early to bed that night and slept like a baby.

There followed days of plaudits. Sir William Coventry called him the man who must be the Speaker of Parliament. Another gentleman said that if he put on a gown and pleaded in law suits at the Chancery Bar he could not earn less than £1,000 a year. The Solicitor General himself said he thought Sam spoke the best of any man in England. We were all happy and light and relieved.

A week later we gave a very grand dinner. Our guests were young Lord Hinchingbrooke and his wife, the young Sir Philip Carteret and his wife Lady Jemima, Cousin Roger, John Creed, and Sir William Godolphin, a most courteous gentleman who'd been Lord Sandwich's secretary in Spain. We'd had a professional table layer in the day before, who made the napkins into the most beautiful shapes of fish and birds and flowers, and Sam bought a large pewter cistern for washing the plates between courses. We had a man-cook in to dress the food.

Since we were all in our different ways part of the Sandwich family, the talk was mostly of my Lord and bits of Court gossip: that Lady Castlemaine is such a gamester she has won £15,000 in a night and lost £25,000 another, that the beautiful Frances Stuart, now the Duchess of Richmond, has smallpox and her face is ruined, that Mary Davis, an actress and the King's new mistress, so charmed him by her singing of 'My Lodging It Is On the Cold Ground' that it raised her from her bed on the cold ground to a bed Royal. They say she was pimped by the Duke of Buckingham to get rid of Lady Castlemaine. The King has given her a ring of £700 and furnished a house most richly for her. And from the King's mistress to the Duke of Buckingham's mistress, Lady Shrewsbury, whose husband challenged the Duke to a duel at Barn Elms. One of Buckingham's seconds was killed and the other, my old admirer Robert Holmes, run through all along his arm, while Lord Shrewsbury was run through the body and is expected to die of his wounds. And a couple of strange things about the Fire: that it burned just as many parish churches as there were hours from the beginning to the end of the fire, and in the part of the City that wasn't burned there were just as many churches left standing as there were taverns, thirteen of each.

Young Lord Hinchingbrooke was very attentive to me (shades of his father) and when I was showing him a picture in my closet he tried very hard for a proper kiss and told me he had thought me a beauty ever since his boyhood. I told him I was honoured but he had a fine wife and I a fine husband and we must find our pleasure there. Flattering, though, to have a twenty-year-old try me. I could see his wife looking alarmed, though God knows she need have no fear on my account. I told Mary and Will about it and Mary was impressed but Will said something about it being no surprise the young man felt like that about me, the surprise was that a newly married man should be trying another lady so soon. I didn't mention it to Sam at all, needless to say.

We're through the worst of the winter now, there are buds on the trees and the rebuilding of the City is proceeding apace. I walked along Thames Street to Billingsgate and where it was only twelve feet wide before it's thirty feet now, with handsome brick houses going up on either side. At last we can begin to believe the whole City will be rebuilt one day, and much better than before.

SPRING

The apprentices decided to celebrate the Easter holidays with a riot. They began by pulling down bawdy houses in Moorfields. Everyone at Court was greatly alarmed and all the soldiers, horse and foot, were ordered to arms by means of alarms beaten on drum and trumpet all over Westminster, as though the French were coming to town. The soldiers assmbled in Lincoln's Inn Fields with Lord Craven riding up and down giving orders like a madman. When some of the prentices were imprisoned in Clerkenwell, the rest came and broke them out. For three days they made fools of the militia, throwing stones at them, and some blood spilt. It was more serious than the usual riot, for they were crying that instead of pulling down the little bawdy houses they should pull down the great one that is Whitehall. Eventually they grew tired and it died out.

At least it made me more eager for the peace and quiet of the country. Will Hewer escorted me, young Betty Turner, Deb and Jane to Brampton where we're staying for a couple of months. Strange how well we all get on when there are no men around (I don't count Sam's father). A couple of nights before we left, Sam made Deb write out a list of the things that still needed to be done and she couldn't do it well enough. She sulked when it was taken notice of so we were both cross with her, though it was made up after she'd undressed Sam for bed. But here life's not as taxing as it is in London.

We walk in the fields and gather wild flowers. The weather is mild, a pale blue sky and a gentle breeze, with the leaves unfurling to a soft haze of green. We sit in a bluebell wood and talk about men and marriage. We make a list of things to do for childlessness, viz:

1. The man not to hug his wife too hard or too much.

2. Don't eat late suppers.

3. Drink sage juice.

4. Take red wine and toast.

5. The man to wear cool Holland-linen drawers.

6. Both to keep the stomach warm and the back cool.

7. Do the deed when you most have a mind to it, whether night or morning.

8. The wife not to be laced too tight.

9. The man to drink strong spiced ale with sugar.

10. Make the bed high at the foot and low at the head.

I said, a little sadly, that I could personally vouchsafe that none of it worked, and they looked at me so tenderly, one stroking my arm and one my dress, that no words were needed for me to know their sympathy. And I looked at Jane, hoping to be married to her Tom, and wondered what the future would bring her. And little Deb, still almost child-like in her form, for whom these things are a long way off yet, and I felt such fondness for them, and hoped that they'd be lucky where I hadn't been.

And the milkmaids walked home singing.

Sam came for a day and a night at the end of May. He brought the gossip — and it all seemed so far away. At the theatre the Queen walked out when Mrs Davis came on to dance, and Lady Castlemaine looked mighty melancholy. After the pulling down of the bawdy houses at Easter, the poor whores have petitioned Lady Castlemaine for relief and addressed her as the most eminent lady of pleasure, and this has mortified her terribly. The Queen has miscarried a perfect child, aged ten weeks. Lord Carnegie deliberately went to the foulest whore he could find so as to give the pox to his wife who was whore to the Duke of York and she duly gave it to him and he to the Duchess and that's why their children have all been sickly. The Duke of Buckingham has installed his whore the Countess of Shrewsbury in his house now that her husband is dead of his wounds in the duel. When his wife protested that it was not for the two of them to live in the same house, he replied that he thought so too, and her coach was waiting outside to take her to her father's. So he turned her out and she had no choice but to go.

In the smaller world, Betty Martin's baby has died aged eighteen months and Kate Joyce has upped and married a tobacconist. She'd asked Sam to enquire about him but didn't wait for his report, which makes him think the man hasn't as much money as he claimed. As she brews, so let her bake.

My news was very little. That Pall was grown fat, pert and proud he could see for himself. Lady Sandwich's money troubles which were evident but not spoken of to me were broached very quickly by their steward, Mr Shipley, and Sam agreed to lend her £100, with no hope of ever seeing it again. I didn't need to tell him either that his father and I were not on the best of terms – he's growing cantankerous and I can do nothing right for him. The next morning we lay together with much mutual pleasure (an increasingly rare event) and Sam left for London promising to return in two weeks when we would take a tour.

He was as good as his word. We both, and Deb and Will Hewer set out by coach for the West Country, staying the first night at Newport Pagnell, a pleasant country town but very few people in it. We were up the next morning by four o'clock and had a guide to take us to Oxford where we saw All Souls College and Christ Church and Brazen Nose College. There we saw the outline of the hand of a giant wrestler which fitted four of mine. We stayed the night at Abingdon, where there was a custard fair and indeed we ate a very fine custard and sang and danced till supper.

The next day we drove to Hungerford where we dined on the trout and crayfish that the town is famous for, and very good. Then on to Salisbury, guided by the spire, to the George Inn for supper and bed. Next morning we looked over the cathedral and then took horse with a guide to see Stonehenge. We had to ride over great hills and when we breasted the last one and looked down at the stones it was as prodigious a sight as we had been told. As we rode our horses around and in between them they appeared huger and more massive than I could ever have imagined. We kept wondering what they were for. I felt that the people who had put these stones up (at what effort) must have known something we've forgotten. But what a testament to leave behind them. In a curious way I felt the stones were alive, but utterly implacable; it was almost frightening.

Back to our inn for dinner and then over Salisbury Plain, getting lost on the way, until at ten o'clock at night we found an inn where there was a pedlar in bed and he was made to rise so we could have the room. Deb and Betty lay in truckle beds beside us. The beds were good but in the morning we found we were all lousy, which caused some merriment. Great joy when we crossed from Wiltshire to Somerset, Deb's home county and to me the start of the West Country, where the light changes somehow, with a bigger sky and the sun higher in it. We arrived at Bath before night and saw the town was all of stone and very clean but we were too weary to do more than sup and go to bed.

The next morning we were carried in Bath chairs to the Cross-Bath, called so because there's a cross in the middle and the men sit on seats around that while the ladies sit at the sides under the arches. It was the coolest bath of them all but even so in places the springs were too hot to endure. After two hours we were wrapped in sheets and carried home and put to bed to sweat for an hour – a lovely cosy feeling – and then musicians came to play to us as we got up.

We set out for Bristol and got there about two o'clock. Deb went to visit her uncle and brought him back for dinner, a sober city merchant with good conversation. Afterwards we all walked round the quay and saw the ships and the new Custom House, and then round the back to the street where Deb was born. There was great joy among the old people there to see Mrs Willet's daughter in her fine clothes and good company. Then her uncle led us to his own house and gave us strawberries and cold venison pasty and the sherry sack that is called Bristol milk, because it's the first liquid that is given to infants in this city, so they say.

In truth I was a little envious of Deb, being the object of so much good will and having a family that could offer Sam the sort of entertainment that he's accustomed to, whereas mine can offer nothing and there is no place I could go back to and be recognised and welcomed. It made me feel a bit as though I'm tossed around on the sea instead of being firmly anchored. Stonehenge kept coming into my mind, making me feel our lives are short and small beside those stones. Strange how pleasure is sometimes the prelude to melancholy.

Stopping at Avebury on the way home, looking at another circle of massive stones, I had the feeling again. I found myself thinking that my life in London was very fragile, my happiness very much at other people's whim. It seems one has to be a beauty and that is a harder struggle with each passing year. Beauty retires, indeed. I look at Deb and see her throat as plump as a dove and notice that my neck is beginning to be thin. Suddenly I think that if I must retire from city life I might just as well live in France, where I would be happy, and I put the thought away as a private dream.

I suspected, from one or two things Sam and Will had let drop, that Sam's life while I'd been in the country at Brampton had been a continuous round of those pleasures (and people) to be found in the city. As soon as we returned to London this was confirmed by Nell when I asked how her master had fared in my absence. She answered that she hardly knew for he had been very little at home. (Pursed lips speaking volumes.)

Mary Mercer came to visit and told me without being asked that Sam had called on her and taken her to the theatre. The thing about Mary is that Sam tries it on with her as he does with any pretty woman, but she doesn't respond. I'm certain of this, seeing them together so many times, unlike Mrs Knepp or even Betty Martin, who sells him linen – and what else? And Elizabeth P. calls on me and says Sam has certainly been enjoying himself, the theatre every day and all the time taking people abroad, and it all becomes too much for me and that night I find myself crying with great sobs. But what a fool to

PORTRAIT OF A MARRIAGE

285

imagine that your husband of thirteen years is going to spend your absence in mourning. Particularly when that husband is Sam.

He doesn't say much, just lets me cry and is gentle to me afterwards. Lord Anglesey disapproves of his absence from the office on holiday while I disapprove of his presence in London disporting himself. Poor Sam, he's caught between the Devil and the deep blue sea. I see all sides, I see that he intends me no harm, but yet . . . I was in the middle of my tears when the cry of 'Fire!' came and it was in Mark Street, right next to us and so near we thought we'd be burnt in our beds, but it was in one of the new brick houses and instead of spreading, it all fell in on itself so we were safe. I know fires happen everywhere but sometimes it seems there's never a night goes by in this town without fear of riot or plague or invasion or fire or burglary.

I cried again and told Sam I wanted to live quietly in France. He hush-hushed me but was utterly perplexed and indeed I couldn't explain it myself, suddenly feeling like this. But the mood passed and life resumed its usual course. I went abroad with Deb – the poor girl had looked so worried when I was crying – to Unthank's, and the theatre, and buying linen. The streets are full of people bringing their wine home from their suppliers before the duty goes up. It's very hot, the meat is stinking. We walk in the garden in the cool of the evening and sing with Mary and Deb and Mr Pelling, who turns out to be as good a singer as he is an apothecary. Sam's eyes torment him.

∽

SUMMER

Cousin Roger Pepys is most insistent that we visit him
at Impington when Stourbridge Fair is on at the end
of September. I'm sitting for my miniature with Mr
Cooper, and Will and Deb and Mary come and sit
with me and we all go to the theatre afterwards, to
see *Henry the Fifth*, and Sam buys us all oranges. And
in front of us a man chokes on his orange and drops
down as though dead and Orange Mall (who sold it
to him) calmly puts her fingers down his throat and
pulls it out and he gets up and no harm done. Then
we go to the Spring Gardens and eat lobster. The
talk is that against the Queen's wishes the Duchess of
Richmond is admitted as a lady of her bedchamber,
and the King minds little else but what to do with
his women. And we observed how rude some of the
young gallants of the town have become, to go into
arbours where there are women sitting without men
and force their company on them – a picture of the
vice of the age.

Once again I have helped deliver Betty Mitchell
of a girl child, another Betty. This time we were
pleased but not as happy as before, not daring to
spend that emotion before knowing if the child will
survive. She says she couldn't bear to lose another
one so soon. Sam has had 13 ounces of blood let to
try to cure his eyes but he says it seems to make
little difference. It's very hot. We visit Elizabeth P.
and she tells us the Duchess of Monmouth broke

her hip in dancing and although recovered will be lame for life.

I have a row with Deb about losing a new hood – it's a bit like mother and daughter, nothing to take to heart. Sam's ashamed still to be seen in a hackney carriage. (Good! All the sooner our own coach.) But when it comes to actually laying out for it, as always, he's slow and reluctant. He's very busy writing a letter for the Duke of York to read to the Commissioners regarding their shortcomings. And he's deeply, deeply vexed to hear that John Creed is to marry Betty Pickering, my Lady's niece – much too close to the family, he says. Well, some make it and some marry it.

Deb and I went with him at an hour's notice when he had to go to Petersfield to talk to Sir Thomas Allen about the instructions for going to Algiers. We stayed at Liphook the first night and Guildford the second, and then home, where we find my miniature is finished, at £30, and the gold and crystal case comes to £8-3s-4d and Sam paid it all at once, so as not to be in debt. And he comes home and Deb combs his head and I read to him and we all have domestic pleasure.

The next day we go to the Gypsies at Norwood, me and Mary Mercer and Deb and Mr Pelling, to have our fortunes told. I sit opposite a swarthy woman with the blackest eyes I've ever seen, a fire smoking beside us, and after I've crossed her palm with silver she tells me I have no children, nor ever will have. And I sigh but it's no surprise. She looks at my palm for a long time, stroking it now and then with her thumb. She says I will have a long life and be happy.

And then she looks up at me and tells me I have a good husband and I must look after him and I say I will do my best. And she tells Deb that she will marry and have five children, and Mary Mercer that she will marry a dark-haired man next year – which rules out Will Hewer, one of my little fantasies. Mr Pelling was promised long life and a prosperous business.

Mr Simpson comes to put up the new chimney-piece in our great chamber, which costs a great deal of money but it will look very fine. Hysterics from Jane Birch: Tom has promised to marry her and now goes back on his word. Sam says he'll get rid of them both if this carries on. The Navy Board is still under attack and Sam and I and Will Hewer have a long talk. The conclusion is that if Sam is turned out of office, it's of no matter, we have enough money and Sam's eyes are so bad he can't work as well as he'd wish to. Will Hewer can be taken care of elsewhere if it comes to it. We all hope it doesn't come to that but we're prepared if it does.

And while these affairs of state go on, so does our daily life. Sam rehangs pictures in our green room to accommodate the new map of Paris he's bought. And I move the hangings from the best chamber to the long chamber, where Deb lies, and teach her how to sew and hang them and I reflect that it might have been my daughter I was teaching now if we'd been blessed with children in our early years. Deb is apt at this craft and I take pride in her achievements. It looks very neat by the time we've finished.

We go to a grand dance at the Bateliers', with Mary, the Pearses, Mrs Knepp, Mr Harris. The Pearses leave early – two o'clock – because she's big with child but the rest of us stay until three. The next day Deb, Mary, Will, and I all go to see *Hamlet* together, very good. Afterwards we go to Bartholomew Fair and Sam joins us and we see *Merry Andrew*, an obscene little puppet play, but quite amusing, and then to see Jacob Hall dancing on the tightropes, an act much followed now. We feel like old hands for we've already been watching him for eight years, but it's heart-warming to see that all his labour is finally bringing its reward.

I remember the nuns at school saying that it didn't matter what you did in life as long as you did it to the greater glory of God – *ad majorem Dei gloriam* – and we had to put it at the top of every piece of written work. A.M.D.G. And it seemed to me that Jacob Hall danced on the ropes to the glory of God. I suppose that if life depended on crossing a bridge strung across a ravine this would be a useful talent. As it is, one can only say that it is part of God's plenty and Jacob Hall does it the best it can be done.

We bumped into Mrs Knepp and went in her coach and lost the others and then we all ended up having supper at Hercules Pillars afterwards, spiced beef – heavily spiced because the weather was so hot.

On the 2nd September the Fast Day for the burning of London was very strictly kept and everyone was quiet and thoughtful of those dreadful events. The next day Sam bought Hobbes's *Leviathan* and it cost 30 shillings where it was 8 shillings before the Fire – the Bishops have not allowed it to be reprinted so copies are very scarce. My little dog Fancy died, full of pups. I do believe she'll be there when it's my time, in years to come.

Meanwhile I set out for Impington with Deb and Mary Mercer and Will Hewer and we are merry company and entertained very well by Cousin Roger when we arrive. Very different from being with Sam's father at Brampton; this is more like London life in the country. Having Will with us makes a difference, and William Batelier comes to visit as well. Sam makes a tour of East Anglia and collects us all on his way back.

We return to find that young William Penn is in Newgate Prison from where he has issued a pamphlet attacking everyone except the Quakers. I still think that he will do great things, though Sam dismisses him as a fool. We both and Deb go out to choose tapestry hangings. We rehang pictures. Sam puts an offer in on a coach. I see it and am mad with joy for it. Deb combs his hair. The plasterers and painters are in the house, all the usual mess. I go to see my mother in Deptford, where she's staying with Balty. My twenty-eighth birthday passes unremarked.

AFTERWARDS.

Once there was a time when I didn't know, hadn't seen.

And now there's the rest of my life.

I'm sitting in my closet. Mice scamper round the room. There are five complete pattern repeats of the fleur-de-lis on the window hangings. They stand an inch proud of the floor. The Turkey rug is red with a pattern of blue trees in it. A blue and white Delft bowl sits on polished wood. The moonlight strikes it.

Occupy your mind with these things and you don't have to think about . . .

I read to him this afternoon. William Batelier came for supper. Sam went to his closet to have Deb comb his hair. I wanted to ask him something and walked in on them.

The thing I never thought to see in my own home.

Her white legs splayed on his lap. Her head thrown back, her throat exposed for him to kiss. His fingers up her cunny. The terrible, shocked, jumping apart as I open the door but not soon enough to stop me seeing. And shakily smoothing their clothes and Deb darting out of the room.

At first I say nothing. And then: 'What was that?'

'Nothing. Just a little hug. Nothing.'

'What was that?'

'I tell you nothing, it means nothing. Just a pretty girl on my lap, nothing.'

'But I saw you.'

'All you saw was me hugging her. I'm sorry, it was foolish.'

'I saw what I saw.'

'You must have imagined it. There was nothing else to see.'

'Don't tell me what I saw. At least I can trust my eyes, if I can't trust you.'

'You were mistaken. Trust me, there was nothing.'

'But I saw it.'

'There was nothing to see. It was just a hug.'

There is no point in trying to talk to a man who is lying in his teeth. I feel shocked and shaken, as though I've been knocked out. We go to bed in silence and he's soon snoring. I get up and sit in my closet with paper and pen, watching the mice.

Awful, vivid imaginings of screaming at him and her. In between, moments of utter blankness.

I go back to our chamber. I want to kill him for sleeping while I suffer. I shake him awake and tell him I've become a Catholic, the most worrying thing I can think of, not true but I want him to be as hurt as I am. And I cry and cry and ask him how he could prefer her to me. And he keeps saying he loves me and is so sorry if he's hurt me but I don't believe him. After a while we stop and he falls asleep again and I stare at the mouldings on the ceiling for an hour.

I can't bear to be lying still. Up and out into the street in my nightgown and I look up at the stars and howl. And nothing stirs, not a face at a window, not a scurrying rat, no sign of the watch or a candle lit. What I was most afraid of confronts me now. Why, it's almost a relief, no more wondering if, when. It's here, now. I'm staring at it open-eyed and it fills my brain to the point where there's nothing else in all the world.

And I think of the stones we saw, massive, unyielding, and see how foolish my certainties were. And I feel the weight of grief will kill me.

Indoors I play a few notes on my flageolet but it sounds too melancholy and I put it aside.

I'm tired but I'm too frightened to go to sleep. Staying awake keeps the old life going. Waking after sleep will mean waking to a new life, the old one gone for ever.

The overwhelming feeling is betrayal. I treated her as a friend, as a daughter, as one who could be trusted.

And I trusted him too. It never occurred to me, whatever his flirtations outside the house, that he would be treacherous in the middle of his own family.

Then I realise that the degree of intimacy means this couldn't have been the first time.

The time Deb and I were at Brampton and I talked about my childlessness and she stroked my arm – had it already begun? Was she already betraying me, if only in her thoughts? And was he aching in her absence?

The watchman calls five of the clock.

Dawn at last, cold and grey. Back to bed and a deep, plunging sleep for half an hour.

Tuesday.

The next day begins, waking to the noise of the prentices banging open their shutters: 'What do you lack, lady, what do you lack?' Why, I lack a heart, for mine is broken.

The milkmaid brings her cow to the door and there are cries in the street for fish and eggs. I feel as though I'll never want to eat again.

I don't speak to Deb and she stays well out of my way. Sam goes to Whitehall to speak to the Duke of York about the Board's business. Then he waits a long time to speak privately to Lord Sandwich on the same matter. Then he comes home and we all have dinner together, a miserable meal. None of us talk. I think of the merry times we've had at this table in the past, the company, the trust that we were in it together. The day seems to have been going on for ever.

We go out afterwards taking Deb with us — nothing's been admitted yet. The other servants don't know. We buy a few household things and nobody talks unless it's necessary. We drag through the day and have supper and go to bed where my anger breaks out again, and I shout at him how he could have kissed her and he says he didn't, it was only a hug. And he promises that he'll never see Mrs Knepp again, or Elizabeth Pearse, and he says again it was only an indiscretion, there was no harm intended. In the end I go to sleep, exhausted, and sleep until five in the morning, when another day begins, too early, and not wanting to know what it will bring.

Wednesday.

Sam is out almost all day on business, of course. I want her to go, he says we must consider things. I make sure he has no chance to speak to her alone. She looks very mopish — so she should. I warn her to stay out of my sight unless she wants to be hit. In the afternoon Mary Mercer comes at my invitation and we weep together in my closet and she says Sam must learn to behave as a grown man, and at least I'm sure, from her reaction to the news, that she hasn't betrayed me and I thank God for a true friend at this time. At night to bed and my anger breaks out again, like a great wave crashing down, and I rant and rave without pause, so many years of shutting my mouth finally unstopped. He talks kindly and makes fair promises: the trip to France, the coach, his unswerving loyalty.

Thursday.

We rise, all milk and honey. A difficult day for me — I have horrid visions of them together — but I also feel Sam does know where his heart lies and he will come out right in the end. One moment there's a feeling of exhilaration — I've won! — and the next moment I'm downcast because the fact is she's still here. And the truth is, I know it in my heart, that he's still besotted with her. That's what makes me rail and rant, because I can do nothing about it. I can force his behaviour to change, but I can't change his heart.

At this moment, of all, the workmen have arrived to work on my closet, so I don't even have that refuge. Sam hides in his at every opportunity. I go out to the market — some cheese, I'll buy some cheese — and it's raining and I'm walking by the wall to avoid the quagmire of the street and I come against a man who not only keeps the wall and doesn't yield it but deliberately pushes me into the gutter in the process. And I don't see why life should be all so hard. I don't see any justice or fairness, nothing, it's all blank.

Friday.

The days are beginning to merge one into another. That must be good, must mean the pain is less finely etched than before. There is a strange, uneasy peace between us.

November

Mr Povey sends his coach for us to see as a model of what we might like for ourselves, and we like it very much indeed but the coachmaker has just sold his only one. The days crawl by until it's Sunday again and I'm thinking 'a week ago, a week ago'. Sam works in his chamber with Will Hewer all morning. After dinner I read to him. To bed quietly.

The next day I ask Deb's aunt round and tell her, in kind terms, that I am no longer able to keep a woman and we must part with Deb. Sam has been deeply reluctant to do this, trying to convince me that we can still all live in the same house, it need be no more than a minor upset in the pattern of our lives. How blind can a man be? I insist that she must go. I watch him like a hawk at dinner to see if he's looking at her, and I swear they do exchange a glance and of course there are two or three silent tears from her. He looks so sad and I feel like giving him a big punch in the mouth to have something real to be sad about.

He finds he has to be out a great deal on business – and indeed there's a great deal going on: Lord Anglesey turned out of office, the Duke of York near being deprived of the Admiralcy. It all seems to be happening in a different world. Sam and I talk of the possibility of him being put out of the office. We'd go and live with Balty in Deptford for a year while he cleared all his accounts. We talked very civilly, we didn't mention Deb, but both treading on eggshells. The painters are aware that something's up – much less banter than usual, and no wish to wait around for the chance of beer in the kitchen.

When we got up in the morning I dressed him myself so he couldn't see her. I wouldn't let him into the blue room where she was working with the upholsterers. He's trying very hard to keep the peace. Sometimes I wonder if he's telling the truth, and I was mistaken in what I thought I saw, but then the picture of them both comes back and I know there was no mistake. Deb asks to go to her family for the day and I'm delighted to have her out of the house. When Sam comes home at night he doesn't know whether she's here or not. He doesn't ask and I don't tell him. When she returns the next morning, he can't stop his face breaking into a great smile, just can't help himself.

Another Sunday. Two weeks ago tonight. Sam hides in his chamber putting papers to rights. If only human hearts could be put to rights so easily. If only I had some escape like that, something that would take my mind off this wretched business for hours at a time. She dines with us – another cold, silent meal. In the evening Mr Pelling comes to supper and is concerned that I'm so dull and melancholy. He suggests various remedies but I'm afraid there's nothing in his pharmacy that will lift my spirits. Deb didn't appear, hiding in her chamber. Another miserable sleepless night.

In the morning I get up in a fearful rage. Overwhelmed with anger that she's ruined my marriage, destroyed my peace of mind, and she's still in the house. As soon as Sam has scuttled out, I grab her (by the lace collar that I gave her) and pull her into my closet and shout at her, 'Tell me the truth. Just admit it. He was kissing you, wasn't he?' She sobs, no, no, it was only a hug. The old story. Have they talked it over together and agreed on what to say? I take her roughly by the shoulders and shake her within an inch of her life, screaming at her like a mad woman

'He was kissing you, wasn't he?'

'Yes, yes.'

'And he had his hand up your cunny?'

'Yes, yes.'

'And it's been going on for months?'

'Yes.'

So, there it is. I push her out of the room and wait for Sam to come home to dinner. I'm in my chamber. He walks in and asks if I'm not coming down to dinner and I say I don't want to, I'm too upset because I talked to Deb this morning and I had the truth from her. I'm watching him closely as I say this and I see a slight start, quickly concealed, but a tension in his body, almost an animal reaction of fear. I know that his heart must be pounding, for mine is, but he says with barely a tremor that I must eat and he'll order dinner to be sent up here for both of us.

So we eat, whatever tasteless stuff it is, and then Mr Hollier passes by and comes in, just for a friendly visit, and it's all in abeyance until he goes, but a relief for a few minutes for both of us.

Mr Hollier goes, and it all comes out. I reproach Sam for his lying. Why couldn't he have just told me the truth in the first place instead of going through this play of nothing happened? And he weeps, so many tears, as though they will deflect my anger, as though they're proof of his finer feelings. And I tell him how loyal and true I've been to him over the years, how much I've done for him, how I refused Captain Ferrer's proposition from Lord Sandwich (that makes him groan) and Lord Hinchingbrooke's (another groan). He weeps without cease. I feel sick at heart.

Then off he goes to work and I pace the house, almost demented. Time hangs so heavily. I'm living minute by miserable minute. Supper, bed, he's asleep in no time. Men, for all their torment, are not easily put off their sleep or their food. I stare at the ceiling for an hour, my anger rising, and then shake him awake and scream at him that I'll never sleep again and he weeps some more and promises that he himself will tell Deb to be gone. We sleep as best we can, exhausted, but too entwined in it all to sleep deeply.

Another day in which he doesn't tell Deb to go. That night I wake up with a start and rave like a lunatic and he weeps as though it was the Flood and we're awake until dawn with the moon shining in on us.

We can't go through many more nights like that. The next day he can't put it off any longer and calls Deb up to my chamber and tells her that she must go as soon as possible and he doesn't want to see her again while she is in the house. There are tears on both sides – but not from me, I feel as though I am wept dry and there's nothing left, just blankness. Let them weep that can. Later, I ask him for her money and he gives me £10 for one year and half a quarter's wages

THE JOURNAL OF MRS PEPYS

and I go into her chamber and count it out to her, paying her for destroying my life. With only me there she's dry-eyed, picks the money up lightly enough, there's almost a glint of defiance in her eye. Almost – she hasn't got over the shaking I gave her yet.

The next day he tries to see her before she leaves but I stop him from going into the kitchen and he's vexed at being thwarted and speaks a few words angrily and I immediately fly into a terrible rage and call him a dog and a rogue with a rotten heart and he backs off and admits he deserves it all.

So she leaves by coach with her things, and we have been quiet since.

What day, what month, what year?

Did we go to Bartholomew Fair this year?

Yes, don't you remember? With Will and Mary and Deb, and then we met Mrs Knepp and our coaches lost each other and we ended up all having supper at Hercules Pillars. Don't you remember?

Yes, of course I remember, it just seems such a long time ago, I wasn't sure if it was this year or last. Or if last year was the Plague year, or the Fire, or the Dutch invasion. Things all seem a long way away, I can't sort them out very well.

Sometimes when I walk along the street the thought comes to me so strongly – it's only one step to go under a coach. And I have to press myself against the wall. And I wonder what I'm saving myself for. Sam would be delighted, he could marry his Deb. No one could say it was self-murder, slipping on a wet street and falling under hooves and wheels.

But the stones at the Henge come back to me.

They've survived, silent, implacable. So will I, and let God know the reason for it, for I don't.

And as an afterthought: we have slept together more in the last few weeks than in the whole of the previous year, and with greater pleasure.

∞

SUNDAY, 15TH NOVEMBER. THREE WEEKS.

A sort of return to the usual way. And I say to him, 'Are we on course?' and he says yes, yes, we're on course. And I begin to think it's all nearly over. Mr Pelling comes to supper and wonders at us both being so dumpish (Sam manifestly misses her). Again, I fear there's nothing Mr Pelling can prescribe for us. But, again, don't say it. It's all put down to me feeling unwell.

The painters have gone at last and the maids and I set to cleaning the house, me with more vigour than ever before because I want to scour out every trace of her presence. Sam brings home *Cassandra*, and some other French books for me. We sleep fairly well. When he goes out the next day I know he's looking for her, he would have looked sadder otherwise, or taken it out on me somehow. But there's a sort of lift in his feet and I know where his mind is. And I spend all day arranging the new hangings while he's out, as though making our house ordered and beautiful will make our feelings for each other like that too. I know while I'm doing it that he's seeing her and what should be a happy fulfilling moment – putting up the hangings that he's worked to pay for and we've chosen together – becomes dead and meaningless and I go through the form of doing it because if I didn't I'd just sit staring at the wall.

So in a way it was no surprise when Mary Mercer came round and told me her mother's maid had seen Sam and Deb in a coach together. She didn't tell me out of malice: she thinks, as I do, that knowledge is the greatest power. And I pressed her was she sure and she said the maid knew them both well and swore to it. And I sit in the dining room, because there's nowhere else that workmen aren't busy, and when he comes home for dinner I call him a rotten-hearted rogue for being with Deb and he tries to deny it but sees there's no point and confesses it – but it was only because she was so terribly upset, it was a way of finishing it all.

How could she be more upset than I am? I threaten to slit her nose and he's in agony. Good. All afternoon it goes on. I say that if he'll give me £400 I'll go, retire to France. Otherwise he can be assured I'll spread it all round town. He groans, he weeps, he howls, and in the end he calls in Will Hewer. And when Will hears of our trouble he cries like a child.

Then Will, whose ears Sam boxed so many times, so many years ago, comes to each of us as the trusted go-between and makes a peace between us on the basis that Sam will never see Deb again, which I half believe. Certainly Sam is shocked enough that it might be so. The upholsterers have finished at last, but there's no joy for either of us in their work.

The next day I insist Will Hewer accompanies

him everywhere in the future unless I can go myself, and Sam's only too ready to agree. But then I'm at home all day on my own and everything preys on my mind and when Sam comes back I revile him in the bitterest terms and fall to striking him and pulling his hair as the only way to make him understand. I want to black his eye, to see on him some visible form of the anguish he's caused me. He stays as calm as he can because he pretends it's all over now, and not something we need to make a fuss about any more. And he tries to coax me to eat my dinner but I swear again that I'll slit her nose – because I know, I know in my heart that it isn't over between them.

He swears it is, I know it isn't. He throws himself on the bed in the blue room. Will Hewer mediates again and we come to the agreement that if Sam writes to her as a whore and that he never wants to see her again, all will be forgiven. Sam excuses himself from writing 'whore' and I tear the letter up. He writes it again, including the word, and we're all satisfied. Will Hewer delivers it with a sharp note from me warning her not to show her face round here again.

And now a period of truce sets in. We're both too exhausted from all the emotion of the last month to do any more than get through our daily lives and be as civil as we can with each other. He says his greatest desire is to please me by his behaviour and every night he kneels down at his bed to call on God's help in living a good life. The house is neat and clean, and I spent a whole Sunday making myself clean, while Tom read *The Life of Archbishop Tennyson* to Sam. We went to the theatre to see *The Duchess of Malfi* and he was very careful not to look round and ogle the ladies. When the Pearses came to dine, he was cool to Elizabeth and took the opportunity to leave early when Will Hewer rushed in to say he'd lost a tally for £1,000.

We have Mr Povey to dine, and Cousin Roger, and Mary Batelier to supper, and always Will Hewer. Sam and I are careful, we step around each other as though we might break.

Our coach arrives and if it's not the unalloyed joy it might have been before Deb, it is still a great balm to wounded pride. Sam insists that I myself must take its maidenhead. The horses are not well-matched and we are getting better ones, but even so I had great pleasure in making a round of visits in my own coach for the first time. The delight of sitting back knowing that a sober, polite coachman in your own livery will take you directly to the right place and will be waiting for you outside at your convenience, that never again will you be troubled because it's raining and there are no hackneys.

We've come a long way, Sam and I. And a long way to go yet, please God.

∞

31ST DECEMBER

I'm sitting by the fire in my closet while Sam and Captain Ferrer dine downstairs. Despite the fact that I love Captain Ferrer's company I thought it wiser to be withdrawn after what I'd told Sam about him and Lord Sandwich's proposition. I don't know whether

Sam will mention it – a passing reference, just to let him know he knows – or whether he's trying to put it out of his mind.

The coach has made a great difference to my life. Quite often now I accompany Sam abroad and wait in it while he attends to his business at Whitehall or the Exchequer or wherever it may be. I waited in it while Sam and Will met Ned Pickering and his horse-dealer friend (Mr Pickering is so much the sort of man who would have a horse-dealer friend) to look at new horses. All men think they know about horses, but Sam admitted afterwards he would never have dreamed of all the craft and cunning there was in the buying and selling of them. For all that, they couldn't decide on anything, though there was a fine black pair which he liked the look of. Then Mr Knepp came in on it as well and in the end it took a week for them all to agree that the fine black pair at £50 were just what was wanted.

There was a hiccup with Deb, of course. Jane comes home from market and I'm looking over the goods when she says she met Deb, gone to market for her aunt. And Deb boasts of having a friend who gives her money, and she's looking mighty fine. Jane says this more in sadness than impudence, she knows the situation of course, though we don't speak of it. So I wait for Sam to come home and then it all explodes and he swears the friend is not him and is most concerned to pacify me and assure me I will never have any new occasion for concern. And I reflect that even if he has given her money he won't like to hear that she's boasting of it, so I've done myself no harm with my outburst.

My sleep is still troubled, and so is his. I heard him call out 'hussy' one night, and wondered which of us he was referring to. He claims not to dream of her. Sometimes I can go an hour or two at a time without thinking of it.

We took Roger's son Talbot, now a well-looked student at the Middle Temple, to Holborn to see the bearded woman. Her beard was bushy and thick and black but her voice made sure she was a woman. As a lady myself I was offered the chance of seeing further proof but I declined. The men weren't given this chance, though they asked for it. Poor woman. We went on to see *Macbeth* and it was sad how the King craned to see his mistress Mary Davis, while Lady Castlemaine beside him blushed when she saw who he was looking at. Lady C. is no longer the freshest of flowers but she's still a beauty. Farewell to Talbot, who goes to Impington for Christmas. He and Will both said (accidentally on purpose within my hearing?) that I was as pretty as any woman there. It's so heartening that people who know of our troubles find ways to make me feel better.

We talk about the possibility of going to France next year, in the late summer before Parliament returns in October. We've talked about it so often before, but next year it looks as though there will be the time and money. But I don't get up my hopes too much. I don't get up my hopes too much for anything any more.

Our Christmas Day was quiet. (Surprise.) Sam went to church in the morning and we dined alone at home. I spent all day altering and lacing a black petticoat while Sam had Tom read to him from *The*

Life of Julius Caesar. Then he made him play on his lute, and so quietly to bed.

The next day we went to the theatre to see Fletcher's *Women Pleased*. Where do these men get their titles? It was indifferent. Later we talked, of generalities and gossip, and I read to him because his eyes are so bad he can't even do his accounts.

And then we managed to have our first row since . . . Which I suppose I should take as a sign of things being back to the way they were. About crumpled table linen – and I haven't given the linen my full concentration, I must admit. I still spend too much time staring at nothing, trying to comprehend all that's happened. And I burst into tears at once and he was kind to me.

He was more upset by having to pay out 40 shillings for a window that had broken in the coach. Then on the way back from seeing *King Harry the 8th*, the near horse kicked himself over the pole and it was a great business to extricate him. Having one's own coach and pair has its problems as well as its pleasures.

Older, sadder, wiser, they say, at the end of the year.

All three in trumps for me.

1669

∞

New Year

Please God this will be a year of calm, both public and private. I pray that we can leave our trouble behind and find a new trust in each other. When all's said and done, I shall try to think of the many blessings I have, rather than dwell on the pains.

So – a New Year's gift to me of a fine walnut wood cabinet for my closet from Sam. And very pretty, I've never seen walnut used before and the pattern is of great beauty. A gift of a noble silver warming pan to both of us from Captain Beckford who sells the Navy their sailors' clothing – and is now petitioning to sell his wartime stock for more than the regulated price. Sam's doubtful about accepting the gift because it must be in the Board's interest to keep the price of slops down. He's more careful these days. And one warming dish less or more hardly matters.

We went to the King's playhouse to see Dryden's *Maiden Queen* and sat in a box, but Mrs Knepp was playing Asteria and whenever she was on stage she looked at us (or Sam) and I found it quite difficult, even though he was very careful not to respond to her. Ever since it happened I find myself much quicker to feel emotion. So it was that when we came to 'discuss' my clothes allowance, I was in tears very quickly when he felt obliged to refuse what I knew he would subsequently grant. As he did of course the next morning – £30 a year. He was out all day, but that night, when Will was there as well for supper, we made out the agreement in writing, with merriment, and Will witnessed it.

John Creed and his new wife Elizabeth came to visit. Sam was able to be cordial to them despite his private feelings. We had them again the next day to a Twelfth Day dinner, as well as Cousin Jane Turner and her daughters. Thea, whom I last saw when she was only ten or so, is eighteen now. And Cousin Dyke, and a friend of theirs – a man at last to even up the numbers. We spent all day at dinner and looking over the house and in the evening had a noble cake which according to the new fashion was cut into neat pieces and we had it with wine. The titles were written on pieces of paper and drawn out of a hat to avoid spoiling the cake hunting for the bean and the pea. Sam drew Queen and Thea drew King and we spent the evening in innocent pleasure. And I thought of the time nine years ago when Pall was Queen and all that's happened since: Pall married, Tom dead, the Plague, the Fire, and I marvelled that we were both still here to see another new year.

A few days later we had a grand dinner for some important colleagues: Lord Brouncker, Captain Cocke, and young James Hoare, the goldsmith banker, whom I hadn't met before. He was charm itself. Everything went well and we were greatly content. There were some words the next day when Sam made some unthinking remark about the maids we used to have and I thought he was talking about Deb, but it smoothed over soon enough.

In great good humour I bought Sam a pair of gloves, as our contract demanded, out of my £30. And then he disappears with no word of where he's going and while he's out one of the servants hears that he has been seen in a coach with Deb.

I'm in the dumps; he goes to bed and waits for me to join him but instead I get more wood for my fire and fresh candles and he begs me to come to bed but I can't, I've had too many nights not sleeping, staring at the ceiling, and he swears he wasn't with her and goes back to bed and I can hear him snoring. After an hour I put the tongs in the fire and let them get red-hot and go to his bedside and pull his bed curtain open and scream at him and make as though to pinch him with the tongs which wakes him up fast enough and forces him to pay attention. And I tell him I can't bear him being out and not knowing where he is, and he says he understands, and after a while there's peace of a sort and I come to bed. Little things that I wouldn't have worried about before are all out of true now.

One day I just sat staring out of the window, feeling blank and numb. I didn't speak to Sam or go to bed when he did. Then I heard him sobbing with grief and I went to him and took his head on my breast and he said he couldn't bear the unhappiness between us any more. I spoke to him tenderly and after a while we both slept.

Our grand dinner for Lord Sandwich took my

mind off things for a while. The day before we had
the table-layer in again, and Sam was so pleased with
the way he folded the napkins he's going to pay him
40 shillings to teach me how to do it. Sam brought
home a new looking-glass for the dining room, and
some more pewter and fine wine. Our guests were
Lords Peterborough and Sandwich and the latter's
sons, Lord Hinchingbrooke and Mr Sidney, and also
Sir Charles Herbert and Sir William Godolphin.
Distinguished company, they stayed from noon until
seven o'clock. We had the meal sent up in the
French fashion, one course after another, and we
have enough silver now for a clean plate for each
course. The food was excellent (man-cook) and the
wines soft and sweet, much talk of their provenance.
I notice that as we become more prosperous, fewer
and fewer wines are fit to drink and more and more
attention is paid to which region and which vineyard
they come from.

After dinner my Lords played cards and the rest
of us looked at our books and pictures, and my own
drawings were looked at and pronounced mighty
good. It's a great pleasure to be the hostess – and
the only woman – on such an occasion. One feels
more feminine than usual, but with the sea-wall of
domestic competence as a bulwark against charges
of frippery. When they'd all gone, in dark and foul
weather, how nice to be at home already, and to have
time to sup together in my closet. Then I cut his hair
and combed it and found some lice and I wondered
if he was thinking of that night when Deb was here
and we set them to running races.

The next day William Batelier came to sup with

us, bringing lots of goods from France: Nanteuil's
engravings of the French King and Colbert for Sam,
and lots of different perfumed gloves for me, but all
too big. Nevertheless I bought quite a few of them
– causing words with Sam, over soon. William told
us that Colbert has caused vast acreages of land in
France to be planted with oak trees so that in three
hundred years' time, in the 1960s, France will be
self-sufficient in the supply of masts for sailing ships
for her Navy.

∞

FEBRUARY (THE HARDEST MONTH)

I was vexed at seeing Mrs Knepp smile and wink at
Sam at the theatre. On the way back a bolt broke
on the coach and the horses ran off and we had to
wait while it was mended. What a great relief to be
home at last.

But I woke – there are whole days when I'm
tearful – thinking he was being false to me with Jane
– stupid, but I did. And I was so despairing I threw
myself on the ground, sobbing, and he came to me
and was understanding and so friends again.

Mr Pelling got us young William Penn's book
against the Trinity – he's been a close prisoner in
the Tower since last year for publishing it, poor
man. I read it to Sam who found it so well-written
he couldn't believe it was his work, but I always
thought there was more to him than Sam allowed.

Bab and Betty, Cousin Roger's girls, came to stay

for a few nights. I took them to Bedlam to see the lunatics which they greatly enjoyed. On the Sunday we had both Williams, Batelier and Hewer, to dine and sup because Sam finds himself not light enough company to be always merry with the girls. We took them to the theatre to see *Bartholomew Fair* and afterwards met the Williams and young Talbot Pepys for supper at Hercules Pillars. I enjoy being with so many young people, in lieu of having any children of our own. Sometimes I think of the children who aren't here, the boy who might have been thirteen or fourteen now, the girl who might have been twelve. The little ones who never managed to find their way to us.

On Shrove Tuesday Sam took us to see the tombs at Westminster Abbey and as a special favour we were shown the body of Queen Katherine of Valois, Henry 5's beautiful wife who died when she was thirty-six, and oddly enough that's how old Sam was on that very day, his birthday. And he was allowed to lift her (she is there from the waist up) and kiss her, which he reflected is the first time he has ever kissed a Queen. I had a confusion of feeling – that he is of sufficient privilege to be accorded this honour, but she's a long-dead Queen; there was something very unsettling in his putting his lips to this fragment of dried, leathery skin stretched over a skull.

It was a relief after that to go to the glass house and watch them making things, in particular some singing glasses for us which were so delicate that a strong breath could break them. As Sam proved. But his eyes were desperately painful afterwards, from the bright light of the candles there.

The next day he lay a long time until his eyes felt better, and he had a terrible cold as well but managed to get to the office and do a great deal of business. In the evening we supped at Will Hewer's lodging, where he has two neatly furnished chambers and it's such a joy to see him doing well. He gave us excellent custards and tarts and fine wine and we had the good talk of old friends.

∞

SPRING

Lady Paulina Mountagu was brought up to London, very ill, and taken to the house in Chelsea where her father dallied during his supposed illness years ago. God knows what memories it had for her, but whatever they were she died of consumption at the beginning of March.

The King has prorogued Parliament until 20th October, which should give us the time for our visit to France. We had a great family dinner and then dancing in the evening with lots of other people, Will, Mary, various Bateliers, Mr Goodgroome, Will Howe, even William Batelier's blackamoor man and maid (who danced most beautifully). A fine supper, more dancing and then, the strangers going home, we slept fifteen people in comfort, viz: Cousin Roger Pepys and his new wife in the blue chamber, Cousin Jane Turner and her sister and daughter in our best chamber, Bab and Betty Pepys and Betty Turner in our own chamber, me and Sam in the maids' bed, the maids in the coachman's bed, and the coachman with the boy in his settle bed.

It is such a secure feeling to be able to do this, I can't quite explain the satisfaction it gives me, and Sam as well. Something about being shored against disasters, I suppose. And then breakfast the next morning is a proper meal instead of the usual piecemeal picking and Sam and I are very content that we can treat our guests so well. But it doesn't stop me falling out with him two days later when he stays out all day until midnight, being entertained by the Duchess of York and her ladies. And it doesn't prevent his eyes popping when I tell him this week's entertainment cost £12, but as he says, it's only once in a while, and after all a man should have such a merry day now and then.

Sir William Coventry is in the Tower, the victim of Lord Buckingham, but he's pretty sanguine about it. We went to the Strudwickes', where we haven't been for a long time, and Sam drank the best part of a pint of the juice of oranges (which I reckoned at sixpence an orange must have cost 5 shillings the glass) but being the first time he'd ever drunk it he was fearful in case it did him harm. It didn't seem to.

The blossom is promising on the cherry trees, and the apples and pears. The weather is warmer and it feels as though a terrible hard winter is beginning to be over. I believe when we make our French tour – and now I really believe we're going to do it – everything will resolve itself, we will be free again, of the anguish and pain. In the meantime buds are growing sticky, and the sun is higher in the sky every day. I've almost taken on a new chambermaid, highly recommended. I told Sam she has one great fault which is that she's very handsome and I made a sort of joke about it being dangerous to have her in the house whereupon he assured me of his resolve to have nothing to do with my maids. Of course I know that secretly he was pleased, but he had more sense than to show it. And I, too, prefer well-looked people around me rather than plain – it doesn't speak well of a household if all the servants are ugly.

A complete change of tack the next day. I was driven into a mad fury when Mary came to visit and told me she'd seen Deb in a coach and she was living very fine, and wearing black spots. And her maid's gossip was that she'd been speaking ill of me, that I was lazy and dirty and insanely jealous of her. I was in my closet alone, so angry I couldn't speak until Sam walked through the door, when the words poured out. He stayed very calm and called her a baggage and understood why I was angry – though he couldn't help his face falling when I said it had made me decide against the pretty maid and take a smallpoxed one instead.

But helping Tom and Jane arrange their wedding took my mind off it. They decided on 26th March – Sam's Stone Day – and Mr Pelling assisted me in getting a licence for them to be married in Lent. Sam had to be away advising on a court martial in Chatham, but I think he was glad of the chance of some time to himself. Ever since the Deb incident his relations with our servants have not been what they were. Even there, trust broke down.

We were merry enough without him, despite the weather turning snowy, but that made it all the cosier in a way. They were married at St Mary's, Islington, with Thea Turner and Mary Batelier as bridemaids and Talbot Pepys and Will Hewer as bridemen. The wedding dinner (which Sam paid for) was at the old place, the King's Head in Islington where we've been so often for air. Afterwards we put them to bed in our blue chamber with great mirth and pulling off of ribbons. Will Hewer and I sat for a long time in the kitchen, talking over the years that have passed since they all first came to us. Nine years for Jane and Will, seven years for Tom. All the other servants who've come and gone, the ups and downs of our lives. As the candles guttered low, it seemed to me that we had seen a lot between us and that it was God's blessing we were still here to talk about it.

The next day Tom looked suitably smug, so I think we can assume all was as it should be. When I asked Jane how she was, she said she was very well – but with a look on her face as though she was still trying to make sense of what had happened.

When Sam came back, we had our usual morning-after long lie and talk in bed, and I told him all about the wedding. I think we're both content that with Tom and Jane gone we will have a new household of servants who don't remember Deb. For Bridget, our cook, is going as well, having given notice but then found to be a thief anyway. In her place we have Doll, a blackamoor from Mr Batelier, who dresses the food mighty well and we're very pleased with her. In the end, of course, I took on the pretty maid, not the smallpoxed one, and she can dress me and my hair beautifully, as she did for our first ride in Hyde Park in our own coach. People observed our coach and horses as being as pretty as any other there.

Sam has brought home a new friend, Mr Sheeres, who's been working on the defences at Tangier. I find he's a poet as well as being a military engineer, and I like the combination and find him good company, to the point that Sam's eyebrows twitch a little but he doesn't say anything. They both called for me and Betty Turner at Unthank's and we went to the Mulberry Garden where Mr Sheeres treated us to dinner cooked by a man who'd been with my Lord in Spain. It was a Spanish stew called Oleo, made of lots of different meats. Very noble, and other good things too that we kept for a collation at night. Meanwhile we drove out five or six miles in our coach to Brentford, where Cosimo de Medici, the Prince of Tuscany who's come to visit our country, had been greeted by the Lord Chamberlain. We glimpsed him in his coach; he looks comely and jolly, though they say the reason for his travels is an unrequited passion for his wife.

We overtook Captain Ferrer on the way, riding a fine Spanish horse he'd brought back with him, and he rode beside us to the park, chatting in his usual roguish way. He left us there and we met Thea and Talbot and the Bateliers and took them to the Mulberry Garden for our supper. The supper was very good but the company round about was thin, mainly rascals and whores, using the wilderness for their own purposes. But we were merry enough — good food and good friends is all it takes for us to be happy.

Very different from when we visited the Creeds

in their new house and they received us as strangers, quite according to the new cold fashion of the Court, and didn't offer us anything to eat or drink. It makes for a difference between us because Sam and I both continue the old English way of freedom and kindness to all our friends. John Creed, the former Puritan, was full of Lady Paulina making a very good end, and said she'd been deeply religious and left notes on sermons. Sam and I listened politely but could hardly reconcile this account with the girl we had always known as peevish.

We took Jane and Tom to dine at the Cock, never mind that they were once our servants. I particularly wanted to have their pea soup which is excellent. Sam has decided to give Tom £40 and Jane £20 toward their setting out in the world, and I shall give Jane £20 more, so they start out equal. Then we all went to the Bear Garden to see a prize fight between a soldier and a countryman who looked much too small to take the soldier on, but he fought so bravely and evenly, smiling in between his blows, that we were all infinitely taken with him and mighty pleased when he beat the soldier and cut him over the head. Mr Sheeres was with us as well, as it happens.

And when I went to the theatre with Will a couple of days later, he was there too and found his way to join us, which caused more twitching in Sam, arriving late.

He had further occasion for jealousy on Easter Sunday, but this time from the Duke of York, quite a different matter. It was the first time the Duke had seen us in the park in our own coach and he eyed me mightily, and I couldn't help smiling and Sam glowed with pride. That same day we saw the most incredible painting of a pot of flowers, done by a Dutchman, which looked so real I had to keep touching the drops of dew to be sure they were paint. Sam offered him £20 for it but he wanted £70. (The next day he came down to £50 but he won't shift from that, and I'm sure he'll get it.)

Again we met Mr Sheeres by accident at the theatre, and when he came to dine by invitation, I had a very good dinner ready for him and there was more twitching – Sam was already vexed that I'd been out till ten with Mary Batelier the night before. But friends soon enough (and no reason not to be; though I'm very fond of Mr Sheeres, and he of me, I think, there's no more to it than that). In the end he came with us to the Exchange and helped Sam choose a new summer suit of coat and breeches, and a vest of flowered watered silk. We get on very well together, the three of us.

In the meantime the coach is being repainted and the window frames gilded against May Day and all the worry is whether it will be done in time. Sam spent all the evening of the last day in April standing over the workmen at the coachmaker's to see it finished.

SUMMER

Nothing is ever quite the way you expect it to be, and because we had such high expectations of May Day I suppose they were bound to be disappointed.

The weather was foul, lowering and grey, but I was determined to go on our tour of Hyde Park, and was dressed in my watered-silk gown, now newly laced, and made Sam change into his new clothes. So we drove through the City with our coachman in his new livery, and the horses' manes and tails tied with red ribbon, and Sam was out of humour because little Betty Turner hadn't joined us as he expected and he knew we were to meet Mr Sheeres in Pall Mall. We did, and Sam was obliged to have him in the coach. I was slightly out of humour because Sam would insist on sitting next to me and crushing my gown.

It was windy and raining, and although there were many private coaches, there were so many hackney coaches that we could hardly see the gentlemen's. We met the Bateliers and dined with them and then resumed our circuit in the procession, all the time Sam a little sullen and me so wanting it to be different – for Mr Sheeres was to leave for Portsmouth that night on his way to Tangier and we both knew it would be a long time before we met again. And I'd pictured our pretty coach in May with dappled sunlight and due courtesies between us all, but in the end it was as though we couldn't wait to get away from each other. We dropped Mr Sheeres at St James's Gate, and went home to our supper. I was sadly out of humour for the rest of the night because the occasion – riding round the park on May Day, and that being his last day in London – will never be repeated, and where it should have been one to put away for years to come, it was spoilt.

But, other places, other times. One must hope. My monthly is so bad I spend the day in bed.

Sam's out all day and I'm cross until he explains all the business he's done. Sometimes I wonder if I'm more prone to quarrel with him when my monthlies are on me. We walk in the garden. Sam has new vizards made, with glasses to put in and out as he will, and he hopes these will do some good, or at least stop his eyes hurting as much.

All on one day: I got up at three in the morning with my new maid Matt to gather May dew. We went in the coach and were back in bed by six. Sam dined with Lord Crewe, my Lady's father, and a long time since they have spoken. There was a countryman there, and they were talking about the decay of gentlemen's families in the country and the countryman said there was an old rule that a family might remain 50 miles from London for a hundred years, and 100 miles from London for two hundred years, and so the further away, the more years. And that in his father's time it was so rare for a country gentleman to come to London that he would make his will before he set out. And Sam hears from John Creed, and Mr Povey, that the gold lace on his sleeves has been taken notice of, and not altogether with approval for someone in his position, and he goes to his tailor and asks him to remove it. And for some reason, in a way I can't explain, I find these three things, the May dew, the country families, the gold lace, all interlinked – oh, if nothing else, all part of the fabric of our life.

Brother John arrives and tells us Pall is with child, and far gone. Sam petitions the Duke of York that he may have three or four months' leave of absence to travel abroad over the water so he can rest his eyes.

He proposes going into Holland to observe things there of the Navy (he can observe the dockyards while I observe the shops). The Duke was very sympathetic about his eyes and approved of his proposition but had to ask the King's leave, and the King said he'd be a good master to Sam, letting his servant go away for the good of his health.

I had a terrible toothache and Sam was so kind, sitting with me until Mr Marsden came. He's drawn my teeth before and advised this one must go as well, fortunately nothing that shows as long as I don't smile too widely. I'm so glad to have a dentist I can trust to do it as fast and gently as possible in the circumstances, though if the pain had got much worse I'd have used a man in the street with a pair of pliers. The next day my cheek was very swollen and Sam took me to Mr Hollier but he wasn't in, so we drove on to Islington to the old house and ate and drank a little and my cheek has gradually got better of its own accord.

On the King's birthday we joined the great store of company in Hyde Park where the Prince of Tuscany had ordered a firework display in celebration, and sent out free casks of Italian wine and beer, which caused even more applause.

Our new maid, Matt, upped and went pretty quickly, but I was pleased because it meant I could concentrate on finding a good French maid, who'll be much more useful on our travels.

Sam has spent most of the summer with Will Hewer here trying to get his personal and office accounts straight. They'd got into a terrible muddle because his eyes were so bad he couldn't bear the pain of doing them. But now, in the middle of August, he declares himself satisfied. He has also decided that Balty should come with us – I think Sam realises his spoken French isn't all that it might be, and it will be a help to him to have a man who's fluent. And I have an excellent French maid, Odile, who it turns out went to the same Ursuline convent in Paris as I did. We've bought maps of France and Holland and spent many happy hours planning our route.

Our friend John Evelyn has travelled extensively and he's given us advice and letters of introduction in Paris and recommendations of the best print sellers, for we intend to buy lots of beautiful things to send home. The Houblons have given more introductions and letters of credit. We'll start with the Dutch naval bases then journey down through Holland and Flanders and northern France to Paris, returning via Brussels. I don't know how I shall manage with keeping my journal; I suppose my mother will be receiving a lot of letters.

A week before we go we hold a dinner for the friends we won't see again for a while. At one point I find myself looking round the table, and there are so many memories gathered here. Captain Ferrer sits on my right – years ago there would have been groping with hand or foot under the table, but we're too old friends for that now. I ask him does he remember the time he jumped off the balcony and couldn't walk for six weeks, and he laughs and says he has no idea why he did it, and in return asks me if I remember a certain ride through Brampton Woods when the milkmaids were coming home, and I laugh and say it was a long time ago.

At the other end of the table Elizabeth Pearse sits next to Sam. She's painted, which he doesn't like, but even so they look friendly enough. She's still a beauty but time is beginning to work its business on her, as indeed it is upon us all. We've had our falling-outs but we've had our merry times too, the times we sang in the studio when my portrait was being painted, the river trip to the Hope, our expeditions to Unthank's and the Exchange. I think in the future, as time makes itself known ever more thoroughly each year, we'll become true friends.

On Sam's other side sits Mrs Knepp. I have even invited her to join us — as a testament to the new trust between Sam and myself which our journey will cement, and which I truly believe, desire, want and wish with all my heart. And in my mood of benevolence (after several glasses of good wine) even Elizabeth Knepp is allowed her virtues of being pretty, and one who sang 'Barbara Allen' as I've never heard it before or since. She introduced us to Nell Gwyn, and if she flirts with Sam, at least I know that her own marriage is a great deal unhappier than mine. She's been part of our life, so it's right she should be here.

As have Tom and Jane who've come back especially tonight to serve us. Tom, the boy who came to us when his voice broke, is now as grave and serious as a young man of twenty-one can be, while Jane, who was our little girl, smiles privately at her swelling belly. God bless them both.

And dear Will Hewer, who was never spared the rod by Sam in his youth, and is now the closest confidant of our public and private lives. So many instances of loyalty and devotion over the years. He introduced Mary Mercer as my companion, who is now my friend and I shall always be grateful for that. The number of times he has escorted me to Brampton. Trusting him, having his confidence. Knowing that if we leave our business in his hands while we're abroad, they're the safest pair of hands we could wish for. Knowing that we'll know him for the rest of our lives.

And Mary Mercer, sitting next to him, how much better a friend than a servant. But we must find her a husband soon. She dances like a dream. She's a loyal friend to me, despite Sam's advances to her over the years. How many times we've walked in the garden, all of us, singing, how many times we've danced impromptu. The long, long talks we've had. The reassurance of knowing that she'll always be my friend, there to talk to, unless she marries a countryman and goes to live far away, which please God she doesn't.

And the Bateliers, William and his sister Mary, both neat, sweet people you love to be with because they're so easy and enhance any occasion with their lovely manners. And I look at John Pelling, who taught me how to make tea and has tried his hardest to prescribe potions for me, over the years, when sometimes I've known that there's been no potion that will work against the pain. But he's done his best, and as well has a lovely singing voice, and he and Sam have soared together.

And I look around the table and I think – fiercely – this is my time, these are my people, this is my life and I love it all. And I look at Sam and I know that he's been thinking the same way, and I'm sure, I'm sure, that we're making for the calm green uplands, where our toil will be over and we'll reap our reward.

But when the toast was 'Absent Friends', so many more memories crowded in, of Sam's brother Tom, and his mother, of Will's and Tom's fathers and Dr Burnet dead in the plague, of Mr Kirton, dead of grief, of so many little babies along the years.

And then I was back in the present and we were all alive and well, and everyone wishing us God speed for our trip. Now it only remains to embark on it. And to hold on to those links of friendship which light our way in what is a dark enough passage, and to trust that we'll see each other through the years. And to trust in God to see us safe over the water and back again.

7TH SEPTEMBER

The sailors kept saying our voyage to Amsterdam wasn't rough at all but it seemed to me that our packet was tossed about dreadfully. The tide was too low for us to get into the harbour so we were rowed ashore in little boats (and getting into them from a heaving ship was no easy business). Most of the passengers were sick on the journey so it was a great relief to be on dry land again and find that our hotel was as clean and well-ordered as we could wish. Indeed, throughout the country there is evidence of almost fanatical cleanliness and orderliness. The rule in Holland is that wherever there are people, there's someone scrubbing floors. Visitors are given straw slippers to change into so that they don't bring a speck of mud into the house. But such standards ensure that the beds are always freshly aired and the linen is immaculate, and there are no bugs. (Which we've been warned to expect in Flanders and France.)

In the dockyards everything was so neatly stowed it made Sam realise how untidy and wasteful our own yards are. We watched them making cable — the Dutch use only a third of the men that we do but they're much more skilful. Amsterdam is very pretty, red brick houses, and the canals full of brightly painted barges. The streets are crowded with sailors, porters, coachmen, women in wooden shoes, hawkers selling fruit or frying pancakes. We've bought a beautiful Rembrandt etching to take home.

We've been staying at English inns where the servants are Dutch but the food is dressed in the English manner. The Dutch tend only to cook once or twice a week and then they keep reheating it or serving it cold with bread and butter and cheese and always gallons of beer. We did try their national dish — hutsepot. It's a stew of meat, vegetables and prunes soaked in lemon juice and vinegar and boiled for a long time in fat and ginger. We didn't care for it.

The whole country is like a beautifully tended garden, the green willows at the side of the canals contrasting with the red gabled roofs, windmills gently creaking as they turn in the sun. Pots of flowers outside the houses, and everywhere evidence of careful husbandry. We have gone sometimes by boat on the canal, and sometimes by coach, but always the same impression of ordered greenery, as though even the big old trees lining the road have been shaped by men over the years. After the trials of the last twelve months it's immensely restful to us both to sit back and see such pretty country and neat towns, to watch storks feeding on river banks, to know that our day's travel will end in a clean bed and that we'll both sleep soundly, after so long a time when good sleep was something we'd almost forgotten. We eat dishes of the freshest cream, and we look at each other across the coach or the boat and we smile and feel, I think, very content together. Balty is an excellent travelling companion, very helpful, and I feel a glow that my family is at last an asset to Sam, not a liability.

We found a Delftware basket just like the one Sam brought me back years ago, the one he kicked and broke in a temper. He bought it and promised me that this one would never be broken. I believe him, for we're both older and wiser now and know we must cherish each other.

So, Rotterdam, Dordrecht, Breda, Antwerp, Ghent. Still six weeks of our journey to go, and the best part – Paris – still to come.

PARIS, 21ST SEPTEMBER

At last. We arrived yesterday to an excellent clean
hotel which was very welcome after some of the
places we'd stayed at on the way. As we journeyed
from Holland into Flanders, the landscape changed.
Instead of canals, now there were fields of wheat
and poppies, with every available soul bringing in the
harvest. I began to remember that journey so many
years ago when I came through this country with my
parents, when I was a little girl and Balty a little boy. It
was a poignant memory of a time when hopes hadn't
been disappointed, when there was all still to play for.
We must make of our lives what we can.

And now in front of us the peasants' children
were sitting on top of the hay carts, singing the
harvest home. Our coach crawled at walking pace
behind them, but we had time enough and Sam was
delighted at their songs, and gave them money. Sitting
back in the coach, with sunlight dappling through the
trees, hearing those childish voices, I had a moment
when everything was perfect, all life was strong and
sweet and good. Sam and Balty smiled at me and I felt
lapped in their love, embraced in a golden world.

But much as I love my father's native land, even
I must admit that there are some inns where mops
and brooms are not in the catalogue of necessaries,
where the food is stinking and the water foul and
brackish. In some places the landlords are so mean
they're pleased when their guests don't eat the food,

where an English host would be offended if food were left. We carry our own bedding with us to use as necessary, sometimes laying a silk coverlet and a sheet over the mattress, to prevent infection from people who've lain there before. In the larger towns the inns are very highly furnished – large gilt glasses, tapestries, paintings, satin beds – but crawling with bugs and hopping with fleas.

But we're very comfortable now, in a hotel in the Marais with three bedchambers and an elegant dining room. Here we drink coffee in the morning and then we generally dine out at a variety of establishments, and sometimes by invitation in a private house. Seeing the way French ladies and gentlemen dress has made it absolutely essential for us to buy a new gown for me and a new suit for Sam, and shoes and buckles and ribbons and Chantilly lace.

At last we've arrived at the point where if I admire something (not too expensive) Sam offers to buy it for me, instead of making me plead for it. I wonder if this is just the effect of the Parisian air, or whether he's finally convinced that I'm not a spendthrift, and his behaviour will continue like this when we return home. Or is he trying to say, in the best way he knows, that all is well now?

∞

PARIS, 28TH SEPTEMBER

The Rue St Jacques was just as noisy and full of people as I remembered so that the deep peace within was even more apparent when Odile and I visited our old convent. Mère Joseph, our Reverend Mother, was still there, her face deeply wrinkled now against the starch of her wimple. She remembered Odile, and me too, the pretty little half-English girl who wept when her family took her away. Those were innocent tears. Had that young girl known how many more were to be shed – thank God that we don't know the future or our hearts might fail us.

I'd always wanted to go back to the convent (I've been to it many times in my dreams) and it was almost like laying a ghost, to smell the incense in the chapel, to see the form room again, the girls sewing silently with their heads bowed over their work, a few of them glancing up shyly.

I took the peace of that place away with me. Something inside me was quieted, a long lasting resentment against my family was gone. They'd loved me and they'd done what they thought was best for me. What more can we ask of our parents?

Sam is utterly delighted by Paris, the buildings, the bridges, the books and pictures, not to mention the many pretty women (though he's very careful of his deportment). My own beauty has been extravagantly admired but I, too, am careful to give him no cause for jealousy. Neither of us has the heart for those games any more.

∞

ıst OCTOBER

It's hard to find time to write. There's so much of interest to do, so many books and prints to look at in the little stalls beside the Seine, so many arcades to wander through and sights to see: Notre Dame, the Louvre Palace, the Tuileries, even the market at Halles. I know most of them already, but what pleasure to see them again and show them off to Sam. He swears that if our prosperity continues we'll come again.

There's a moment, watching sunlight dance on the river, when I feel I've come full circle. I was a young girl here once and now I'm a woman in the prime of my life. I think that long-ago girl would have been happy enough to see herself here, as I am all these years later. A lot of water has gone under the bridge, and more to come, please God.

∞

BRUSSELS, 14TH OCTOBER

As beautiful a city as everyone says, and wonderfully clean inns with excellent furnishings and food. I don't feel very well so I haven't seen all I might have done

– an impression of lovely squares and fountains, of polite and pleasant people. Sam and Balty have seen all the sights on my behalf. I'm quite happy to lie in bed. People say the road to Ostend is good. I pray it is.

∞

23RD OCTOBER, SEETHING LANE, LONDON

When you're ill, when you're in pain, when you're weary beyond belief, there is nothing as comforting and restorative as your own bed. I began to feel ill about ten days ago and the last week of our journey, through Flanders, was something of an ordeal. I had a headache all the time and didn't feel like eating anything. I'd sit back in the coach watching the leaves fall, the sun low in the sky, and I felt as though I were falling myself, into a world of fever. I could see the concern on Sam's face – he and Balty spared no effort to make the journey less troublesome to me but there was nothing they could do about bumpy roads or the noise and bustle of the port or the dreadful pitching of the boat.

The fever helps a little in a way to ease the griping pain in my bowel, makes me feel I'm cut off from my body. I've never felt this ill before, as though I'll never have the strength to get out of bed again.

I'm beginning to be afraid it may be typhus.

Today is my birthday and I'm twenty-nine.

If my illness is what I fear, it could be the last one. We never know when is the last time we'll do something. We didn't go to Bartholomew Fair this year because we were away. Was last year the last time? We went with Mary Mercer and Will Hewer and Deb and we saw Jacob Hall dancing on the ropes and we met Mrs Knepp there and dined at Hercules Pillars, and it was before I knew about Deb. Looking back it seems like such an innocent time, before my trust was broken and not knowing this was the last time I'd ever see the booths twinkling in the dark and the puppet show and the monkeys, and eat pork.

I don't know it for certain. All I know is I've never felt this ill in this way before. I've never really felt that I might die. I try to push the thought away when it comes because it frightens me so much.

Our house looked so warm and welcoming when we arrived home. And all the things that will arrive in due course from our travels to make it even more beautiful. So much still to come . . .

Mr Hollier has visited and given me a syrup to bring down the fever. I can tell from his manner that he thinks it's serious. Poor Sam, as soon as we returned, was plunged into defending the Navy Board and himself from yet more charges of corruption. All his time is taken up either going through his papers or sitting with me. I wonder if I'll ever hear him play the lute again. I'll ask him to play at my bedside.

There's beginning to be a pattern to the fever, worse in the evening, better in the morning, but never absent.

The fever's worse. My mouth very dry. I drink milk and water. Growing very thin but my belly swollen. Sam reads to me from *Cyrus* and I'm floating through an Arcadian world of young men and women and in their beauty and their friendship they're like a host of angels. Sometimes when the pain's not too bad I close my eyes and drift into that company and I feel surrounded by love.

Time moves in a different way. An hour can be very long or very short. I think of latitude and longitude. I suppose I'll never understand longitude now.

Odile is a dear girl and a blessing at this time.

Father Fogarty. If you were here. Pray, Father, bless me, for I have sinned. Occasional acts of impurity by thought. Occasional acts of flirtatious behaviour designed to encourage impure thoughts. Occasional lies to my husband about the price of lace or gloves or a gown. Impatience with my servants. Pride at where we've got to.

Poor wretch, that's small beer. Three Hail Marys and an Our Father.

I wish he could be with me, but I must make do with Mr Milles's cold comfort. There's no choice, I must be shriven if it comes to it.

But that it should come to this, barely twenty-nine years old and childless. I wonder what part my life played in God's purpose.

Then I reflect that I've had a glimpse of the glories of His creation, and more than many, many others have enjoyed. And I hope that in the manner of my life I've given some testament of having seen it – in the delight of hearing a bird sing, the pleasure of entertaining friends, the satisfaction of a neatly-folded pile of clean linen, sweet-smelling.

In the end that's all I can say, except that the last ten years with Sam were the best years of my life and I thank God for those many occasions of our mutual joy.

I don't know how much time there is left. If I must die I will record it as far as I can. That's something I can seize from it at least, while I can still write. Sam has spoken of sending for my mother and I'll give her my last pages.

Ah, I know it's serious if he's sending for my mother.

Every morning there's a little time after Odile has attended to me when although the fever is there, it's so much less than it was in the night that my mind feels almost clear. I know, if it's typhus, what the course of the disease will be, for I helped my mother nurse a friend of hers to the grave. I know that if a rash of bright pink spots appears on the chest, that is a bad sign. I know that the fever will grow more intense and the pain worse until there is a kind of sleep that's like death and then death itself. So there's more to go through yet. We must labour to be born and we must labour to die.

I surprise myself that I can write so calmly. But I've forgotten what it's like not to have a fever, I can't remember what it's like to be alive and be well,

I can't imagine it any more. Already. After however many days it's been, I'm losing count.

I keep thinking of Mrs Knepp singing 'Barbara Allen' – Now Mother, Mother make my bed, for Mother I am dying.

I could still get better and be reading this in a year's time, laughing at my fears, but I know it in my heart, my bones, my water, that I won't.

DON'T KNOW THE DATE.

A few days since I wrote. The fever worse. The time when I can sit up and write very short. More and more time with the Arcadian people. The pain very bad. But not so afraid any more.

In my Father's house there are many mansions. I go to prepare a place for you.

I love Sam so much I can't bear the thought of losing him for ever. In the end there's only love, nothing else is worth a fig. And we fumble our way towards it the best we can. God help us all.

I suppose he'll find a widow, too old for children, he wouldn't want that now, but someone to look after him and keep him warm in bed. I don't begrudge him that for a moment. But can't bear to think of myself lying cold in the church, with all the plague graves outside the door.

∞

All Souls' Day (Odile told me)

Yesterday the rash appeared and I watched Mr Hollier's eyes and they widened for a moment when he saw it and Dr Williams came and the same thing and then I knew for sure that I was dying. Why, it seems as though I've hardly begun. Just when we'd both learnt enough to live so happily together.

Sometimes I see a girl sitting under a tree and leaves are falling on her and the moment will come that the leaves are all over her and she'll never get up again.

God bless my dear Sam and his poor eyes.

Hail Mary, full of Grace, the Lord is with thee. Blessed art thou among women and blessed is the fruit of thy womb, Jesus. Holy Mary, Mother of God, pray for us sinners now and at the hour of our death. Amen.

Tunnels Go Underground

Tunnels Go Underground

a building block book

Lee Sullivan Hill

Carolrhoda Books, Inc./Minneapolis

To engineer David Shilling, who generously shared his tunneling experience, knowledge, and enthusiasm with me—L. S. H.

For metric conversion, when you know the number of feet, multiply by 0.30 to find the number of meters. When you know the number of miles, multiply by 1.61 to find the number of kilometers. When you know the number of gallons, multiply by 3.785 to find the number of liters.

The photographs in this book are reproduced through the courtesy of: © Howard Ande, front cover, back cover, pp. 1, 7, 28; © Betty Crowell, pp. 2, 27; © Jerry Hennen, pp. 5, 6, 22; © Eugene G. Schulz, p. 8; **Tony Stone Images:** (© Gavriel Jecan) p. 9, (© Connie Coleman) p. 12, (© Ken Biggs) p. 15, (© George Hunter) p. 20, (© Phil Schermeister) p. 25; © CORBIS/ Philip Gould, p. 10; © The Metropolitan Water Reclamation District of Greater Chicago, p. 11; **TRIP:** (© R. Belbin) pp. 13, 29, (© Streano/Havens) p. 17, (© M. Stevenson) p. 23; © Stephen Graham Photography, p. 14; © Terry C. Hazen/Visuals Unlimited, p. 16; © David Shilling, pp. 18, 19, 26; © CORBIS/Pablo Corral V, p. 21; © CORBIS/Richard Hamilton Smith, p. 24.

Text copyright © 2001 by Lee Sullivan Hill

Carolrhoda Books, Inc.
A division of Lerner Publishing Group
241 First Avenue North
Minneapolis, MN 55401 U.S.A.

Website address: www.lernerbooks.com

Library of Congress Cataloging-in-Publication Data

Hill, Lee Sullivan, 1958–
    Tunnels go underground / Lee Sullivan Hill.
      p.   cm. — (A building block book)
    Summary: Describes different kinds of tunnels, how they are built, and what they are used for.
      ISBN 1-57505-429-9
      1. Tunnels—Juvenile literature. 2. Tunneling—Juvenile literature. [1. Tunnels.]
I. Title. II. Series: Hill, Lee Sullivan, 1958– Building block book.
    TA807.H55 2001
    624.1'93—dc21
                                                                                    99-33045

Manufactured in the United States of America
1 2 3 4 5 6 – JR – 06 05 04 03 02 01

Tunnels disappear into darkness. They go
under mountains or rivers or busy city streets.

Some tunnels take people from one place to
another. Ride into a tunnel. Right away,
darkness drops like a blanket.

At the tunnel's end,
you are in the sun again.
It's so bright!

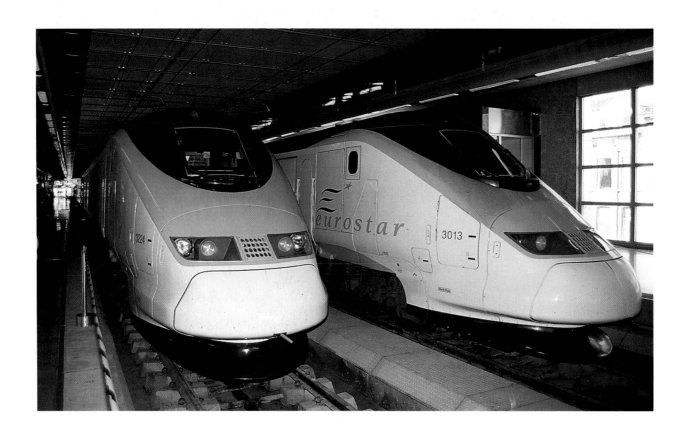

Some tunnels go under water. The Chunnel is
a tunnel that runs between France and England.
Stormy seas may stop boats from crossing the
English Channel, but not the trains that travel in
the tunnel far below.

Tunnels cut through mountains. Instead of going up and over the top, trains take a shortcut through the mountain.

Some tunnels carry water, not cars and trains. Small tunnels carry water under roads. Creep through a culvert. Splash and shout. HELLO . . . HELLO . . . HELLO . . . Sounds echo off the walls.

Miles of underground pipes can hold millions of gallons of storm water. When it rains, water pours into the tunnels instead of flooding city streets and basements.

Some tunnels take miners underground to dig for iron, gold, or diamonds. Take a tour of an old mine. Wooden beams hold up the roof. Water drips from the roof and walls. The earth above seems to press down. (Ready for the tour to end? Let's get out of here!)

Some tunnels lead to secret places. This door in the ground leads to miles of tunnels. Soldiers used the tunnels as hiding places during the war in Vietnam.

Tunnels can surprise you. You cannot always
see them from where you are. Are you standing
above one now? Ride down an escalator from the
street to a subway tunnel.

Whoosh! A subway train roars into the underground station.

It takes years of planning before people can build a tunnel. First, engineers test the dirt. Is it rocky or soft? Is it wet or dry? They also find out what is above the ground. Will the tunnel go under a field or an elementary school?

Next, engineers decide how to dig a tunnel.
The easiest way to build a tunnel is called cut and
cover. Workers dig a deep trench. They build a
tunnel structure at the bottom. Then they cover
the tunnel with dirt.

A second way to build a tunnel is called machine bore. Miners dig with a tunnel-boring machine that eats dirt like a giant earthworm in a garden. Sharp blades at the front cut the earth as the machine pushes forward. A long belt at the back takes the dirt away.

Every few feet, the machine stops digging.
A shield holds back the soft dirt. Miners build
tunnel walls piece by piece. Five pieces form one
ring. Rings join end to end to make tunnel walls.

A third way to dig a tunnel is called drill and blast. Miners drill small holes in rock. Then they load explosives into the holes. Everyone gets out of the way. BOOM!

After the blast, miners clear away the broken rocks. They put steel arches in place to hold back the rock. Then they drill and blast again. The tunnel creeps deeper with each blast.

Not all tunnels are built by machines. It took thousands of years for wind and water to carve this tunnel out of rock along Lake Superior.

People made this snow tunnel with shovels
and their own hands.

You can dig your own tunnel in a sandbox or a snowbank. Watch out for cave-ins!

When you grow up, you could be a miner and search for gold.

You could be an engineer and plan tunnels.

Or you could run a giant tunnel-boring machine.

Tunnels cut through mighty mountains. They dive down deep beneath the sea.

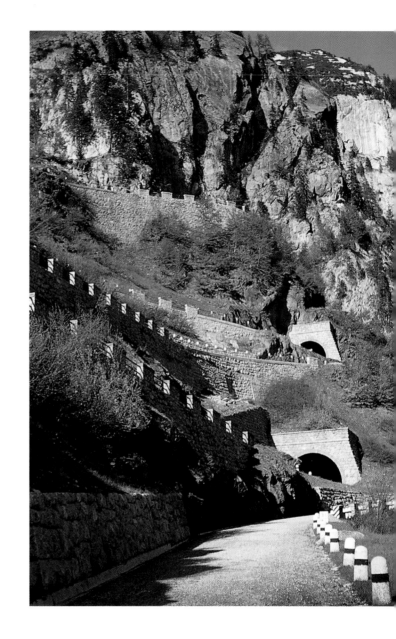

They help cars and trains take shortcuts and
carry water underground. They make you
wonder what lies under your own two feet.

Tunnels go underground,
all over the world.

A Photo Index to the Tunnels in This Book

Cover A Southern Pacific Railroad train roars out of a tunnel near Price River Canyon in Utah.

Page 1 This tunnel on the Burlington Northern Santa Fe Railroad near Bealville, California, looks similar to the tunnel on the cover. Both tunnels have an arch shape. Ancient Romans were the first builders to understand the strength of the arch. Many modern tunnels use the same design.

Page 2 These arches are like the windows of a tunnel that runs alongside the mountains in Austria's Flexen Pass. The tunnel was built into the side of the mountain to protect trains from falling rocks and snow.

Page 5 Railroad tracks used to run through this tunnel on the Elroy-Sparta bike trail in Wisconsin.

Page 6 A van on Gold Camp Road goes through a lighted tunnel near Cripple Creek, Colorado.

Page 7 How is this tunnel near Port-Cartier, Quebec, different from the other tunnels in this book? Look at the shape. Engineers have discovered that egg-shaped tunnels hold back dirt and rocks even better than arches with straight walls.

Page 8 A train called the Eurostar travels in the Chunnel between Calais, France, and Folkestone, England. The Chunnel runs for 31 miles under the English Channel.

Page 9 This train is traveling through the rugged Swiss Alps. Tunnels and bridges allow trains to take shortcuts through mountains and over valleys.

Page 10 This culvert is part of a larger water-control project being built in Plaquemines Parish, Louisiana. When it rains, water from the nearby Mississippi River often floods the land. Tunnels can reduce flooding by carrying storm water away from towns.

 **Page 11** Chicago, Illinois, has 131 miles of storm sewers in the Tunnel and Reservoir Plan, also called the Deep Tunnel. The sewers connect with huge underground caverns that can hold up to 41 billion gallons of storm water.

 **Page 12** Wooden beams and columns hold back the dirt at Empire Mine State Historic Park in Grass Valley, California.

 **Page 13** A tour guide is opening the hatch that leads to the Cu Chi Tunnels in Vietnam. During the Vietnam War, these tunnels connected to secret hospitals, kitchens, and places for soldiers to sleep underground.

 **Page 14** The subway in London, England, is called the Underground or the Tube. This escalator is carrying passengers between the street above and Tube #3.

 **Page 15** This subway station is part of the Metrorail Red Line in Los Angeles, California. Subway trains whisk people from place to place without getting stuck in traffic.

 **Page 16** Soil engineers use a machine called an auger to take core samples from the ground. Engineers must understand the layers of dirt and rock below to dig a tunnel safely.

 Page 17 Tunnels will carry the Southeast Expressway under Boston, Massachusetts. The machine in this photograph is placing tie-backs into the ground. These rods keep the walls from caving in while the tunnel is being built.

 **Page 18** This tunnel-boring machine, or TBM, is working on a Metro subway tunnel in Washington, D.C. The overall length of the machine is more than 100 feet and includes the ramps and tracks shown in this photograph.

 **Page 19** The TBM at the Metro project fits sections of concrete rings together. Once all the rings are in place, workers will cover them with plastic to keep out water. Another layer of concrete will complete the tunnel walls.

31

 **Page 20** Dust billows as gold miners in Ontario, Canada, drill small holes in boulders. Later, explosives will break up the rocks and form the tunnel deep into the ground.

 **Page 21** Workers are building steel arches to support the walls of a tunnel near Baños in Ecuador. Rock walls are strong, but they can crack. The steel adds extra support.

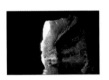 **Page 22** Lake Superior flows in and out of the tunnels at the Apostle Islands National Lakeshore in Wisconsin.

 **Page 23** This snow tunnel was dug in the mountains near Aiguille du Midi in France. Sometimes mountain climbers cut tunnels through ice and snow to make their way to the top of a mountain.

 **Page 24** These children in Saint Paul, Minnesota, can dig snow tunnels all winter long. Minnesota's cold winters last for many months. Do you dig tunnels in sand or snow?

 **Page 25** Safety is important in mines. A miner's hard hat protects his or her head from falling rocks. A lamp on the hat lights the way if the tunnel is too dark.

 **Page 26** This TBM operator on the Metro project in Washington, D.C., uses computer monitors and digital controls to steer the TBM. It looks more like a spaceship than an underground drilling rig!

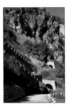 **Page 27** Many tunnels cut through the mountains of the Monte Croce Pass in Italy. These tunnels were built so that cars could travel through the mountains.

 **Page 28** Amtrak train #242 is coming out of a short railroad tunnel in Cold Spring, New York.

 **Page 29** These tunnels on Madeira Island near Portugal go under both a mountain and a city. Where are the tunnels in your hometown? What do they go under?